Charles John Tibbits

Folk-Lore and Legends

Vol. 12

Charles John Tibbits

Folk-Lore and Legends
Vol. 12

ISBN/EAN: 9783337391966

Printed in Europe, USA, Canada, Australia, Japan

Cover: Foto ©Andreas Hilbeck / pixelio.de

More available books at **www.hansebooks.com**

FOLK-LORE

AND

LEGENDS

GERMANY

J. B. LIPPINCOTT COMPANY

PHILADELPHIA·

1892

PREFATORY NOTE

IT is proposed that this shall be the first of a series of little volumes in which shall be presented in a handy form selections from the Folklore and legends of various countries. It has been well said that "the legendary history of a nation is the recital of the elements that formed the character of that nation; it contains the first rude attempts to explain natural phenomena, the traditions of its early history, and the moral principles popularly adopted as the rules for reward and punishment; and generally the legends of a people may be regarded as embodying the popular habits of thought and popular motives of action." The following legends of Germany cannot, we think, fail to interest those who read them. Some of the stories are invested with a charming simplicity of thought which cannot but excite admiration. Others are of a weird, fantastic character fitted to a land of romantic natural features, of broad river, mountain, and deep forest. The humorous, the pathetic, the terrible, all find place in the German folk-tales, and it would be difficult to rise from their perusal without having received both amusement and instruction. The general lesson they convey is the sure punishment of vice and the reward of virtue; some way or another the villain always meets with his desert. In future volumes we shall deal with the legends of other countries, hoping that the public will bear us company in our excursions.

CONTENTS

INTRODUCTION

THE value of national stories and legends has in late years become very widely recognised. Folklore has recently received a large amount of attention, and the thought and labour bestowed upon the subject have been rewarded by results which prove that its investigators have entered upon no unfruitful, however long neglected, field.

This book, and its successors in the series which it is proposed to issue, may come into the hands of some who, having little opportunity afforded them to consider how the legends and tales it contains may be of the value we claim for them, may be glad to have the "case" for legends and national stories presented to them in a few words.

The peasant's tale, the story preserved through centuries on the lips of old wives, the narrative which has come down to us having done duty as a source of amusement in the fireside groups of preceding generations, may seem to some to afford slight matter for reflection, and may even appear so grotesque in its incidents as to be fitted only to excite a smile of wonder at the simplicity of those among whom such stories could obtain reception, and surprise at the fantastic imagination in which such tales could find their origin. Modern thought has, however, been busy asking itself what is the meaning of these stories, and it has done much to supply itself with an answer. This, at least, it has done: it has discovered that these legends and tales, which so many have been inclined to cast aside as worthless, are of a singular value, as throwing a light which little else can afford upon the mind of primitive man. At first the collection of national stories was undertaken merely for the purpose of affording amusement. Folk-tales were diverting, so they found their way into print, and were issued as curious literary matter fitted to supply diversion for a vacant hour. Many of the tales are very beautiful, and their mere literary merit sufficed to make them sought for. But legendary lore was soon observed to possess much more value than could attach to its merely amusing features. It was obvious that in these legends were preserved the fragments of the beliefs of the ancient folk.

"The mythology of one period," remarked Sir Walter Scott, "would appear to pass into the romance of the next century, and that into the nursery tale of the subsequent ages." "Fiction," said Sir John Malcolm, "resolves itself into its primitive elements, as, by the slow and unceasing action of the wind and rain, the solid granite is crumbled into sand. The creations embodied by the vivid imagination of man in the childhood of his race incorporate themselves in his fond and mistaken faith. Sanctity is given to his day-dreams by the altar of the idol. Then, perhaps, they acquire a deceitful truth from the genius of the bard. Blended with the mortal hero, the aspect of the god glances through the visor of the helmet, or adds a holy dignity to the royal crown. Poetry borrows its ornaments from the lessons of the priests. The ancient god of strength of the Teutons, throned in his chariot of the stars, the Northern Wain, invested the Emperor of the Franks and the paladins who surrounded him with superhuman might. And the same constellation, darting down its rays upon the head of the long-lost Arthur, has given to the monarch of the Britons the veneration which once belonged to the son of 'Uthry

Bendragon,' 'Thunder, the supreme leader,' and 'Eygyr, the generating power.' Time rolls on; faith lessens; the flocks are led to graze within the rocky circle of the giants, even the bones of the warriors moulder into dust; the lay is no longer heard; and the fable, reduced again to its original simplicity and nudity, becomes the fitting source of pastime to the untutored peasant and the listening child. Hence we may yet trace no small proportion of mystic and romantic lore in the tales which gladden the cottage fireside, or, century after century, soothe the infant to its slumbers." The works of the brothers Grimm, the appearance of the *Kinder-und-Haus-Mährchen*, in 1812, and of the *Deutsche Mythologie*, in 1835, threw a new light on the importance of national tales, and awoke the spirit of scientific comparison which has made the study of Folklore productive of such valuable results.

With regard to the diffusion of national stories, it is remarkable that we find substantially identical narratives flourishing in the most widely separated countries, and this fact has given rise to several explanatory theories, none of which seems perfectly satisfactory. The philological discovery of the original unity of all the Aryan races may account for the possession by the Aryan peoples of similar stories. It may be, as Sir George Cox suggests, a common inheritance of such tales as were current when the Aryans "still lived as a single people." We find, however, that these tales are also current among people whom, accepting this theory, we should least expect to find possessing them, and so the wide diffusion of the stories yet remains unsatisfactorily accounted for. Identity of imagination, inheritance, transmission, may each have played its part.

As to the origin of the tales much debate has arisen. It is obvious from the nature of the incidents of many of them that they could only have originated in a most primitive state of man. "Early man," says Sir George Cox, "had life, and therefore all things must have life also. The sun, the moon, the stars, the ground on which he trod, the clouds, storms, lightnings were all living beings; could he help thinking that, like himself, they were all conscious beings also?" Such, according to this authority, was the origin of primary myths, secondary and tertiary myths arising in the course of time from the gradual misunderstanding of phrases applied by primitive man to personified objects. According to Professor Max Müller, animism, or the investing all things with life, springs not in the first place from man's thought, but from the language in which he clothes it. Man, he says, found himself speaking of all things in words having "a termination expressive of gender, and this naturally produced in the mind the corresponding idea of sex." He thus came to invest all objects with "something of an individual, active, sexual, and at last personal character." However hard it may be to discover the reason for the origin of the tendency to animism, the fact is certain that the tendency is to be found generally existing among savage peoples, and it would seem that we must accept the national stories which have come down to us embodying this tendency in grotesque incidents as relics handed down from the savage days of the people with whom the tales originated, as the expression of portions of their thought when they had as yet only attained to such a degree of civilisation as exists among savages of the present day.

Strange and grotesque as some of the national stories are, they may be regarded as embodying the fragments of some of man's most primitive beliefs; and recognising this, it will be impossible to

dismiss the folk-tale as unworthy of careful consideration, nor may it be regarded as unfitted to
afford us, if studied aright, very much more than
merely such amusement as may be derived from its
quaint incident and grotesque plot.

C. J. T.

GAFFER DEATH.

THERE was once a poor man who had twelve children, and he was obliged to labour day and night
that he might earn food for them.   When at length,
as it so happened, a thirteenth came into the world,
the poor man did not know how to help himself,
so he ran out into the highway, determined to
ask the first person he met to be godfather to the
boy.

There came stalking up to him Death, who said—

"Take me for a godfather."

"Who are you?" asked the father.

"I am Death, who makes all equal," replied the
stranger.

Then said the man—

"You are one of the right sort: you seize on rich
and poor without distinction; you shall be the child's
godfather."

Death answered—

"I will make the boy rich and renowned through-
out the world, for he who has me for a friend can
want nothing."

A

Said the man—

"Next Sunday will he be christened, mind and come at the right time."

Death accordingly appeared as he had promised, and stood godfather to the child.

When the boy grew up his godfather came to him one day, and took him into a wood, and said—

"Now shall you have your godfather's present. I will make a most famous physician of you. Whenever you are called to a sick person, I will take care and show myself to you. If I stand at the foot of the bed, say boldly, 'I will soon restore you to health,' and give the patient a little herb that I will point out to you, and he will soon be well. If, however, I stand at the head of the sick person, he is mine; then say, 'All help is useless; he must soon die.'"

Then Death showed him the little herb, and said—

"Take heed that you never use it in opposition to my will."

It was not long before the young fellow was the most celebrated physician in the whole world.

" The moment he sees a person," said every one, "he knows whether or not he 'll recover."

Accordingly he was soon in great request. People came from far and near to consult him, and they gave him whatever he required, so that he made an immense fortune. Now, it so happened that the king was taken ill, and the physician was called upon to say whether he must die. As he went up to the bed he saw Death standing at the sick man's head, so that there was no chance of his recovery. The physician thought, however, that if he outwitted Death, he would not, perhaps, be much offended, seeing that he was his godfather, so he caught hold of the king and turned him round, so that by that means Death was standing at his feet. Then he gave him some of the herb, and the king recovered, and was once more well. Death came up to the physician with a very angry and gloomy countenance, and said—

"I will forgive you this time what you have done, because I am your godfather, but if you ever venture to betray me again, you must take the consequences."

Soon after this the king's daughter fell sick, and nobody could cure her. The old king wept night and day, until his eyes were blinded, and at last he proclaimed that whosoever rescued her from Death should be rewarded by marrying her and inheriting his throne. The physician came, but Death was standing at the head of the princess. When the physician saw the beauty of the king's daughter, and thought of the promises that the king had made, he forgot all the warnings he had received, and, although Death frowned heavily all the while, he turned the patient so that Death stood at her feet, and gave her some of the herb, so that he once more put life into her veins.

When Death saw that he was a second time cheated out of his property, he stepped up to the physician, and said—

"Now, follow me."

He laid hold of him with his icy cold hand, and led him into a subterranean cave, in which there were thousands and thousands of burning candles, ranged in innumerable rows. Some were whole, some half burnt out, some nearly consumed. Every instant some went out, and fresh ones were lighted, so that the little flames seemed perpetually hopping about.

"Behold," said Death, "the life-candles of mankind. The large ones belong to children, those half consumed to middle-aged people, the little ones to the aged. Yet children and young people have oftentimes but a little candle, and when that is burnt out, their life is at an end, and they are mine."

The physician said—

"Show me my candle."

Then Death pointed out a very little candle-end, which was glimmering in the socket, and said—

"Behold!"

Then the physician said—

"O dearest godfather, light me up a new one, that I may first enjoy my life, be king, and husband of the beautiful princess."

"I cannot do so," said Death; "one must burn out before I can light up another."

"Place the old one then upon a new one, that that may burn on when this is at an end," said the physician.

Death pretended that he would comply with this wish, and reached a large candle, but to revenge himself, purposely failed in putting it up, and the little piece fell and was extinguished. The physician sank with it, so he himself fell into the hands of Death.

THE LEGEND OF PARACELSUS.

It once happened that Paracelsus was walking
through a forest, when he heard a voice calling to
him by name. He looked around, and at length
discovered that it proceeded from a fir-tree, in the
trunk of which there was a spirit enclosed by a
small stopper, sealed with three crosses.

The spirit begged of Paracelsus to set him free.
This he readily promised, on condition that the
spirit should bestow upon him a medicine capable
of healing all diseases, and a tincture which would
turn everything it touched to gold. The spirit
acceded to his request, whereupon Paracelsus took
his penknife, and succeeded, after some trouble, in
getting out the stopper. A loathsome black spider
crept forth, which ran down the trunk of the tree.
Scarcely had it reached the ground before it was
changed, and became, as if rising from the earth, a
tall haggard man, with squinting red eyes, wrapped
in a scarlet mantle.

He led Paracelsus to a high, overhanging, craggy
mount, and with a hazel twig, which he had broken

off by the way, he smote the rock, which, splitting
with a crash at the blow, divided itself in twain,
and the spirit disappeared within it. He, however,
soon returned with two small phials, which he
handed to Paracelsus—a yellow one, containing the
tincture which turned all it touched to gold, and
a white one, holding the medicine which healed all
diseases. He then smote the rock a second time,
and thereupon it instantly closed again.

Both now set forth on their return, the spirit
directing his course towards Innsprück, to seize
upon the magician who had banished him from that
city. Now Paracelsus trembled for the consequences which his releasing the Evil One would
entail upon him who had conjured him into the
tree, and bethought how he might rescue him.
When they arrived once more at the fir-tree, he
asked the spirit if he could possibly transform himself again into a spider, and let him see him creep
into the hole. The spirit said that it was not only
possible, but that he would be most happy to make
such a display of his art for the gratification of his
deliverer.

Accordingly he once more assumed the form
of a spider, and crept again into the well-known
crevice. When he had done so, Paracelsus, who
had kept the stopper all ready in his hand for the
purpose, clapped it as quick as lightning into the hole,
hammered it in firmly with a stone, and with his

knife made three fresh crosses upon it. The spirit, mad with rage, shook the fir-tree as though with a whirlwind, that he might drive out the stopper which Paracelsus had thrust in, but his fury was of no avail. It held fast, and left him there with little hope of escape, for, on account of the great drifts of snow from the mountains, the forest will never be cut down, and, although he should call night and day, nobody in that neighbourhood ever ventures near the spot.

Paracelsus, however, found that the phials were such as he had demanded, and it was by their means that he afterwards became such a celebrated and distinguished man.

HANS IN LUCK.

Hans had served his master seven years, and at last said to him—

"Master, my time is up; I should like to go home and see my mother, so give me my wages."

And the master said—

"You have been a faithful and good servant, so your pay shall be handsome."

Then he gave him a piece of silver that was as big as his head. Hans took out his pocket-handkerchief, put the piece of silver into it, threw it over his shoulder, and jogged off homewards. As he went lazily on, dragging one foot after another, a man came in sight, trotting along gaily on a capital horse.

"Ah!" said Hans aloud, "what a fine thing it is to ride on horseback! There he sits as if he were at home in his chair. He trips against no stones, spares his shoes, and yet gets on he hardly knows how."

The horseman heard this, and said—

"Well, Hans, why do you go on foot, then?"

"Ah!" said he, "I have this load to carry; to be sure, it is silver, but it is so heavy that I can't hold up my head, and it hurts my shoulder sadly."

"What do you say to changing?" said the horseman. "I will give you my horse, and you shall give me the silver."

"With all my heart," said Hans, "but I tell you one thing: you will have a weary task to drag it along."

The horseman got off, took the silver, helped Hans up, gave him the bridle into his hand, and said—

"When you want to go very fast, you must smack your lips loud and cry, 'Jip.'"

Hans was delighted as he sat on the horse, and rode merrily on. After a time he thought he should like to go a little faster, so he smacked his lips and cried "Jip." Away went the horse full gallop, and before Hans knew what he was about, he was thrown off, and lay in a ditch by the wayside, and his horse would have run off if a shepherd, who was coming by driving a cow, had not stopped it. Hans soon came to himself, and got upon his legs again. He was sadly vexed, and said to the shepherd—

"This riding is no joke when a man gets on a beast like this, that stumbles and flings him off as if he would break his neck. However, I'm off now once for all. I like your cow a great deal better; one can walk along at one's leisure behind her, and have milk, butter, and cheese every day into the bargain. What would I give to have such a cow!"

"Well," said the shepherd, "if you are so fond of her I will change my cow for your horse."

"Done!" said Hans merrily.

The shepherd jumped upon the horse and away he rode. Hans drove off his cow quietly, and thought his bargain a very lucky one.

"If I have only a piece of bread (and I certainly shall be able to get that), I can, whenever I like, eat my butter and cheese with it, and when I am thirsty I can milk my cow and drink the milk. What can I wish for more?" said he.

When he came to an inn he halted, ate up all his bread, and gave away his last penny for a glass of beer. Then he drove his cow towards his mother's village. The heat grew greater as noon came on, till at last he found himself on a wide heath that it would take him more than an hour to cross, and he began to be so hot and parched that his tongue cleaved to the roof of his mouth.

"I can find a cure for this," thought he; "now will I milk my cow and quench my thirst." So he tied her to the stump of a tree, and held his leathern cap to milk into, but not a drop was to be had.

While he was trying his luck, and managing the matter very clumsily, the uneasy beast gave him a kick on the head that knocked him down, and there he lay a long while senseless. Luckily a butcher came by driving a pig in a wheelbarrow.

"What is the matter with you?" said the butcher, as he helped him up.

Hans told him what had happened, and the butcher gave him a flask, saying—

"There, drink and refresh yourself. Your cow will give you no milk; she is an old beast, good for nothing but the slaughter-house."

"Alas, alas!" said Hans, "who would have thought it? If I kill her, what will she be good for? I hate cow-beef; it is not tender enough for me. If it were a pig, now, one could do something with it; it would at any rate make some sausages."

"Well," said the butcher, "to please you I'll change and give you the pig for the cow."

"Heaven reward you for your kindness!" said Hans, as he gave the butcher the cow and took the pig off the wheelbarrow and drove it off, holding it by a string tied to its leg.

So on he jogged, and all seemed now to go right with him. He had met with some misfortunes, to be sure, but he was now well repaid for all. The next person he met was a countryman carrying a fine white goose under his arm. The countryman stopped to ask what was the hour, and Hans told him all his luck, and how he had made so many good bargains. The countryman said he was going to take the goose to a christening.

"Feel," said he, "how heavy it is, and yet it is only eight weeks old. Whoever roasts and eats it may cut plenty of fat off, it has lived so well."

"You 're right," said Hans, as he weighed it in his hand ; "but my pig is no trifle."

Meantime the countryman began to look grave, and shook his head.

"Hark ye," said he, "my good friend. Your pig may get you into a scrape. In the village I have just come from the squire has had a pig stolen out of his sty. I was dreadfully afraid when I saw you that you had got the squire's pig. It will be a bad job if they catch you, for the least they 'll do will be to throw you into the horse-pond."

Poor Hans was sadly frightened.

"Good man," cried he, "pray get me out of this scrape. You know this country better than I; take my pig and give me the goose."

"I ought to have something into the bargain," said the countryman ; "however, I 'll not bear hard upon you, as you are in trouble."

Then he took the string in his hand and drove off the pig by a side path, while Hans went on his way homeward free from care.

"After all," thought he, "I have the best of the bargain. First there will be a capital roast, then the fat will find me in goose-grease for six months, and then there are all the beautiful white feathers. I will put them into my pillow, and then I am sure

I shall sleep soundly without rocking. How happy my mother will be ! "

As he came to the last village he saw a scissors-grinder, with his wheel, working away and singing—

> " O'er hill and o'er dale so happy I roam,
> Work light and live well, all the world is my home ;
> Who so blythe, so merry as I ? "

Hans stood looking for a while, and at last said—
" You must be well off, master grinder, you seem so happy at your work."

" Yes," said the other, " mine is a golden trade. A good grinder never puts his hand in his pocket without finding money in it—but where did you get that beautiful goose ? "

" I did not buy it, but changed a pig for it."

" And where did you get the pig ? "

" I gave a cow for it."

" And the cow ? "

" I gave a horse for it."

" And the horse ? "

" I gave a piece of silver as big as my head for that."

" And the silver ? "

" Oh ! I worked hard for that seven long years."

" You have thriven well in the world hitherto," said the grinder, " now if you could find money in your pocket whenever you put your hand into it your fortune would be made."

" Very true, but how is that to be managed ? "

" You must turn grinder like me," said the other.
" You only want a grindstone, the rest will come of
itself. Here is one that is only a little the worse
for wear. I would not ask more than the value of
your goose for it. Will you buy it ? "

" How can you ask such a question ? " said Hans.
" I should be the happiest man in the world if I
could have money whenever I put my hand in my
pocket. What could I want more ? There 's the
goose."

" Now," said the grinder, as he gave him a
common rough stone that lay by his side, " this is
a most capital stone. Do but manage it cleverly
and you can make an old nail cut with it."

Hans took the stone, and went off with a light
heart. His eyes sparkled with joy, and he said to
himself—

" I must have been born in a lucky hour. Everything I want or wish comes to me of itself."

Meantime he began to be tired, for he had been
travelling ever since daybreak. He was hungry too,
for he had given away his last penny in his joy at
getting the cow. At last he could go no further,
and the stone tired him terribly, so he dragged himself to the side of the pond that he might drink some
water and rest a while. He laid the stone carefully
by his side on the bank, but as he stooped down to
drink he forgot it, pushed it a little, and down it

went, plump into the pond.   For a while he watched it sinking in the deep, clear water, then sprang up for joy, and again fell upon his knees and thanked Heaven with tears in his eyes for its kindness in taking away his only plague, the ugly, heavy stone.

"How happy am I!" cried he ; "no mortal was ever so lucky as I am."

Then he got up with a light and merry heart, and walked on, free from all his troubles, till he reached his mother's house.

THE GREY MARE IN THE GARRET.

In the portal of the Church of the Apostles, near
the new market in Cologne, hung a picture, the
portraits of a certain Frau Richmodis von Aducht
and her two children, of whom the following singular story is related. The picture was covered with
a curtain which she worked with her own hands.

Her husband, Richmuth von Aducht, was, in the
year of grace 1400, a rich burgomaster of Cologne,
and lived at the sign of the Parroquet in the New
Marckt. In that year a fearful plague desolated all
quarters of the city. She fell sick of the pest, and,
to all appearance, died. After the usual period had
elapsed she was buried in the vaults of the Apostles'
Church. She was buried, as the custom then was,
with her jewelled rings on her fingers, and most of
her rich ornaments on her person. These tempted
the cupidity of the sexton of the church. He
argued with himself that they were no use to the
corpse, and he determined to possess them. Accordingly he proceeded in the dead of night to the vault
where she lay interred, and commenced the work

B

of sacrilegious spoliation. He first unscrewed the coffin lid. He then removed it altogether, and proceeded to tear away the shroud which interposed between him and his prey. But what was his horror to perceive the corpse clasp her hands slowly together, then rise, and finally sit erect in the coffin. He was rooted to the earth. The corpse made as though it would step from its narrow bed, and the sexton fled, shrieking, through the vaults. The corpse followed, its long white shroud floating like a meteor in the dim light of the lamp, which, in his haste, he had forgotten. It was not until he reached his own door that he had sufficient courage to look behind him, and then, when he perceived no trace of his pursuer, the excitement which had sustained him so far subsided, and he sank senseless to the earth.

In the meantime Richmuth von Aducht, who had slept scarcely a moment since the death of his dear wife, was surprised by the voice of his old man-servant, who rapped loudly at his chamber door, and told him to awake and come forth, for his mistress had arisen from the dead, and was then at the gate of the courtyard.

"Bah!" said he, rather pettishly, "go thy ways, Hans; you dream, or are mad, or drunk. What you see is quite impossible. I should as soon believe my old grey mare had got into the garret as that my wife was at the courtyard gate."

Trot, trot, trot, trot, suddenly resounded high over his head.

"What's that?" asked he of his servant.

"I know not," replied the man, "an' it be not your old grey mare in the garret."

They descended in haste to the courtyard, and looked up to the window of the attic. Lo and behold! there was indeed the grey mare with her head poked out of the window, gazing down with her great eyes on her master and his man, and seeming to enjoy very much her exalted station, and their surprise at it.

Knock, knock, knock went the rapper of the street gate.

"It is my wife!" "It is my mistress!" exclaimed master and man in the same breath.

The door was quickly unfastened, and there, truly, stood the mistress of the mansion, enveloped in her shroud.

"Are you alive or dead?" exclaimed the astonished husband.

"Alive, my dear, but very cold," she murmured faintly, her teeth chattering the while, as those of one in a fever chill; "help me to my chamber."

He caught her in his arms and covered her with kisses. Then he bore her to her chamber, and called up the whole house to welcome and assist her. She suffered a little from fatigue and fright, but in a few days was very much recovered.

The thing became the talk of the town, and hundreds flocked daily to see, not alone the lady that was rescued from the grave in so remarkable a manner, but also the grey mare which had so strangely contrived to get into the garret.

The excellent lady lived long and happily with her husband, and at her death was laid once more in her old resting-place. The grey mare, after resting in the garret three days, was got down by means of scaffolding, safe and sound. She survived her mistress for some time, and was a general favourite in the city, and when she died her skin was stuffed, and placed in the arsenal as a curiosity. The sexton went mad with the fright he had sustained, and in a short time entered that bourn whence he had so unintentionally recovered the burgomaster's wife.

Not only was this memorable circumstance commemorated in the Church of the Apostles, but it was also celebrated in *bassi relievi* figures on the walls of the burgomaster's residence—the sign of the Parroquet in the New Marckt. The searcher after antiquities will, however, look in vain for either. They are not now to be found. Modern taste has defaced the porch where stood the one, and erected a shapeless structure on the site of the other.

THE WATER SPIRIT.

ABOUT the middle of the sixteenth century, when
Zündorf was no larger than it is at present, there
lived at the end of the village, hard by the church,
one of that useful class of women termed midwives.
She was an honest, industrious creature, and what
with ushering the new-born into life, and then
assisting in making garments for them, she contrived to creep through the world in comfort, if not
in complete happiness.

The summer had been one of unusual drought,
and the winter, of a necessity, one of uncommon
scarcity, so that when the spring arrived the good
woman had less to do than at any period in the
preceding seven years. In fact she was totally
unemployed. As she mused one night, lying abed,
on the matter, she was startled by a sharp, quick
knock at the door of her cottage. She hesitated for
a moment to answer the call, but the knocking was
repeated with more violence than before. This
caused her to spring out of bed without more delay,
and hasten to ascertain the wish of her impatient

visitor. She opened the door in the twinkling of an eye, and a man, tall of stature, enveloped in a large dark cloak, stood before her.

"My wife is in need of thee," he said to her abruptly; "her time is come. Follow me."

"Nay, but the night is dark, sir," replied she. "Whither do you desire me to follow?"

"Close at hand," he answered, as abruptly as before. "Be ye quick and follow me."

"I will but light my lamp and place it in the lantern," said the woman. "It will not cost me more than a moment's delay."

"It needs not, it needs not," repeated the stranger; "the spot is close by. I know every foot of ground. Follow, follow!"

There was something so imperative, and at the same time so irresistible, in the manner of the man that she said not another word, but drawing her warm cloak about her head followed him at once. Ere she was aware of the course he had taken, so dark was the night, and so wrapt up was she in the cloak and in her meditations, she found herself on the bank of the Rhine, just opposite to the low fertile islet which bears the same name as the village, and lies at a little distance from the shore.

"How is this, good sir?" she exclaimed, in a tone of surprise and alarm. "You have missed the way—you have left your road. Here is no further path."

"Silence, and follow," were the only words he spoke in reply ; but they were uttered in such a manner as to show her at once that her best course was obedience.

They were now at the edge of the mighty stream ; the rushing waters washed their feet. The poor woman would fain have drawn back, but she could not, such was the preternatural power exercised over her by her companion.

"Fear not; follow!" he spoke again, in a kinder tone, as the current kissed the hem of her garments.

He took the lead of her. The waters opened to receive him. A wall of crystal seemed built up on either side of the vista. He plunged into its depths; she followed. The wild wave gurgled over them, and they were walking over the shiny pebbles and glittering sands which strewed the bed of the river.

And now a change came over her indeed. She had left all on earth in the thick darkness of a starless spring night, yet all around her was lighted up like a mellow harvest eve, when the sun shines refulgent through masses of golden clouds on the smiling pastures and emerald meadows of the west. She looked up, but she could see no cause for this illumination. She looked down, and her search was equally unsuccessful. She seemed to herself to traverse a great hall of surpassing transparency, lighted up by a light resembling that given out by a huge globe of ground glass. Her conductor still preceded her. They approached a little door. The chamber within it contained the object of their solicitude. On a couch of mother-of-pearl, surrounded by sleeping fishes and drowsy syrens, who could evidently afford her no assistance, lay the sick lady.

"Here is my wife," spake the stranger, as they entered this chamber. "Take her in hand at once, and hark ye, mother, heed that she has no injury through thee, or——"

With these words he waved his hand, and, preceded by the obedient inhabitants of the river, who had until then occupied the chamber, left the apartment.

The midwife approached her patient with fear and trembling; she knew not what to anticipate. What was her surprise to perceive that the stranger was like any other lady. The business in hand was soon finished, and midwife and patient began to talk together, as women will when an opportunity is afforded them.

"It surprises me much," quoth the former, "to see such a handsome young lady as you are buried down here in the bottom of the river. Do you never visit the land? What a loss it is to you!"

"Hush, hush!" interposed the Triton's lady, placing her forefinger significantly on her lips; "you peril your life by talking thus without guard.

Go to the door; look out, that you may see if there be any listeners, then I will tell something to surprise you."

The midwife did as she was directed. There was no living being within earshot.

" Now, listen," said the lady.

The midwife was all ear.

" I am a woman; a Christian woman like yourself," she continued, " though I am here now in the home of my husband, who is the spirit of these mighty waters."

" God be praised!" ejaculated her auditor.

" My father was the lord of the hamlet of Rheidt, a little above Lülsdorf, and I lived there in peace and happiness during my girlish days. I had nothing to desire, as every wish was gratified by him as soon as it was formed. However, as I grew to womanhood I felt that my happiness had departed. I knew not whither it had gone, or why, but gone it was. I felt restless, melancholy, wretched. I wanted, in short, something to love, but that I found out since. Well, one day a merry-making took place in the village, and every one was present at it. We danced on the green sward which stretches to the margin of the river; for that day I forgot my secret grief, and was among the gayest of the gay. They made me the queen of the feast, and I had the homage of all. As the sun was going down in glory in the far west, melting the masses of clouds into liquid gold, a stranger of a noble mien appeared in the midst of our merry circle. He was garbed in green from head to heel, and seemed to have crossed the river, for the hem of his rich riding-cloak was dripping with wet. No one knew him, no one cared to inquire who he was, and his presence rather awed than rejoiced us. He was, however, a stranger, and he was welcome. When I tell you that stranger is my husband, you may imagine the rest. When the dance then on foot was ended, he asked my hand. I could not refuse it if I would, but I would not if I could. He was irresistible. We danced and danced until the earth seemed to reel around us. I could perceive, however, even in the whirl of tumultuous delight which forced me onward, that we neared the water's edge in every successive figure. We stood at length on the verge of the stream. The current caught my dress, the villagers shrieked aloud, and rushed to rescue me from the river.

"'Follow!' said my partner, plunging as he spoke into the foaming flood.

"I followed. Since then I have lived with him here. It is now a century since, but he has communicated to me a portion of his own immortality, and I know not age, neither do I dread death any longer. He is good and kind to me, though fearful to others. The only cause of complaint I have is his invariable custom of destroying every babe to which I give birth on the third day after my delivery. He says it is for my sake, and for their sakes, that he does so, and he knows best."

She sighed heavily as she said this.

"And now," resumed the lady, "I must give you one piece of advice, which, if you would keep your life, you must implicitly adopt. My husband will return. Be on your guard, I bid you. He will offer you gold, he will pour out the countless treasures he possesses before you, he will proffer you diamonds and pearls and priceless gems, but—heed well what I say to you—take nothing more from him than you would from any other person. Take the exact sum you are wont to receive on earth, and take not a kreutzer more, or your life is not worth a moment's purchase. It is forfeit."

"He must be a cruel being, indeed," ejaculated the midwife. "God deliver me from this dread and great danger."

"See you yon sealed vessels?" spake the lady, without seeming to heed her fright, or hear her ejaculations.

The midwife looked, and saw ranged on an upper shelf of the apartment about a dozen small pots, like pipkins, all fast sealed, and labelled in unknown characters.

"These pots," pursued she, "contain the souls of those who have been, like you, my attendants in childbirth, but who, for slighting the advice I gave them, as I now give you, and permitting a spirit of unjust gain to take possession of their hearts, were deprived of life by my husband. Heed well what I say. He comes. Be silent and discreet."

As she spake the water spirit entered. He first asked his wife how she did, and his tones were like the rushing sound of a current heard far off. Learning from her own lips that all was well with her, he turned to the midwife and thanked her most graciously.

"Now, come with me," he said, "I must pay thee for thy services."

She followed him from the sick-chamber to the treasury of the palace. It was a spacious crystal vault, lighted up, like the rest of the palace, from without, but within it was resplendent with treasures of all kinds. He led her to a huge heap of shining gold which ran the whole length of the chamber.

"Here," said he, "take what you will. I put no stint upon you."

The trembling woman picked up a single piece of the smallest coin she could find upon the heap.

"This is my fee," she spake. "I ask no more than a fair remuneration for my labour."

The water spirit's brow blackened like a tempestuous night, and he showed his green teeth for a moment as if in great ire, but the feeling, whatever it was, appeared to pass away as quickly as it came, and he led her to a huge heap of pearls.

"Here," he said, "take what you will. Perhaps you like these better? They are all pearls of great price, or may be you would wish for some memento of me. Take what you will."

But she still declined to take anything more, although he tempted her with all his treasures. She had not forgotten the advice of her patient.

"I desire nothing more from you, great prince as you are, than I receive from one of my own condition." This was her uniform answer to his entreaties—

"I thank you, but I may not take aught beside my due."

"If," said he, after a short pause, "you had taken more than your due, you would have perished at my hands. And now," proceeded the spirit, "you shall home, but first take this. Fear not."

As he spake he dipped his hand in the heap of gold and poured forth a handful into her lap.

"Use that," he continued, "use it without fear. It is my gift. No evil will come of it; I give you my royal word."

He beckoned her onward without waiting for her reply, and they were walking once again through the corridors of the palace.

"Adieu!" he said, waving his hand to her, "adieu!"

Darkness fell around her in a moment. In a moment more she awoke, as from a dream, in her warm bed.

PETER KLAUS.

Peter Klaus, a goatherd of Sittendorf, who tended
herds on the Kyffhauser mountain, used to let them
rest of an evening in a spot surrounded by an old
wall, where he always counted them to see if they
were all right. For some days he noticed that one
of his finest goats, as they came to this spot,
vanished, and never returned to the herd till late.
He watched him more closely, and at length saw
him slip through a rent in the wall. He followed
him, and caught him in a cave, feeding sumptuously
upon the grains of oats which fell one by one from
the roof. He looked up, shook his head at the
shower of oats, but, with all his care, could discover
nothing further. At length he heard overhead the
neighing and stamping of some mettlesome horses,
and concluded that the oats must have fallen from
their mangers.

While the goatherd stood there, wondering about
these horses in a totally uninhabited mountain, a
lad came and made signs to him to follow him
silently. Peter ascended some steps, and, crossing

a walled court, came to a glade surrounded by rocky cliffs, into which a sort of twilight made its way through the thick-leaved branches. Here he found twelve grave old knights playing at skittles, at a well-levelled and fresh plot of grass. Peter was silently appointed to set up the ninepins for them.

At first his knees knocked together as he did this, while he marked, with half-stolen glances, the long beards and goodly paunches of the noble knights. By degrees, however, he grew more confident, and looked at everything about him with a steady gaze—nay, at last, he ventured so far as to take a draught from a pitcher which stood near him, the fragrance of which appeared to him delightful. He felt quite revived by the draught, and as often as he felt at all tired, received new strength from application to the inexhaustible pitcher. But at length sleep overcame him.

When he awoke, he found himself once more in the enclosed green space, where he was accustomed to leave his goats. He rubbed his eyes, but could discover neither dog nor goats, and stared with surprise at the height to which the grass had grown, and at the bushes and trees, which he never remembered to have noticed. Shaking his head, he proceeded along the roads and paths which he was accustomed to traverse daily with his herd, but could nowhere see any traces of his goats. Below him he saw Sittendorf; and at last he descended with quickened step, there to make inquiries after his herd.

The people whom he met at his entrance to the town were unknown to him, and dressed and spoke differently from those whom he had known there. Moreover, they all stared at him when he inquired about his goats, and began stroking their chins. At last, almost involuntarily, he did the same, and found to his great astonishment that his beard had grown to be a foot long. He began now to think himself and the world altogether bewitched, and yet he felt sure that the mountain from which he had descended was the Kyffhauser; and the houses here, with their fore-courts, were all familiar to him. Moreover, several lads whom he heard telling the name of the place to a traveller called it Sittendorf.

Shaking his head, he proceeded into the town straight to his own house. He found it sadly fallen to decay. Before it lay a strange herd-boy in tattered garments, and near him an old worn-out dog, which growled and showed his teeth at Peter when he called him. He entered by the opening, which had formerly been closed by a door, but found all within so desolate and empty that he staggered out again like a drunkard, and called his wife and children. No one heard; no voice answered him.

Women and children now began to surround the

strange old man, with the long hoary beard, and to contend with one another in inquiring of him what he wanted. He thought it so ridiculous to make inquiries of strangers, before his own house, after his wife and children, and still more so, after himself, that he mentioned the first neighbour whose name occurred to him, Kirt Stiffen. All were silent, and looked at one another, till an old woman said—

"He has left here these twelve years. He lives at Sachsenberg; you 'll hardly get there to-day."

" Velten Maier ? "

"God help him ! " said an old crone leaning on a crutch. "He has been confined these fifteen years in the house, which he 'll never leave again."

He recognised, as he thought, his suddenly aged neighbour ; but he had lost all desire of asking any more questions. At last a brisk young woman, with a boy of a twelvemouth old in her arms, and with a little girl holding her hand, made her way through the gaping crowd, and they looked for all the world like his wife and children.

" What is your name ? " said Peter, astonished.

" Maria."

" And your father ? "

" God have mercy on him, Peter Klaus. It is twenty years since we sought him day and night on the Kyffhauser, when his goats came home without him. I was only seven years old when it happened."

The goatherd could no longer contain himself.

"I am Peter Klaus," he cried, "and no other," and he took the babe from his daughter's arms.

All stood like statues for a minute, till one and then another began to cry—

"Here 's Peter Klaus come back again! Welcome, neighbour, welcome, after twenty years; welcome, Peter Klaus!"

THE LEGEND OF RHEINECK.

Graf Ulric von Rheineck was a very wild youth.
Recklessly and without consideration did he plunge
into every excess. Dissipation grew to be the habit
of his life, and no sensual indulgence did he deny
himself which could be procured by any means
whatever. Amply provided for as he was, the
revenues of his wide possessions, which comprehended Thal Rheineck, and the adjacent country, to
the shore of the Rhine, and as far as the mouth of
the Aar, were soon discovered to be insufficient for
all his absorbing necessities. One by one his broad
lands were alienated from him, piece after piece of
that noble possession fell from his house, until
finally he found himself without a single inch of
ground which he could call his own, save the small
and unproductive spot on which Rheineck stood.
This he had no power to transfer, or perhaps it
would have gone with the remainder. The castle
had fallen sadly into disrepair, through his protracted absence from home, and his continual
neglect of it,—indeed there was scarcely a habitable

room within its precincts, and he now had no means to make it the fitting abode of any one, still less of a nobleman of his rank and consequence. All without, as well as all within it, was desolate and dreary to the last degree. The splendid garden, previously the pride of his ancestors, was overrun with weeds, and tangled with parasites and creepers. The stately trees, which once afforded shelter and shade, as well as fruits of the finest quality and rarest kinds, were all dying or withered, or had their growth obstructed by destroying plants. The outer walls were in a ruinous condition, the fortifications were everywhere fallen into decay, and the alcoves and summer-houses had dropped down, or were roofless, and exposed to the weather. It was a cheerless prospect to contemplate, but he could not now help himself, even if he had the will to do so. Day after day the same scene of desolation presented itself to his eyes, night after night did the same cheerless chamber present itself to his view. It was his own doing. That he could not deny, and bitterly he rued it. To crown his helplessness and misery, his vassals and domestic servants abandoned him by degrees, one after another, and at last he was left entirely alone in the house of his fathers—a hermit in that most dismal of all solitudes, the desolate scene of one's childish, one's happiest recollections.

One evening about twilight, as he sat at the

outer gate, looking sadly on the broad, bright river which flowed calmly beneath, he became aware of the presence of a stranger, who seemed to toil wearily up the steep acclivity on the summit of which the castle is situated. The stranger—an unusual sight within those walls then—soon reached the spot where Ulric sat, and, greeting the youth in the fashion of the times, prayed him for shelter during the night, and refreshment after his most painful journey.

"I am," quoth the stranger, " a poor pilgrim on my way to Cologne, where, by the merits of the three wise kings—to whose shrine I am bound—I hope to succeed in the object of my journey."

Graf Ulric von Rheineck at once accorded him the hospitality he required, for though he had but scant cheer for himself, and nought of comfort to bestow, he had still some of the feeling of a gentleman left in him.

"I am alone here now," said he to the pilgrim, with a deep sigh. "I am myself as poor as Job. Would it were not so! My menials have left me to provide for themselves, as I can no longer provide for them. 'Twas ever the way of the world, and I blame them not for it. The last departed yesterday. He was an old favourite of my father's, and he once thought that he would not leave my service but with his life. We must now look to ourselves, however,—at least so he said. But that has nothing to do with the matter, so enter, my friend."

They entered. By their joint exertions a simple evening meal was soon made ready, and speedily spread forth on a half-rotten plank, their only table.

"I have no better to offer you," observed the young Count, "but I offer you what I have with right goodwill. Eat, if you can, and be merry."

They ate in silence, neither speaking during the meal.

"Surely," said the pilgrim, when it was over,— "surely it may not be that the extensive cellars of this great castle contain not a single cup of wine for the weary wayfarer."

The Count was at once struck by the idea. It seemed to him as if he had never thought of it before, though in reality he had ransacked every corner of the cellars more than once.

"Come, let us go together and try," continued the pilgrim; "it will go hard with us if we find nought to wash down our homely fare."

Accompanied by his persuasive guest, the Count descended to the vaults, where the wines of Rheineck had been stored for ages. Dark and dreary did they seem to him. A chill fell on his soul as he strode over the mouldy floor.

"Here," said the pilgrim, with great glee,—"here, here! Look ye, my master, look ye! See! I have found a cup of the best."

The Count passed into a narrow cellar whither the pilgrim had preceded him. There stood his companion beside a full butt of burgundy, holding in his hand a massive silver cup, foaming over with the generous beverage, and with the other he pointed exultingly to his prize. The scene seemed like a dream to Ulric. The place was wholly unknown to him. The circumstances were most extraordinary. He mused a moment, but he knew not what to do in the emergency.

"We will enjoy ourselves here," said the pilgrim. "Here, on this very spot, shall we make us merry! Ay, here, beside this noble butt of burgundy. See, 'tis the best vintage! Let us be of good cheer!"

The Count and his boon companion sat down on two empty casks, and a third served them for a table. They plied the brimming beakers with right goodwill; they drank with all their might and main. The Count became communicative, and talked about his private affairs, as men in liquor will. The pilgrim, however, preserved a very discreet silence, only interrupting by an occasional interjection of delight, or an opportune word of encouragement to his garrulous friend.

"I'll tell you what," began the pilgrim, when the Count had concluded his tale,—"I'll tell you what. Listen: I know a way to get you out of your difficulties, to rid you of all your embarrassments."

The Count looked at him incredulously for a moment; his eye could not keep itself steady for a longer space of time. There was something in the pilgrim's glance as it met his that greatly dissipated his unbelief, and he inquired of him how these things could be brought about.

" But, mayhap," continued the pilgrim, apparently disregarding the manifest change in his companion's impressions regarding him,—" mayhap you would be too faint-hearted to follow my advice if I gave it you."

The Count sprang on his feet in a trice, and half-unsheathed his sword to avenge this taunt on his manhood, but the pilgrim looked so unconcerned, and evinced so little emotion at this burst of anger, that the action and its result were merely momentary. Ulric resumed his seat, and the pilgrim proceeded—

" You tell me that you once heard from your father, who had it from his father, that your great-grandfather, in the time when this castle was beleaguered by the Emperor Conrad, buried a vast treasure in some part of it, but which part his sudden death prevented him from communicating to his successor ?"

The Count nodded acquiescence.

" It is even so," he said.

" In Eastern lands have I learned to discover where concealed treasures are hidden," pursued the pilgrim; "and—— "

The Count grasped him by the hand.

"Find them," he cried,—"find them for me, and a full half is thine! Oh, there is gold, and there are diamonds and precious stones of all kinds. They are there in abundance. My father said so! 'Tis true, 'tis true! Find them, find them, and then shall this old hall ring once more with the voice of merriment. Then shall we live! ay, we shall live! that we shall."

The pilgrim did not attempt to interrupt his ecstasies, or to interpose between him and the excess of his glee, but let him excite himself to the highest pitch with pictures of the pleasing future, until they had acquired almost the complexion of fact and the truth of reality for his distracted imagination. When he had exhausted himself, the wily tempter resumed—

"Oh yes, I know it all. I know where the treasure is. I can put your finger on it if I like. I was present when the old man buried it in the——"

"You present!" exclaimed Ulric, his hair standing on end with horror, for he had no doubts of the truth of the mysterious stranger's statements,—"you present!"

"Yes," resumed the pilgrim; "I was present."

"But he is full a hundred years dead and buried," continued the Count.

"No matter for that, no matter for that," replied

the guest abruptly; "many and many a time have we drunk and feasted and revelled together in this vault—ay, in this very vault."

The Count knew not what to think, still less what to reply to this information. He could not fail to perceive its improbability, drunk as he was, but still he could not, for the life of him, discredit it.

"But," added the pilgrim, "trouble not yourself with that at present which you have not the power to comprehend, and speculate not on my proceedings, but listen to my words, and follow my advice, if you will that I should serve you in the matter."

The Count was silent when the stranger proceeded.

"This is Walpurgis night," he said. "All the spirits of earth and sea and sky are now abroad on their way to the Brocken. Hell is broke loose, you know, for its annual orgies on that mountain. When the castle clock tolls twelve go you into the chapel, and proceed to the graves of your grandfather, your great-grandfather, and your great-great-grandfather; take from their coffins the bones of their skeletons—take them all, mind ye. One by one you must then remove them into the moonlight, outside the walls of the building, and there lay them softly on the bit of green sward which faces to the south. This done, you must next place them in the order in which they lay in their last resting-place. When you have completed that task, you must return to the chapel, and in their coffins you will find the treasures of your forefathers. No one has power over an atom of them, until the bones of those who in spirit keep watch and ward over them shall have been removed from their guardianship. So long as they rest on them, or oversee them, to the dead they belong. It is a glorious prize. 'Twill be the making of you, man, for ever!"

Ulric was shocked at the proposal. To desecrate the graves of his fathers was a deed which made him shudder, and, bad as he was, the thought filled him with the greatest horror, but the temptation was irresistible.

At the solemn hour of midnight he proceeded to the chapel, accompanied by the pilgrim. He entered the holy place with trembling, for his heart misgave him. The pilgrim stayed without, apparently anxious and uneasy as to the result of the experiment about to be made. To all the solicitations of the Count for assistance in his task he turned a deaf ear; nothing that he could say could induce him to set foot within the chapel walls.

Ulric opened the graves in the order in which they were situated, beginning with the one first from the door of the chapel. He proceeded to remove the rotting remains from their mouldering coffins. One by one did he bear their bleached bones into the open air, as he had been instructed, and placed them as they had lain in their narrow beds, under the pale moonbeams, on the plot of green sward facing the south, outside the chapel walls. The coffins were all cleared of their tenants, except one which stood next to the altar, at the upper end of the aisle. Ulric approached this also to perform the wretched task he had set himself, the thoughts of the treasure he should become possessed of but faintly sustaining his sinking soul in the fearful operation. Removing the lid of this last resting-place of mortality, his heart failed him at the sight he beheld. There lay extended, as if in deep sleep, the corpse of a fair child, fresh and comely, as if it still felt and breathed and had lusty being. The weakness Ulric felt was but momentary. His companion called aloud to him to finish his task quickly, or the hour would have passed when his labour would avail him. As he touched the corpse of the infant the body stirred as if it had sensation. He shrank back in horror as the fair boy rose gently in his coffin, and at length stood upright within it.

"Bring back yon bones," said the phantom babe,— "bring back yon bones; let them rest in peace in the last home of their fathers. The curse of the dead will be on you otherwise. Back! back! bring them back ere it be too late."

The corpse sank down in the coffin again as it uttered these words, and Ulric saw a skeleton lying in its place. Shuddering, he averted his gaze, and turned it towards the chapel door, where he had left his companion. But, horror upon horror! as he looked he saw the long, loose, dark outer garment fall from the limbs of the pilgrim. He saw his form dilate and expand in height and in breadth, until his head seemed to touch the pale crescent moon, and his bulk shut out from view all beyond itself. He saw his eyes firing and flaming like globes of lurid light, and he saw his hair and beard converted into one mass of living flame. The fiend stood revealed in all his hideous deformity.

His hands were stretched forth to fasten on the hapless Count, who, with vacillating step, like the bird under the eye of the basilisk, involuntarily, though with a perfect consciousness of his awful situation, and the fearful fate which awaited him, every moment drew nearer and nearer to him. The victim reached the chapel door—he felt all the power of that diabolical fascination—another step and he would be in the grasp of the fiend who grinned to clutch him. But the fair boy who spoke from the grave suddenly appeared once more, and, flinging himself between the wretched Count and the door, obstructed his further progress.

"Avaunt, foul fiend!" spake the child, and his voice was like a trumpet-note; "avaunt to hell! He is no longer thine. Thou hast no power over him. Your hellish plot has failed. He is free, and shall live and repent."

As he said this he threw his arms around Ulric,

and the Count became, as it were, at once surrounded by a beatific halo, which lighted up the chapel like day. The fiend fled howling like a wild beast disappointed of its prey.

The remains of his ancestors were again replaced in their coffins by the Count, long ere the morning broke, and on their desecrated graves he poured forth a flood of repentant tears. With the dawn of day he quitted the castle of Rheineck. It is said that he traversed the land in the garb of a lowly mendicant, subsisting on the alms of the charitable, and it is likewise told that he did penance at every holy shrine from Cologne to Rome, whither he was bound to obtain absolution for his sins. Years afterwards he was found dead at the foot of the ancient altar in the ruined chapel. The castle went to ruin, and for centuries nought ever dwelt within its walls save the night-birds and the beasts of prey.

Of the original structure the ruins of one old tower are all that now remain. It is still firmly believed by the peasants of the neighbourhood, that in the first and the last quarter of the moon the spirit of Ulric, the last of the old lords of Rheineck, still sweeps around the ruin at the hour of midnight, and is occasionally visible to belated wanderers.

THE CELLAR OF THE OLD KNIGHTS IN THE KYFFHAUSER.

THERE was a poor, but worthy, and withal very merry, fellow at Tilleda, who was once put to the expense of a christening, and, as luck would have it, it was the eighth. According to the custom of the time, he was obliged to give a plain feast to the child's sponsors. The wine of the country which he put before his guests was soon exhausted, and they began to call for more.

" Go," said the merry father of the newly baptized child to his eldest daughter, a handsome girl of sixteen,—" go, and get us better wine than this out of the cellar."

" Out of what cellar ? "

" Why, out of the great wine-cellar of the old Knights in the Kyffhauser, to be sure," said her father jokingly.

The simple-minded girl did as he told her, and taking a small pitcher in her hand went to the mountain. In the middle of the mountain she found an aged housekeeper, dressed in a very old-fashioned style, with a large bundle of keys at her girdle, sitting at the ruined entrance of an immense cellar. The girl was struck dumb with amazement, but the old woman said very kindly—

"Of a surety you want to draw wine out of the Knights' cellar?"

"Yes," said the girl timidly, "but I have no money."

"Never mind that," said the old woman; "come with me, and you shall have wine for nothing, and better wine too than your father ever tasted."

So the two went together through the half-blocked-up entrance, and as they went along the old woman made the girl tell her how affairs were going on at that time in Tilleda.

"For once," said she, "when I was young, and good-looking as you are, the Knights stole me away in the night-time, and brought me through a hole in the ground from the very house in Tilleda which now belongs to your father. Shortly before that they had carried away by force from Kelbra, in broad daylight, the four beautiful damsels who occasionally still ride about here on horses richly caparisoned, and then disappear again. As for me, as soon as I grew old, they made me their butler, and I have been so ever since."

They had now reached the cellar door, which the old woman opened. It was a very large roomy cellar, with barrels ranged along both sides. The old woman rapped against the barrels—some were quite full, some were only half full. She took the little pitcher, drew it full of wine, and said—

"There, take that to your father, and as often as you have a feast in your house you may come here again; but, mind, tell nobody but your father where you get the wine from. Mind, too, you must never sell any of it—it costs nothing, and for nothing you must give it away. Let any one but come here for wine to make a profit off it and his last bread is baked."

The girl took the wine to her father, whose guests were highly delighted with it, and sadly puzzled to think where it came from, and ever afterwards, when there was a little merry-making in the house, would the girl fetch wine from the Kyffhauser in her little pitcher. But this state of things did not continue long. The neighbours wondered where so poor a man contrived to get such delicious wine that there was none like it in the whole country round. The father said not a word to any one, and neither did his daughter.

Opposite to them, however, lived the publican who sold adulterated wine. He had once tasted the Old Knights' wine, and thought to himself that one might mix it with ten times the quantity of water and sell it for a good price after all. Accordingly, when the girl went for the fourth time with her little pitcher to the Kyffhauser, he crept after her, and concealed himself among the bushes, where he watched until he saw her come out of the entrance which led to the cellar, with her pitcher filled with wine.

On the following evening he himself went to the mountain, pushing before him in a wheelbarrow the largest empty barrel he could procure. This he thought of filling with the choicest wine in the cellar, and in the night rolling it down the mountain, and in this way he intended to come every day, as long as there was any wine left in the cellar.

When, however, he came to the place where he had the day before seen the entrance to the cellar, it grew all of a sudden totally dark. The wind began to howl fearfully, and a monster threw him, his barrow, and empty butt, from one ridge of rocks to another, and he kept falling lower and lower, until at last he fell into a cemetery.

There he saw before him a coffin covered with black, and his wife and four of her gossips, whom he knew well by their dress and figures, were following a bier. His fright was so great that he swooned away.

After some hours he came to himself again, and saw, to his horror, that he was still in the dimly lighted vaults, and heard just above his head the well-known town clock of Tilleda strike twelve, and thereby he knew that it was midnight, and that he was then under the church, in the burying-place of the town. He was more dead than alive, and scarcely dared to breathe.

Presently there came a monk, who led him up a long, long flight of steps, opened a door, placed, without speaking, a piece of gold in his hand, and deposited him at the foot of the mountain. It was a cold frosty night. By degrees the publican recovered himself, and crept, without barrel or wine, back to his own home. The clock struck one as he reached the door. He immediately took to his bed, and in three days was a dead man, and the piece of gold which the wizard monk had given him was expended on his funeral.

THE FISHERMAN AND HIS WIFE.

THERE was once a fisherman who lived with his
wife in a ditch close by the seaside.   The fisherman
used to go out all day long a-fishing, and one day
as he sat on the shore with his rod, looking at the
shining water and watching his line, all of sudden
his float was dragged away deep under the sea.   In
drawing it up he pulled a great fish out of the water.
The fish said to him—

"Pray let me live.   I am not a real fish.   I am
an enchanted prince.   Put me in the water again
and let me go."

"Oh!" said the man, "you need not make so
many words about the matter.   I wish to have
nothing to do with a fish that can talk, so swim
away as soon as you please."

Then he put him back into the water, and the
fish darted straight down to the bottom, and left a
long streak of blood behind him.

When the fisherman went home to his wife in
the ditch, he told her how he had caught a great
fish, and how it had told him it was an enchanted

prince, and that on hearing it speak he had let it go again.

"Did you not ask it for anything?" said the wife.

"No," said the man; "what should I ask it for?"

"Ah!" said the wife, "we live very wretchedly here in this nasty miserable ditch, do go back and tell the fish we want a little cottage."

The fisherman did not much like the business; however, he went to the sea, and when he came there the water looked all yellow and green. He sat at the water's edge and said—

> "O man of the sea,
> Come listen to me,
> For Alice my wife,
> The plague of my life,
> Hath sent me to beg a boon of thee!"

Then the fish came swimming to him and said— "Well, what does she want?"

"Ah!" answered the fisherman, "my wife says that when I had caught you, I ought to have asked you for something before I let you go again. She does not like living any longer in the ditch, and wants a little cottage.

"Go home, then," said the fish; "she is in the cottage already."

So the man went home, and saw his wife standing at the door of a cottage.

"Come in, come in," said she. "Is not this much better than the ditch?"

There was a parlour, a bedchamber, and a kitchen ; and behind the cottage there was a little garden with all sorts of flowers and fruits, and a courtyard full of ducks and chickens.

"Ah," said the fisherman, "how happily we shall live ! "

" We will try to do so, at least," said his wife.

Everything went right for a week or two, and then Dame Alice said—

"Husband, there is not room enough in this cottage, the courtyard and garden are a great deal too small.   I should like to have a large stone castle to live in, so go to the fish again and tell him to give us a castle."

"Wife," said the fisherman, "I don't like to go to him again, for perhaps he will be angry.   We ought to be content with the cottage."

"Nonsense ! " said the wife, " he will do it very willingly.   Go along and try."

The fisherman went, but his heart was very heavy, and when he came to the sea it looked blue and gloomy, though it was quite calm.   He went close to it, and said—

<blockquote>

"O man of the sea,
Come listen to me,
For Alice my wife,
The plague of my life,
Hath sent me to beg a boon of thee ! "

</blockquote>

" Well, what does she want now ? " said the fish.

"Ah!" said the man very sorrowfully, "my wife wants to live in a stone castle."

"Go home, then," said the fish; "she is standing at the door of it already."

Away went the fisherman, and found his wife standing before a great castle.

"See," said she, "is not this grand?"

With that they went into the house together, and found a great many servants there, the rooms all richly furnished, and full of golden chairs and tables; and behind the castle was a garden, and a wood half a mile long, full of sheep, goats, hares, and deer; and in the courtyard were stables and cow-houses.

"Well," said the man, "now will we live contented and happy for the rest of our lives."

"Perhaps we may," said the wife, "but let us consider and sleep upon it before we make up our minds;" so they went to bed.

The next morning when Dame Alice awoke it was broad daylight, and she jogged the fisherman with her elbow, and said—

"Get up, husband, and bestir yourself, for we must be king of all the land."

"Wife, wife," said the man, "why should we wish to be king? I will not be king."

"Then I will," said Alice.

"But, wife," answered the fisherman, "how can you be king? The fish cannot make you king."

"Husband," said she, "say no more about it, but go and try. I will be king."

So the man went away quite sorrowful, to think that his wife should want to be king. The sea looked a dark grey colour, and was covered with foam, as he called the fish to come and help him.

"Well, what would she have now?" asked the fish.

"Alas!" said the man, "my wife wants to be king."

"Go home," said the fish, "she is king already."

Then the fisherman went home, and as he came close to the palace he saw a troop of soldiers, and heard the sound of drums and trumpets; and when he entered, he saw his wife sitting on a high throne of gold and diamonds, with a golden crown upon her head, and on each side of her stood six beautiful maidens.

"Well, wife," said the fisherman, "are you king!"

"Yes," said she, "I am king."

When he had looked at her for a long time, he said—

"Ah! wife, what a fine thing it is to be king! now we shall never have anything more to wish for."

"I don't know how that may be," said she. "Never is a long time. I am king, 'tis true; but I begin to be tired of it, and I think I should like to be emperor."

"Alas! wife, why should you wish to be emperor?" said the fisherman.

"Husband," said she, "go to the fish. I say I will be emperor."

"Ah! wife," replied the fisherman, "the fish cannot make an emperor; and I should not like to ask for such a thing."

"I am king," said Alice; "and you are my slave, so go directly."

So the fisherman was obliged to go, and he muttered as he went along—

"This will come to no good. It is too much to ask. The fish will be tired at last, and then we shall repent of what we have done."

He soon arrived at the sea, and the water was quite black and muddy, and a mighty whirlwind blew over it; but he went to the shore, and repeated the words he had used before.

"What would she have now?" inquired the fish.

"She wants to be emperor," replied the fisherman.

"Go home," said the fish, "she is emperor already."

So he went home again, and as he came near, he saw his wife sitting on a very lofty throne made of solid gold, with a crown on her head, full two yards high; and on each side of her stood her guards and attendants in a row, ranged according to height, from the tallest giant to a little dwarf, no bigger than one's finger. And before her stood princes, and dukes, and earls; and the fisherman went up to her, and said—

"Wife, are you emperor?"

"Yes," said she, "I am emperor."

"Ah!" said the man, as he gazed on her, "what a fine thing it is to be emperor!"

"Husband," said she, "why should we stay at being emperor? We will be pope next."

"O wife, wife!" said he. "How can you be pope? There is but one pope at a time in Christendom."

"Husband," said she, "I will be pope this very day."

"But," replied the husband, "the fish cannot make you pope."

"What nonsense!" said she. "If he can make an emperor, he can make a pope; go and try him."

So the fisherman went; but when he came to the shore the wind was raging, the sea was tossed up and down like boiling water, and the ships were in the greatest distress and danced upon the waves most fearfully. In the middle of the sky there was a little blue; but towards the south it was all red, as if a dreadful storm was rising. The fisherman repeated the words, and the fish appeared before him.

"What does she want now?" asked the fish.

"My wife wants to be pope," said the fisherman.

"Go home," said the fish; "she is pope already."

Then the fisherman went home, and found his wife sitting on a throne, with three crowns on her head, while around stood all the pomp and power of the Church. On each side were two rows of burning lights of all sizes; the greatest as large as a tower, and the smallest no larger than a rush-light.

"Well, wife," said the fisherman, as he looked at all this grandeur, "are you pope?"

"Yes," said she; "I am pope."

"Well," replied he, "it is a grand thing to be pope; and now you must be content, for you can be nothing greater."

"I will consider about that," replied the wife.

Then they went to bed; but Dame Alice could not sleep all night for thinking what she should be next. At last morning came, and the sun rose.

"Ha!" thought she, as she looked at it through the window, "cannot I prevent the sun rising?"

At this she was very angry, and wakened her husband, and said—

"Husband, go to the fish, and tell him I want to be lord of the sun and moon."

The fisherman was half asleep; but the thought frightened him so much that he started and fell out of bed.

"Alas! wife," said he, "cannot you be content to be pope?"

"No," said she, "I am very uneasy, and cannot

bear to see the sun and moon rise without my leave. Go to the fish directly."

Then the man went trembling for fear. As he was going down to the shore a dreadful storm arose, so that the trees and the rocks shook, the heavens became black, the lightning played, the thunder rolled, and the sea was covered with black waves like mountains, with a white crown of foam upon them. The fisherman came to the shore, and said—

> "O man of the sea,
> Come listen to me,
> For Alice, my wife,
> The plague of my life,
> Hath sent me to beg a boon of thee!"

"What does she want now?" asked the fish.

"Ah!" said he, "she wants to be lord of the sun and moon."

"Go home," replied the fish, "to your ditch again."

And there they live to this very day.

THE MOUSE TOWER.

To the traveller who has traversed the delightful
environs of the Rhine, from the city of Mentz as far
as Coblentz, or from the clear waves of this old
Germanic stream gazed upon the grand creations of
Nature, all upon so magnificent a scale, the appearance of the old decayed tower which forms the
subject of the ensuing tradition forms no uninterest-
ing object. It rises before him as he mounts the
Rhine from the little island below Bingen, toward
the left shore. He listens to the old shipmaster as
he relates with earnest tone the wonderful story of
the tower, and, shuddering at the description of the
frightful punishment of priestly pride and cruelty,
exclaims in strong emotion—

"The Lord be with us!"

For, as the saying runs, it was about the year of
Our Lord 968, when Hatto II., Duke of the Ostro-
franks, surnamed Bonosus, Abbot of Fulda, a man
of singular skill and great spiritual endowments,
was elected Archbishop of Mentz. He was also a
harsh man, and being extremely avaricious, heaped

up treasure which he guarded with the utmost care.

It so happened, under his spiritual sway, that a cruel famine began to prevail in the city of Mentz and its adjacent parts, insomuch that in a short time numbers of the poorer people fell victims to utter want. Crowds of wretches were to be seen assembled before the Archbishop's palace in the act of beseeching with cries and prayers for some mitigation of their heavy lot.

But their harsh lord refused to afford relief out of his own substance, reproaching them at the same time as the authors of their own calamity by their indolence and want of economy. But the poor souls were mad for food, and in frightful and threatening accents cried out—

"Bread, bread!"

Fearing the result, Bishop Hatto ordered a vast number of hungry souls to range themselves in order in one of his empty barns under the pretence of supplying them with provisions. Then, having closed the doors, he commanded his minions to fire the place, in which all fell victims to the flames. When he heard the death shouts and shrieks of the unhappy poor, turning towards the menial parasites who abetted his crime he said—

"Hark you! how the mice squeak!"

But Heaven that witnessed the deed did not permit its vengeance to sleep. A strange and unheard of death was preparing to loose its terrors upon the sacrilegious prelate. For behold, there arose out of the yet warm ashes of the dead an innumerable throng of mice which were seen to approach the Bishop, and to follow him whithersoever he went. At length he flew into one of his steepest and highest towers, but the mice climbed over the walls. He closed every door and window, yet after him they came, piercing their way through the smallest nooks and crannies of the building. They poured in upon him, and covered him from head to foot, in numberless heaps. They bit, they scratched, they tortured his flesh, till they nearly devoured him. So great was the throng that the more his domestics sought to beat them off, the more keen and savagely, with increased numbers, did they return to the charge. Even where his name was found placed upon the walls and tapestries they gnawed it in their rage away.

In this frightful predicament the Bishop, finding that he could obtain no help on land, bethought of taking himself to the water. A tower was hastily erected upon the Rhine. He took ship and shut himself up there. Enclosed within double walls, and surrounded by water, he flattered himself that the rushing stream would effectually check the rage of his enemies. Here too, however, the vengeance of offended Heaven gave them entrance. Myriads of mice took to the stream, and swam and swam, and though myriads of them were swept away, an innumerable throng still reached the spot. Again they climbed and clattered up the walls. The Bishop heard their approach. It was his last retreat. They rushed in upon him with more irresistible fury than before, and, amidst stifled cries of protracted suffering, Bishop Hatto at length rendered up his cruel and avaricious soul.

THE DANCERS.

THE Sabbath-day drew to a close in the summer-tide of the year of grace one thousand and one, and the rustics of Ramersdorf amused themselves with a dance, as was their wont to do, in the courtyard of the monastery. It was a privilege that they had enjoyed time immemorial, and it had never been gainsaid by the abbots who were dead and gone, but Anselm von Lowenberg, the then superior of the convent, an austere, ascetic man, who looked with disdain and dislike on all popular recreations, had long set his face against it, and had, moreover, tried every means short of actual prohibition to put an end to the profane amusement. The rustics, however, were not to be debarred by his displeasure from pursuing, perhaps, their only pleasure; and though the pious abbot discountenanced their proceedings, they acquiesced not in his views, and their enjoyment was not one atom the less.

The day had been very beautiful, and the evening was, if possible, more so. Gaily garbed maidens of the village and stalwart rustics filled the courtyard of the convent. A blind fiddler, who had fiddled three generations off the stage, sat in front of a group of elders of either sex, who, though too old and too stiff to partake in the active and exciting amusement, were still young enough to enjoy looking on. A few shaven crowns peered from the latticed casements which looked out on to the merry scene. The music struck up, the dance began. Who approaches? Why are so many anxious glances cast in yonder direction? It is the Abbot.

"Cease your fooling," he spake to them, in a solemn tone; "profane not the place nor the day with your idle mirth. Go home, and pray in your own homes for the grace of the Lord to govern ye, for ye are wicked and wilful and hard of heart as the stones!"

He waved his hand as if to disperse them, but his words and his action were equally unheeded by the dancers and the spectators.

"Forth, vile sinners!" he pursued. "Forth from these walls, or I will curse ye with the curse."

Still they regarded him not to obey his behest, although they so far noticed his words as to return menacing look for look, and muttered threats for threat with him. The music played on with the same liveliness, the dancers danced as merrily as ever, and the spectators applauded each display of agility.

"Well, then," spake the Abbot, bursting with

rage, " an ye cease not, be my curse on your head—
there may ye dance for a year and a day !"

He banned them bitterly; with uplifted hands
and eyes he imprecated the vengeance of Heaven on
their disobedience. He prayed to the Lord to punish
them for the slight of his directions. Then he
sought his cell to vent his ire in solitude.

From that hour they continued to dance until a
year and a day had fully expired. Night fell, and
they ceased not; day dawned, and they danced still.
In the heat of noon, in the cool of the evening, day
after day there was no rest for them, their saltation
was without end. The seasons rolled over them.
Summer gave place to autumn, winter succeeded
summer, and spring decked the fields with early
flowers, as winter slowly disappeared, yet still they
danced on, through coursing time and changing
seasons, with unabated strength and unimpaired
energy. Rain nor hail, snow nor storm, sunshine
nor shade, seemed to affect them. Round and
round and round they danced, in heat and cold, in
damp and dry, in light and darkness. What were
the seasons—what the times or the hour or the
weather to them? In vain did their neighbours
and friends try to arrest them in their wild evolu-
tions; in vain were attempts made to stop them in
their whirling career; in vain did even the Abbot
himself interpose to relieve them from the curse
he had laid on them, and to put a period to the

punishment of which he had been the cause. The
strongest man in the vicinity held out his hand and
caught one of them, with the intention of arresting
his rotation, and tearing him from the charmed
circle, but his arm was torn from him in the attempt,
and clung to the dancer with the grip of life till
his day was done. The man paid his life as the
forfeit of his temerity. No effort was left untried
to relieve the dancers, but every one failed. The
sufferers themselves, however, appeared quite unconscious of what was passing. They seemed to be
in a state of perfect somnambulism, and to be altogether unaware of the presence of any persons, as
well as insensible to pain or fatigue. When the
expiration of their punishment arrived, they were
all found huddled together in the deep cavity which
their increasing gyrations had worn in the earth
beneath them. It was a considerable time before
sense and consciousness returned to them, and
indeed they never after could be said to enjoy them
completely, for, though they lived long, they were
little better than idiots during the remainder of their
lives.

THE LITTLE SHROUD.

THERE was once a woman who had a little son of about seven years old, who was so lovely and beautiful that no one could look upon him without being kind to him, and he was dearer to her than all the world beside. It happened that he suddenly fell ill and died, and his mother would not be comforted, but wept for him day and night. Shortly after he was buried he showed himself at night in the places where he had been used in his lifetime to sit and play, and if his mother wept, he wept also, and when the morning came he departed. Since his mother never ceased weeping, the child came one night in the little white shroud in which he had been laid in his coffin, and with the chaplet upon his head, and seating himself at her feet, upon the bed, he cried—

"O mother, mother, give over crying, else I cannot stop in my coffin, for my shroud is never dry because of your tears, for they fall upon it."

When his mother heard this she was sore afraid, and wept no more. And the babe came upon another night, holding in his hand a little taper, and he said—

"Look, mother, my shroud is now quite dry, and I can rest in my grave."

Then she bowed to the will of Providence, and bore her sorrow with silence and patience, and the little child returned not again, but slept in his underground bed.

THERE once lived, years ago, a man known only by the name of the Arch Rogue. By dint of skill in the black art, and all arts of imposition, he drove a more flourishing trade than all the rest of the sorcerers of the age. It was his delight to travel from one country to another merely to play upon mankind, and no living soul was secure, either in house or field, nor could properly call them his own.

Now his great reputation for these speedy methods of possessing himself of others' property excited the envy of a certain king of a certain country, who considered them as no less than an invasion of his royal prerogative. He could not sleep a wink for thinking about it, and he despatched troops of soldiers, one after another, with strict orders to arrest him, but all their search was in vain. At length, after long meditation, the king said to himself—

"Only wait a little, thou villain cutpurse, and yet I will have thee."

Forthwith he issued a manifesto, stating that the

royal mercy would be extended to so light-fingered a genius, upon condition that he consented to appear at court and give specimens of his dexterity for his majesty's amusement.

One afternoon, as the king was standing at his palace window enjoying the fine prospect of woods and dales, over which a tempest appeared to be then just gathering, some one suddenly clapped him upon the shoulder, and on looking round he discovered a very tall, stout, dark-whiskered man close behind him, who said—

" Here I am."

" Who are you ?" inquired the king.

" He whom you look for."

The king uttered an exclamation of surprise, not unmixed with fear, at such amazing assurance. The stranger continued, " Don't be alarmed. Only keep your word with me, and I will prove myself quite obedient to your orders."

This being agreed on, the king acquainted his royal consort and the whole court that the great sleight-of-hand genius had discovered himself, and soon, in a full assembly, his majesty proceeded to question him, and lay on him his commands.

" Mark what I say," he said, " nor venture to dispute my orders. To begin, do you see yon rustic, not far from the wood, busy ploughing ?"

The conjurer nodded assent.

" Then go," continued the king,—" go and rob him

of his plough and oxen without his knowing anything about it."

The king flattered himself that this was impossible, for he did not conceive how the conjurer could perform such a task in the face of open day, —and if he fail, thought he, I have him in my power, and will make him smart.

The conjurer proceeded to the spot, and as the storm appeared to increase, the rain beginning to pour down in torrents, the countryman, letting his oxen rest, ran under a tree for shelter, until the rain should have ceased. Just then he heard some one singing in the wood. Such a glorious song he had never heard before in all his life. He felt wonderfully enlivened, and, as the weather continued dull, he said to himself—

" Well, there's no harm in taking a look. Yes ; I'll see what sport is stirring," and away he slipped into the wood, still further and further, in search of the songster.

In the meanwhile the conjurer was not idle. He changed places with the rustic, taking care of the oxen while their master went searching through the wood. Darting out of the thicket, in a few moments he had slashed off the oxen's horns and tails, and stuck them, half hid, in the ploughman's last furrow. He then drove off the beasts pretty sharply towards the palace. In a short time the rustic found his way back, and looking towards the spot for his

oxen could see nothing of them. Searching on all
sides, he came at last to examine the furrow, and
beheld, to his horror, the horns and tails of his poor
beasts sticking out of the ground. Imagining that
a thunderbolt must have struck the beasts, and the
earth swallowed them up, he poured forth a most
dismal lamentation over his lot, roaring aloud until
the woods echoed to the sound. When he was
tired of this, he bethought him of running home to
find a pick and a spade to dig his unlucky oxen out
of the earth as soon as possible.

As he went he was met by the king and the conjurer, who inquired the occasion of his piteous
lamentation.

"My oxen! my poor oxen!" cried the boor, and
then he related all that had happened to him,
entreating them to go with him to the place. The
conjurer said—

"Why don't you see if you cannot pull the oxen
out again by the horns or by the tail?"

With this the rustic, running back, seized one of
the tails, and, pulling with all his might, it gave way
and he fell backward.

"Thou hast pulled thy beast's tail off," said the
conjurer. "Try if thou canst succeed better with
his horns. If not, thou must even dig them out."

Again the rustic tried with the same result, while
the king laughed very heartily at the sight. As the
worthy man now appeared excessively troubled at

his misfortunes, the king promised him another pair of oxen, and the rustic was content.

"You have made good your boast," said the king to the conjurer, as they returned to the palace ; " but now you will have to deal with a more difficult matter, so muster your wit and courage. To-night you must steal my favourite charger out of his stable, and let nobody know who does it."

Now, thought the king, I have trapped him at last, for he will never be able to outwit my master of the horse, and all my grooms to boot. To make the matter sure, he ordered a strong guard under one of his most careful officers to be placed round the stable court. They were armed with stout battle-axes, and were enjoined every half-hour to give the word, and pace alternately through the court. In the royal stables others had the like duty to perform, while the master of the horse himself was to ride the favourite steed the whole time, having been presented by the king with a gold snuff-box, from which he was to take ample pinches in order to keep himself awake, and give signal by a loud sneeze. He was also armed with a heavy sword, with which he was to knock the thief on the head if he approached.

The rogue first arrayed himself in the master of the bedchamber's clothes, without his leave. About midnight he proceeded to join the guards, furnished with different kinds of wine, and told them that the king had sent him to thank them for so cheerfully complying with his orders. He also informed them that the impostor had been already caught and secured, and added that the king had given permission for the guards to have a glass or two, and requested that they would not give the word quite so loudly, as her majesty had not been able to close her eyes. He then marched into the stables, where he found the master of the horse astride the royal charger, busily taking snuff and sneezing at intervals. The master of the bedchamber poured him out a sparkling glass to drink to the health of his majesty, who had sent it, and it looked too excellent to resist. Both master and guards then began to jest over the Arch Rogue's fate, taking, like good subjects, repeated draughts—all to his majesty's health. At length they began to experience their effects. They gaped and stretched, sank gradually upon the ground, and fell asleep. The master, by dint of fresh pinches, was the last to yield, but he too blinked, stopped the horse, which he had kept at a walk, and said—

"I am so confoundedly sleepy I can hold it no longer. Take you care of the charger for a moment. Bind him fast to the stall—and just keep watch."

Having uttered these words, he fell like a heavy sack upon the floor and snored aloud. The conjurer took his place upon the horse, gave it whip and spur, and galloped away through the sleeping guards, through the court gates, and whistled as he went.

Early in the morning the king, eager to learn the result, hastened to his royal mews, and was not a little surprised to find the whole of his guards fast asleep upon the ground, but he saw nothing of his charger.

"What is to do here?" he cried in a loud voice. "Get up; rouse, you idle varlets!"

At last one of them, opening his eyes, cried out—

"The king! the king!"

"Ay, true enough, I am here," replied his majesty, "but my favourite horse is not. Speak, answer on the instant."

While the affrighted wretches, calling one to another, rubbed their heavy eyes, the king was examining the stalls once more, and, stumbling over his master of the horse, turned and gave him some hearty cuffs about the ears. But the master only turned upon the other side, and grumbled—

"Let me alone, you rascal, my royal master's horse is not for the like of you."

"Rascal!" exclaimed the king, "do you know who it is?" and he was just about to call his attendants, when he heard hasty footsteps, and the conjurer stood before him.

"My liege," he said, "I have just returned from an airing on your noble horse. He is, indeed, a fine animal, but once or so I was obliged to give him the switch."

The king felt excessively vexed at the rogue's success, but he was the more resolved to hit upon something that should bring his fox skin into jeopardy at last. So he thought, and the next day he addressed the conjurer thus—

"Thy third trial is now about to take place, and if you are clever enough to carry it through, you shall not only have your life and liberty, but a handsome allowance to boot. In the other case you know your fate. Now listen. This very night I command you to rob my queen consort of her bridal ring, to steal it from her finger, and let no one know the thief or the way of thieving."

When night approached, his majesty caused all the doors in the palace to be fast closed, and a guard to be set at each. He himself, instead of retiring to rest, took his station, well armed, in an easy chair close to the queen's couch.

It was a moonlight night, and about two in the morning the king plainly heard a ladder reared up against the window, and the soft step of a man mounting it. When the king thought the conjurer must have reached the top, he called out from the window—

"Let fall."

The next moment the ladder was dashed away, and something fell with a terrible crash to the ground. The king uttered an exclamation of alarm, and ran down into the court, telling the queen, who was half asleep, that he was going to see if the conjurer were dead. But the rogue had borrowed a dead body from the gallows, and having dressed it in his own clothes, had placed it on the ladder. Hardly had the king left the chamber before the conjurer entered it and said to the queen in the king's voice—

"Yes, he is stone dead, so you may now go quietly to sleep, only hand me here your ring. It is too costly and precious to trust it in bed while you sleep."

The queen, imagining it was her royal consort, instantly gave him the ring, and in a moment the conjurer was off with it on his finger. Directly afterwards the king came back.

"At last," he said, "I have indeed carried the joke too far. I have repaid him. He is lying there as dead as a door nail. He will plague us no more."

"I know that already," replied the queen. "You have told me exactly the same thing twice over."

"How came you to know anything about it?" inquired his majesty.

"How? From yourself to be sure," replied his consort. "You informed me that the conjurer was dead, and then you asked me for my ring."

"I ask for the ring!" exclaimed the king. "Then I suppose you must have given it to him," continued his majesty, in a tone of great indignation;

"and is it even so at last? By all the saints, this is one of the most confounded, unmanageable knaves in existence. I never knew anything to equal it."

Then he informed the queen of the whole affair, though before he arrived at the conclusion of his tale she was fast asleep.

Soon after it was light in the morning the wily conjurer made his appearance. He bowed to the earth three times before the queen and presented her with the treasure he had stolen. The king, though excessively chagrined, could not forbear laughing at the sight.

"Now hear," said he, "thou king of arch rogues. Had I only caught a sight of you through my fingers as you were coming, you would never have come off so well. As it is, let what is past be forgiven and forgotten. Take up your residence at my court, and take care that you do not carry your jokes too far, for in such a case I may find myself compelled to withdraw my favour from you if nothing worse ensue."

BROTHER MERRY.

In days of yore there was a war, and when it was at an end a great number of the soldiers that had been engaged in it were disbanded. Among the rest Brother Merry received his discharge, and nothing more for all he had done than a very little loaf of soldier's bread, and four halfpence in money. With these possessions he went his way. Now a saint had seated himself in the road, like a poor beggar man, and when Brother Merry came along. he asked him for charity to give him something. Then the soldier said—

"Dear beggar man, what shall such as I give you? I have been a soldier, and have just got my discharge, and with it only a very little loaf and four halfpence. When that is gone I shall have to beg like yourself."

However, he divided the loaf into four parts, and gave the saint one, with a halfpenny. The saint thanked him, and having gone a little further along the road seated himself like another beggar in the way of the soldier. When Brother Merry came up

the saint again asked alms of him, and the old
soldier again gave him another quarter of the loaf
and another halfpenny.

The saint thanked him, and seated himself in the
way a third time, like another beggar, and again addressed Brother Merry. Brother Merry gave him
a third quarter of the loaf, and the third halfpenny.

The saint thanked him, and Brother Merry journeyed on with all he had left—one quarter of the
loaf and a single halfpenny. When he came to a
tavern, being hungry and thirsty, he went in and
ate the bread, and spent the halfpenny in beer to
drink with it. When he had finished, he continued
his journey, and the saint, in the disguise of a disbanded soldier, met him again and saluted him.

"Good day, comrade," said he; "can you give me
a morsel of bread, and a halfpenny to get a drop
of drink ? "

"Where shall I get it ? " answered Brother
Merry. " I got my discharge, and nothing with it
but a loaf and four halfpence, and three beggars
met me on the road and I gave each of them a
quarter of the loaf and a halfpenny. The last
quarter I have just eaten at the tavern, and I have
spent the last halfpenny in drink. I am quite
empty now. If you have nothing, let us go begging
together."

"No, that will not be necessary just now," said
the saint. " I understand a little about doctoring,

and I will in time obtain as much as I need by that."

"Ha!" said Brother Merry, "I know nothing about that, so I must go and beg by myself."

"Only come along," replied the saint, "and if I can earn anything, you shall go halves."

"That will suit me excellently," replied Brother Merry.

So they travelled on together.

They had not gone a great distance before they came to a cottage in which they heard a great lamenting and screaming. They went in to see what was the matter, and found a man sick to the death, as if about to expire, and his wife crying and weeping loudly.

"Leave off whining and crying," said the saint. "I will make the man well again quickly enough," and he took a salve out of his pocket and cured the man instantly, so that he could stand up and was quite hearty. Then the man and his wife, in great joy, demanded—

"How can we repay you? What shall we give you?"

The saint would not, however, take anything, and the more the couple pressed him the more firmly he declined. Brother Merry, who had been looking on, came to his side, and, nudging him, said—

"Take something; take something. We want it badly enough."

At length the peasant brought a lamb, which he desired the saint to accept, but he declined it still. Then Brother Merry jogged his side, and said—

"Take it, you foolish fellow; take it. We want it badly enough."

At last the saint said—

"Well, I'll take the lamb, but I shall not carry it. You must carry it."

"There's no great hardship in that," cried Brother Merry. "I can easily do it;" and he took it on his shoulder.

After that they went on till they came to a wood, and Brother Merry, who was very hungry, and found the lamb a heavy load, called out to the saint—

"Hallo! here is a nice place for us to dress and eat the lamb."

"With all my heart," replied his companion; "but I don't understand anything of cooking, so do you begin, and I will walk about until it is ready. Don't begin to eat until I return. I will take care to be back in time."

"Go your ways," said Brother Merry; "I can cook it well enough. I'll soon have it ready."

The saint wandered away, while Brother Merry lighted the fire, killed the lamb, put the pieces into the pot, and boiled them. In a short time the lamb was thoroughly done, but the saint had not returned; so Merry took the meat up, carved it, and found the heart.

"That is the best part of it," said he; and he kept tasting it until he had finished it.

At length the saint came back, and said—

"I only want the heart. All the rest you may have, only give me that."

Then Brother Merry took his knife and fork, and turned the lamb about as if he would have found the heart, but of course he could not discover it. At last he said, in a careless manner—

"It is not here."

"Not there? Where should it be, then?" said the saint.

"That I don't know," said Merry; "but now I think of it, what a couple of fools we are to look for the heart of a lamb. A lamb, you know, has not got a heart."

"What?" said the saint; "that's news, indeed. Why, every beast has a heart, and why should not the lamb have one as well as the rest of them?"

"No, certainly, comrade, a lamb has no heart. Only reflect, and it will occur to you that it really has not."

"Well," replied his companion, "it is quite sufficient. There is no heart there, so I need none of the lamb. You may eat it all."

"Well, what I cannot eat I'll put in my knapsack," said Brother Merry.

Then he ate some, and disposed of the rest as he had said. Now, as they continued their journey, the saint contrived that a great stream should flow right across their path, so that they must be obliged to ford it. Then said he—

"Go you first."

"No," answered Brother Merry; "go you first," thinking that if the water were too deep he would stay on the bank where he was. However, the saint waded through, and the water only reached to his knees; but when Brother Merry ventured, the stream seemed suddenly to increase in depth, and he was soon up to his neck in the water.

"Help me, comrade," he cried.

"Will you confess," said the saint, "that you ate the lamb's heart?"

The soldier still denied it, and the water got still deeper, until it reached his mouth. Then the saint said again—

"Will you confess, then, that you ate the lamb's heart?"

Brother Merry still denied what he had done, and as the saint did not wish to let him drown he helped him out of his danger.

They journeyed on until they came to a kingdom where they heard that the king's daughter lay dangerously ill.

"Holloa! brother," said the soldier, "here's a

catch for us. If we can only cure her we shall be made for ever."

The saint, however, was not quick enough for Brother Merry.

"Come, Brother Heart," said the soldier, "put your best foot forward, so that we may come in at the right time."

But the saint went still slower, though his companion kept pushing and driving him, till at last they heard that the princess was dead.

"This comes of your creeping so," said the soldier.

"Now be still," said the saint, "for I can do more than make the sick whole ; I can bring the dead to life again."

"If that's true," said Brother Merry, "you must at least earn half the kingdom for us."

At length they arrived at the king's palace, where everybody was in great trouble, but the saint told the king he would restore his daughter to him. They conducted him to where she lay, and he commanded them to let him have a caldron of water, and when it had been brought, he ordered all the people to go away, and let nobody remain with him but Brother Merry. Then he divided the limbs of the dead princess, and throwing them into the water, lighted a fire under the caldron, and boiled them. When all the flesh had fallen from the bones, the saint took them, laid them on a table, and placed them together in their natural order. Having done this, he walked before them, and said—

"Arise, thou dead one!"

As he repeated these words the third time the princess arose, alive, well, and beautiful.

The king was greatly rejoiced, and said to the saint—

"Require for thy reward what thou wilt. Though it should be half my empire, I will give it you."

But the saint replied—

"I desire nothing for what I have done."

"O thou Jack Fool!" thought Brother Merry to himself. Then, nudging his comrade's side, he said—

"Don't be so silly. If you won't have anything, yet I need somewhat."

The saint, however, would take nothing, but as the king saw that his companion would gladly have a gift, he commanded the keeper of his treasures to fill his knapsack with gold, at which Brother Merry was right pleased.

Again they went upon their way till they came to a wood, when the saint said to his fellow-traveller—

"Now we will share the gold."

"Yes," replied the soldier, "that we can."

Then the saint took the gold and divided it into three portions.

"Well," thought Brother Merry, "what whim has he got in his head now, making three parcels, and only two of us?"

"Now," said the saint, "I have divided it fairly, one for me, and one for you, and one for him who ate the heart."

"Oh, I ate that," said the soldier, quickly taking up the gold. "I did, I assure you."

"How can that be true?" replied the saint. "A lamb has no heart."

"Ay! what, brother? What are you thinking of? A lamb has no heart? Very good! When every beast has why should that one be without?"

"Now that is very good," said the saint. "Take all the gold yourself, for I shall remain no more with you, but will go my own way alone."

"As you please, Brother Heart," answered the soldier. "A pleasant journey to you, my hearty."

The saint took another road, and as he went off—

"Well," thought the soldier, " it 's all right that he has marched off, for he is an odd fellow."

Brother Merry had now plenty of money, but he did not know how to use it, so he spent it and gave it away, till in the course of a little time he found himself once more penniless. At last he came into a country where he heard that the king's daughter was dead.

"Ah!" thought he, "that may turn out well. I 'll bring her to life again."

Then he went to the king and offered his services. Now the king had heard that there was an old soldier who went about restoring the dead to life, and he thought that Brother Merry must be just the man. However, he had not much confidence in him, so he first consulted his council, and they agreed that as the princess was certainly dead, the old soldier might be allowed to see what he could do. Brother Merry commanded them to bring him a caldron of water, and when every one had left the room he separated the limbs, threw them into the caldron, and made a fire under it, exactly as he had seen the saint do. When the water boiled and the flesh fell from the bones, he took them and placed them upon the table, but as he did not know how to arrange them he piled them one upon another. Then he stood before them, and said—

"Thou dead, arise!" and he cried so three times, but all to no purpose.

"Stand up, you vixen! stand up, or it shall be the worse for you," he cried.

Scarcely had he repeated these words ere the saint came in at the window, in the likeness of an old soldier, just as before, and said—

"You impious fellow! How can the dead stand up when you have thrown the bones thus one upon another?"

"Ah! Brother Heart," answered Merry, "I have done it as well as I can."

"I will help you out of your trouble this time," said the saint; "but I tell you this, if you ever again undertake a job of this kind, you will repent it, and for this you shall neither ask for nor take the least thing from the king."

Having placed the bones in their proper order, the saint said three times—

"Thou dead, arise!" and the princess stood up, sound and beautiful as before. Then the saint immediately disappeared again out of the window, and Brother Merry was glad that all had turned out so well. One thing, however, grieved him sorely, and that was that he might take nothing from the king.

"I should like to know," thought he, "what Brother Heart had to grumble about. What he gives with one hand he takes with the other. There is no wit in that."

The king asked Brother Merry what he would have, but the soldier durst not take anything. However, he managed by hints and cunning that the king should fill his knapsack with money, and with that he journeyed on. When he came out of the palace door, however, he found the saint standing there, who said—

"See what a man you are. Have I not forbidden you to take anything, and yet you have your knapsack filled with gold?"

"How can I help it," answered the soldier, "if they would thrust it in?"

"I tell you this," said the saint, "mind that you don't undertake such a business a second time. If you do, it will fare badly with you."

"Ah! brother," answered the soldier, "never fear. Now I have money, why should I trouble myself with washing bones?"

"That will not last a long time," said the saint; "but, in order that you may never tread in a forbidden path, I will bestow upon your knapsack this power, that whatsoever you wish in it shall be there. Farewell! you will never see me again."

"Adieu," said Brother Merry, and thought he, "I am glad you are gone. You are a wonderful fellow. I am willing enough not to follow you."

He forgot all about the wonderful property bestowed upon his knapsack, and very soon he had spent and squandered his gold as before. When he had but fourpence left, he came to a public-house, and thought that the money must go. So he called for three pennyworth of wine and a pennyworth of bread. As he ate and drank, the flavour of roasting geese tickled his nose, and, peeping and prying about, he saw that the landlord had placed two geese in the oven. Then it occurred to him what his companion had told him about his knapsack, so he determined to put it to the test. Going out, he stood before the door, and said—

"I wish that the two geese which are baking in the oven were in my knapsack."

When he had said this, he peeped in, and, sure enough, there they were.

"Ah! ah!" said he, "that is all right. I am a made man."

He went on a little way, took out the geese, and commenced to eat them. As he was thus enjoying himself, there came by two labouring men, who looked with hungry eyes at the one goose which was yet untouched. Brother Merry noticed it, and thought that one goose would be enough for him. So he called the men, gave them the goose, and bade them drink his health. The men thanked him, and going to the public-house, called for wine and bread, took out their present, and commenced to eat. When the hostess saw what they were dining on, she said to her goodman—

"Those two men are eating a goose. You had better see if it is not one of ours out of the oven."

The host opened the door, and lo! the oven was empty.

"O you pack of thieves!" he shouted. "This is the way you eat geese, is it? Pay for them directly, or I will wash you both with green hazel juice."

The men said—

"We are not thieves. We met an old soldier on the road, and he made us a present of the goose."

"You are not going to hoax me in that way," said the host. "The soldier has been here, but went out of the door like an honest fellow. I took care of that. You are the thieves, and you shall pay for the geese."

However, as the men had no money to pay him with, he took a stick and beat them out of doors.

Meanwhile, as Brother Merry journeyed on, he came to a place where there was a noble castle, and not far from it a little public-house. Into this he went, and asked for a night's lodging, but the landlord said that his house was full of guests, and he could not accommodate him.

"I wonder," said Brother Merry, "that the people should all come to you, instead of going to that castle."

"They have good reason for what they do," said the landlord, "for whoever has attempted to spend the night at the castle has never come back to show how he was entertained."

"If others have attempted it, why shouldn't I?" said Merry.

"You had better leave it alone," said the host; "you are only thrusting your head into danger."

"No fear of danger," said the soldier, "only give me the key and plenty to eat and drink."

The hostess gave him what he asked for, and he went off to the castle, relished his supper, and when he found himself sleepy, laid himself down on the floor, for there was no bed in the place. He soon went to sleep, but in the night he was awoke by a great noise, and when he aroused himself he discovered nine very ugly devils dancing in a circle which they had made around him.

"Dance as long as you like," said Brother Merry; "but don't come near me."

But the devils came drawing nearer and nearer, and at last they almost trod on his face with their misshapen feet.

"Be quiet," said he, but they behaved still worse.

At last he got angry, and crying—

"Holla! I'll soon make you quiet," he caught hold of the leg of a stool and struck about him.

Nine devils against one soldier were, however, too much, and while he laid about lustily on those before him, those behind pulled his hair and pinched him miserably.

"Ay, ay, you pack of devils, now you are too hard for me," said he; "but wait a bit. I wish all the nine devils were in my knapsack," cried he, and it was no sooner said than done.

There they were. Then Brother Merry buckled it up close, and threw it into a corner, and as all was now still he lay down and slept till morning, when the landlord of the inn and the nobleman to whom the castle belonged came to see how it had fared with him. When they saw him sound and lively, they were astonished, and said—

"Did the ghosts, then, do nothing to you?"

"Why, not exactly," said Merry; "but I have got them all nine in my knapsack. You may dwell quietly enough in your castle now; from henceforth they won't trouble you."

The nobleman thanked him and gave him great rewards, begging him to remain in his service, saying that he would take care of him all the days of his life.

"No," answered he; "I am used to wander and rove about. I will again set forth."

He went on until he came to a smithy, into which he went, and laying his knapsack on the anvil, bade the smith and all his men hammer away upon it as hard as they could. They did as they were directed, with their largest hammers and all their might, and the poor devils set up a piteous howling. When the men opened the knapsack there were eight of them dead, but one who had been snug in a fold was still alive, and he slipped out and ran away to his home in a twinkling.

After this Brother Merry wandered about the world for a long time; but at last he grew old, and began to think about his latter end, so he went to a hermit who was held to be a very pious man and said—

"I am tired of roving, and will now endeavour to go to heaven."

"There stand two ways," said the hermit; "the one, broad and pleasant, leads to hell; the other is rough and narrow, and that leads to heaven."

"I must be a fool indeed," thought Brother Merry, "if I go the rough and narrow road;" so he went the broad and pleasant way till he came at last to a great black door, and that was the door of hell.

He knocked, and the door-keeper opened it, and when he saw that it was Merry he was sadly frightened, for who should he be but the ninth devil who had been in the knapsack, and he had thought himself lucky, for he had escaped with nothing worse than a black eye. He bolted the door again directly, and running to the chief of the devils, said—

"There is a fellow outside with a knapsack on his back, but pray don't let him in, for he can get all hell into his knapsack by wishing it. He once got me a terribly ugly hammering in it."

So they called out to Brother Merry, and told him that he must go away, for they should not let him in.

"Well, if they will not have me here," thought Merry, "I'll e'en try if I can get a lodging in heaven. Somewhere or other I must rest."

So he turned about and went on till he came to the door of heaven, and there he knocked. Now the saint who had journeyed with Merry sat at the door, and had charge of the entrance. Brother Merry recognised him, and said—

"Are you here, old acquaintance? Then things will go better with me."

The saint replied—

"I suppose you want to get into heaven?"

"Ay, ay, brother, let me in; I must put up somewhere."

"No," said the saint; "you don't come in here."

"Well, if you won't let me in, take your dirty knapsack again. I'll have nothing that can put me in mind of you," said Merry carelessly.

"Give it me, then," said the saint.

Brother Merry handed it through the grating into heaven, and the saint took it and hung it up behind his chair.

"Now," said Brother Merry, "I wish I was in my own knapsack."

Instantly he was there; and thus, being once actually in heaven, the saint was obliged to let him stay there.

FASTRADA.

By the side of the "Beautiful Doorway," leading into the cloisters of the cathedral at Mainz, stands, worked into the wall, a fragment of the tomb of Fastrada, the fourth wife of the mighty monarch Charlemagne according to some authorities, the third according to others. Fastrada figures in the following tradition related by the author of the Rhyming Chronicle.

When the Kaiser, Karl, abode at Zurich, he dwelt in a house called "The Hole," in front of which he caused a pillar to be erected with a bell on the top of it, to the end that whoever demanded justice should have the means of announcing himself. One day, as he sat at dinner in his house, he heard the bell ring, and sent out his servants to bring the claimant before him; but they could find no one. A second and a third time the bell rang, but no human being was still to be seen. At length the Kaiser himself went forth, and he found a large serpent, which had twined itself round the shaft of the pillar, and was then in the very act of pulling the bell rope.

"This is God's will," said the monarch. "Let the brute be brought before me. I may deny justice to none of God's creatures—man or beast."

The serpent was accordingly ushered into the imperial presence; and the Kaiser spoke to it as he would to one of his own kind, gravely asking what it required. The reptile made a most courteous reverence to Charlemagne, and signed in its dumb way for him to follow. He did so accordingly, accompanied by his court; and the creature led them on to the water's edge, to the shores of the lake, where it had its nest. Arrived there, the Kaiser soon saw the cause of the serpent's seeking him, for its nest, which was full of eggs, was occupied by a hideous toad of monstrous proportions.

"Let the toad be flung into the fire," said the monarch solemnly, "and let the serpent have possession of its nest restored to it."

This sentence was carried at once into execution. The toad was burnt, and the serpent placed in possession. Charlemagne and his court then returned to the palace.

Three days afterwards, as the Kaiser again sat at dinner, he was surprised at the appearance of the serpent, which this time glided into the hall unnoticed and unannounced.

"What does this mean?" thought the king.

The reptile approached the table, and raising itself on its tail, dropped from its mouth, into an empty plate which stood beside the monarch, a precious diamond. Then, again abasing itself before him, the crawling creature glided out of the hall as it had entered, and was speedily lost to view. This diamond the monarch caused to be set in a costly chased ring of the richest gold; and he then presented the trinket to his fair wife, the much-beloved Fastrada.

Now this stone had the virtue of attraction, and whoso received it from another, so long as they wore it, received also the intensest love of that individual. It was thus with Fastrada, for no sooner did she place the ring on her finger than the attachment of Charlemagne, great before, no longer knew any bounds. In fact his love was more like madness than any sane passion. But though this talisman had full power over love, it had no power over death; and the mighty monarch was soon to experience that nothing may avert the fiat of destiny.

Charlemagne and his beloved bride returned to Germany, and, at Ingelheim palace, Fastrada died. The Kaiser was inconsolable. He would not listen to the voice of friendship, and he sorrowed in silence over the dead body of his once beautiful bride. Even when decay had commenced, when the remains, late so lovely, were now loathsome to look on, he could not be induced to leave the corpse for a moment, or to quit the chamber of death in which it lay. The court were all astounded. They knew not what to make of the matter. At length Turpin, Archbishop of Rheims, approached the corpse, and being made aware of the cause, by some supernatural communication contrived to engage the emperor's attention while he removed the charm. The magic ring was found by him in the mouth of the dead empress, concealed beneath her tongue.

Immediately that the talisman was removed the spell was broken, and Charlemagne now looked on the putrid corpse with all the natural horror and loathing of an ordinary man. He gave orders for its immediate interment, which were at once carried into execution, and he then departed from Ingelheim for the forest of the Ardennes. Arrived at Aix-la-Chapelle, he took up his abode in the ancient castle of Frankenstein, close by that famous city. The esteem, however, that he had felt for Fastrada was now transferred to the possessor of the ring, Archbishop Turpin; and the pious ecclesiastic was so persecuted by the emperor's affection that he finally cast the talisman into the lake which surrounds the castle.

An immediate transference of the royal liking took place, and the monarch, thenceforth and for ever after during his lifetime, loved Aix-la-Chapelle as a man might love his wife. So much did he become attached to it, that he directed that he should be buried there; and there accordingly his remains rest unto this day.

THE JEW IN THE BUSH.

A FAITHFUL servant had worked hard for his master, a thrifty farmer, for three long years, and had been paid no wages. At last it came into the man's head that he would not go on thus any longer, so he went to his master and said—

"I have worked hard for you a long time, and without pay, too. I will trust you to give me what I ought to have for my trouble, but something I must have, and then I must take a holiday."

The farmer was a sad miser, and knew that his man was simple-hearted, so he took out three crowns, and thus gave him a crown for each year's service. The poor fellow thought it was a great deal of money to have, and said to himself—

"Why should I work hard and live here on bad fare any longer? Now that I am rich I can travel into the wide world and make myself merry."

With that he put the money into his purse, and set out, roaming over hill and valley. As he jogged along over the fields, singing and dancing, a little dwarf met him, and asked him what made him so merry.

"Why, what should make me down-hearted?" replied he. "I am sound in health and rich in purse; what should I care for? I have saved up my three years' earnings, and have it all safe in my pocket."

"How much may it come to?" said the mannikin.

"Three whole crowns," replied the countryman.

"I wish you would give them to me," said the other. "I am very poor."

Then the good man pitied him, and gave him all he had; and the dwarf said—

"As you have such a kind heart, I will grant you three wishes—one for each crown,—so choose whatever you like."

The countryman rejoiced at his luck, and said—

"I like many things better than money. First, I will have a bow that will bring me down everything I shoot at; secondly, a fiddle that will set every one dancing that hears me play upon it; and, thirdly, I should like to be able to make every one grant me whatever I ask."

The dwarf said he should have his three wishes, gave him the bow and the fiddle, and went his way.

Our honest friend journeyed on his way too, and if he was merry before, he was now ten times more so. He had not gone far before he met an old Jew. Close by them stood a tree, and on the topmost twig sat a thrush, singing away most joyfully.

"Oh what a pretty bird!" said the Jew. "I would give a great deal of my money to have such a one."

"If that's all," said the countryman, "I will soon bring it down."

He took up his bow, off went his arrow, and down fell the thrush into a bush that grew at the foot of the tree. The Jew, when he saw that he could have the bird, thought he would cheat the man, so he put his money into his pocket again, and crept into the bush to find the prize. As soon as he had got into the middle, his companion took up his fiddle and played away, and the Jew began to dance and spring about, capering higher and higher in the air. The thorns soon began to tear his clothes, till they all hung in rags about him, and he himself was all scratched and wounded, so that the blood ran down.

"Oh, for heaven's sake!" cried the Jew. "Mercy, mercy, master! Pray stop the fiddle! What have I done to be treated in this way?"

"What hast thou done? Why, thou hast shaved many a poor soul close enough," said the other. "Thou art only meeting thy reward;" and he played up another tune yet merrier than the first.

Then the Jew began to beg and pray, and at last he said he would give plenty of his money to be set free. He did not, however, come up to the musician's price for some time, so he danced him along brisker and brisker. The higher the Jew danced, the higher he bid, till at last he offered a round hundred crowns that he had in his purse, and had just gained by cheating some poor fellow. When the countryman saw so much money, he said—

" I agree to the bargain," and, taking the purse and putting up his fiddle, he travelled on well pleased.

Meanwhile the Jew crept out of the bush, half naked, and in a piteous plight, and began to ponder how he should take his revenge and serve his late companion some trick. At length he went to a judge, and said that a rascal had robbed him of his money, and beaten him soundly into the bargain, and that this fellow carried a bow at his back, and had a fiddle hanging round his neck. The judge sent out his bailiffs to bring up the man whenever they should find him. The countryman was soon caught, and brought up to be tried.

The Jew began his tale, and said he had been robbed of his money.

" Robbed, indeed ! " said the countryman ; "why, you gave it me for playing you a tune, and teaching you to dance."

The judge said that was not likely; that the Jew, he was sure, knew better what to do with his money ; and he cut the matter short by sending the countryman off to the gallows.

Away he was taken, but as he stood at the foot of the ladder, he said—

"My Lord Judge, may it please your worship to grant me but one boon?"

"Anything but thy life," replied the other.

"No," said he; "I do not ask my life. Only let me play upon my fiddle for the last time."

The Jew cried out—

"Oh, no! no! no! for heaven's sake don't listen to him! don't listen to him!"

But the judge said—

"It is only for this once, poor fellow! He will soon have done."

The fact was he could not say no, because the dwarf's third gift enabled the countryman to make every one grant whatever he asked.

Then the Jew said—

"Bind me fast, bind me fast, for pity's sake!"

The countryman seized his fiddle and struck up a merry tune, and at the first note judge, clerks, and jailer were set agoing. All began capering, and no one could hold the Jew. At the second note the hangman let his prisoner go and danced also, and by the time the first bar of the tune was played all were dancing together—judge, court, Jew, and all the people who had followed to look on. At first the thing went merrily and joyously enough, but when it had gone on a while, and there seemed to be no end of either playing or dancing, all began to cry out and beg the countryman to leave off. He stopped, however, not a whit the more for their begging, till the judge not only gave him his life, but paid him back the hundred crowns.

Then the countryman called the Jew, and said—

"Tell us now, you rogue, where you got that gold, or I shall play on for your amusement only."

"I stole it," replied the Jew, before all the people. "I acknowledge that I stole it, and that you earned it fairly."

Then the countryman stopped his fiddling, and left the Jew to take his place at the gallows.

THE ELVES.

The happy day at length arrived on which Count Hermann von Rosenberg was married to his beloved Catherine, a princess of the house of Gonzaca. The event was celebrated by a magnificent banquet and festival, and it was late before the Count and Countess could leave their guests. The young Countess was already asleep, and Hermann was sinking into a slumber, when he was aroused by hearing the sounds of soft and gentle music, and, the door of his apartment flying open, a joyous bridal procession entered the room. The figures engaged in this extraordinary scene were not more than two or three spans high. The bride and bridegroom were in the centre of the procession, and the musicians preceded it.

Hermann rose up in bed, and demanded what brought them there, and why they had aroused him, whereupon one of the company stepped up to him, and said—

" We are attendant spirits of that peaceful class who dwell in the earth. We have dwelt for many years beneath this thy birthplace, and have ever watched over thy dwelling to preserve it from misfortune. Already have we taken good care of the ashes of your forefathers that they should not fall into the power of hostile and evil spirits, and as faithful servants we watch over the welfare of your house. Since thou hast this day been married for the continuance of thy name and ancient race, we have represented to you this bridal ceremony, in hopes that you will grant us full permission to keep and celebrate this joyous festival, in return for which we promise to serve you and your house with the greatest readiness."

"Very well," said Hermann, laughing; "make yourselves as merry in my castle as you please."

They thanked him, and took their departure. Hermann could not, however, banish from his mind this remarkable scene, and it was daybreak before he fell asleep. In the morning his thoughts were still occupied with it, yet he never mentioned one word of the occurrence to his wife.

In the course of time the Countess presented him with a daughter. Scarcely had Hermann received intelligence of this event before a very diminutive old crone entered the apartment and informed him that the elfin bride, whom he had seen in the miniature procession on the night of his nuptials, had given birth to a daughter. Hermann was very friendly to the visitor, wished all happiness to the mother and child, and the old woman took her departure.

The Count did not, however, mention this visit to his wife.

A year afterwards, on the approach of her second confinement, the Countess saw the elves on the occasion of her husband receiving another of their unexpected visits. The little people entered the chamber in a long procession in black dresses, carrying lights in their hands, and the little women were clothed in white. One of these stood before the Count holding up her apron, while an old man thus addressed her—

"No more, dear Hermann, can we find a resting-place in your castle. We must wander abroad. We are come to take our departure from you."

"Wherefore will you leave my castle?" inquired Hermann. "Have I offended you?"

"No, thou hast not; but we must go, for she whom you saw as a bride on your wedding-night lost, last evening, her life in giving birth to an heir, who likewise perished. As a proof that we are thankful for the kindness you have always shown us, take a trifling proof of our power."

When the old man had thus spoken, he placed a little ladder against the bed, which the old woman who had stood by ascended. Then she opened her apron, held it before Hermann, and said—

"Grasp and take."

He hesitated. She repeated what she had said. At last he did what she told him, took out of her apron what he supposed to be **a** handful of sand, and laid it in a basin which stood upon a table by his bedside. The little woman desired him to take another handful, and he did once more as she bade him. Thereupon the woman descended the ladder; and the procession, weeping and lamenting, departed from the chamber.

When day broke, Hermann saw that the supposed sand which he had taken from the apron of the little woman was nothing less than pure and beautiful grains of gold.

But what happened? On that very day he lost his Countess in childbirth, and his new-born son. Hermann mourned her loss so bitterly that he was very soon laid beside her in the grave. With him perished the house of Rosenberg.

THE CONCLAVE OF CORPSES.

Some three hundred years since, when the convent of Kreutzberg was in its glory, one of the monks who dwelt therein, wishing to ascertain something of the hereafter of those whose bodies lay all undecayed in the cemetery, visited it alone in the dead of night for the purpose of prosecuting his inquiries on that fearful subject. As he opened the trap-door of the vault a light burst from below; but deeming it to be only the lamp of the sacristan, the monk drew back and awaited his departure concealed behind the high altar. The sacristan emerged not, however, from the opening; and the monk, tired of waiting, approached, and finally descended the rugged steps which led into the dreary depths. No sooner had he set foot on the lowermost stair, than the well-known scene underwent a complete transformation in his eyes. He had long been accustomed to visit the vault, and whenever the sacristan went thither, he was almost sure to be with him. He therefore knew every part of it as well as he did the interior of his own narrow cell,

114

and the arrangement of its contents was perfectly familiar to his eyes. What, then, was his horror to perceive that this arrangement, which even but that morning had come under his observation as usual, was altogether altered, and a new and wonderful one substituted in its stead.

A dim lurid light pervaded the desolate abode of darkness, and it just sufficed to give to his view a sight of the most singular description.

On each side of him the dead but imperishable bodies of the long-buried brothers of the convent sat erect in their lidless coffins, their cold, starry eyes glaring at him with lifeless rigidity, their withered fingers locked together on their breasts, their stiffened limbs motionless and still. It was a sight to petrify the stoutest heart; and the monk's quailed before it, though he was a philosopher, and a sceptic to boot. At the upper end of the vault, at a rude table formed of a decayed coffin, or something which once served the same purpose, sat three monks. They were the oldest corses in the charnel-house, for the inquisitive brother knew their faces well; and the cadaverous hue of their cheeks seemed still more cadaverous in the dim light shed upon them, while their hollow eyes gave forth what looked to him like flashes of flame. A large book lay open before one of them, and the others bent over the rotten table as if in intense pain, or in deep and fixed attention. No word was said; no sound was heard; the vault was as silent as the grave, its awful tenants still as statues.

Fain would the curious monk have receded from this horrible place; fain would he have retraced his steps and sought again his cell; fain would he have shut his eyes to the fearful scene; but he could not stir from the spot, he felt rooted there; and though he once succeeded in turning his eyes to the entrance of the vault, to his infinite surprise and dismay he could not discover where it lay, nor perceive any possible means of exit. He stood thus for some time. At length the aged monk at the table beckoned him to advance. With slow tottering steps he made his way to the group, and at length stood in front of the table, while the other monks raised their heads and glanced at him with a fixed, lifeless look that froze the current of his blood. He knew not what to do; his senses were fast forsaking him; Heaven seemed to have deserted him for his incredulity. In this moment of doubt and fear he bethought him of a prayer, and as he proceeded he felt himself becoming possessed of a confidence he had before unknown. He looked on the book before him. It was a large volume, bound in black, and clasped with bands of gold, with fastenings of the same metal. It was inscribed at the top of each page

"*Liber Obedientiæ.*"

He could read no further. He then looked, first in the eyes of him before whom it lay open, and then in those of his fellows. He finally glanced around the vault on the corpses who filled every visible coffin in its dark and spacious womb. Speech came to him, and resolution to use it. He addressed himself to the awful beings in whose presence he stood, in the words of one having authority with them.

" *Pax vobis*," 'twas thus he spake—"Peace be to ye."

" *Hic nulla pax*," replied an aged monk, in a hollow, tremulous tone, baring his breast the while—"Here is no peace."

He pointed to his bosom as he spoke, and the monk, casting his eye upon it, beheld his heart within surrounded by living fire, which seemed to feed on it but not consume it. He turned away in affright, but ceased not to prosecute his inquiries.

" *Pax vobis, in nomine Domini*," he spake again—"Peace be to ye, in the name of the Lord."

" *Hic non pax*," the hollow and heartrending tones of the ancient monk who sat at the right of the table were heard to answer.

On glancing at the bared bosom of this hapless being also the same sight was exhibited—the heart surrounded by a devouring flame, but still remaining fresh and unconsumed under its operation. Once more the monk turned away and addressed the aged man in the centre.

" *Pax vobis, in nomine Domini*," he proceeded.

At these words the being to whom they were addressed raised his head, put forward his hand, and closing the book with a loud clap, said—

"Speak on. It is yours to ask, and mine to answer."

The monk felt reassured, and his courage rose with the occasion.

"Who are ye?" he inquired; "who may ye be?"

"We know not!" was the answer, "alas! we know not!"

"We know not, we know not!" echoed in melancholy tones the denizens of the vault.

"What do ye here?" pursued the querist.

"We await the last day, the day of the last judgment! Alas for us! woe! woe!"

"Woe! woe!" resounded on all sides.

The monk was appalled, but still he proceeded.

"What did ye to deserve such doom as this? What may your crime be that deserves such dole and sorrow?"

As he asked the question the earth shook under him, and a crowd of skeletons uprose from a range of graves which yawned suddenly at his feet.

"These are our victims," answered the old monk. "They suffered at our hands. We suffer now, while they are at peace; and we shall suffer."

"For how long?" asked the monk.

"For ever and ever!" was the answer.

"For ever and ever, for ever and ever!" died along the vault.

"May God have mercy on us!" was all the monk could exclaim.

The skeletons vanished, the graves closing over them. The aged men disappeared from his view, the bodies fell back in their coffins, the light fled, and the den of death was once more enveloped in its usual darkness.

On the monk's revival he found himself lying at the foot of the altar. The grey dawn of a spring morning was visible, and he was fain to retire to his cell as secretly as he could, for fear he should be discovered.

From thenceforth he eschewed vain philosophy, says the legend, and, devoting his time to the pursuit of true knowledge, and the extension of the power, greatness, and glory of the Church, died in the odour of sanctity, and was buried in that holy vault, where his body is still visible.

Requiescat in pace!

LEGENDS OF RUBEZAHL, OR NUMBER-NIP.

ONCE upon a time a glazier who was travelling across the mountains, feeling very tired from the heavy load of glass which he was carrying, began to look about to discover a place where he might rest it. Rubezahl, who had been watching for some time, no sooner saw this than he changed himself into a little mound, which the glazier not long afterwards discovered in his way, and on which, well pleased, he proposed to seat himself. But his joy was not of long continuance, for he had not sat there many minutes before the heap vanished from under him so rapidly, that the poor glazier fell to the ground with his glass, which was by the fall smashed into a thousand pieces.

The poor fellow arose from the ground and looked around him, but the mound of earth on which he had before seated himself was no longer visible. Then he began bitterly to lament, and to sigh with heartfelt sorrow over his untoward fate. At length he started once more on his journey.

120

Upon this Rubezahl, assuming the appearance of a traveller, accosted him, and inquired why he so lamented, and what was the great sorrow with which he was afflicted. The glazier related to him the whole affair, how that, being weary, he had seated himself upon a mound by the wayside, how this had suddenly overthrown him, and broken to pieces his whole stock of glass, which was well worth eight dollars, and how, in short, the mound itself had suddenly disappeared. He declared that he knew not in the least how to recover his loss and bring the business to a good ending. The compassionate mountain sprite comforted him, told him who he was, and that he himself had played him the trick, and at the same time bade him be of good cheer, for his losses should be made good to him.

Upon this Rubezahl transformed himself into an ass, and directed the glazier to sell him at the mill which lay at the foot of the mountain, and to be sure to make off with the purchase-money as quickly as possible. The glazier accordingly immediately bestrode the transformed mountain sprite, and rode him down the mountain to the mill, where he offered him for sale to the miller at the price of ten dollars. The miller offered nine, and the glazier, without further haggling, took the money and went his way.

When he was gone the miller sent his newly purchased beast to the stable, and the boy who had charge of him immediately filled his rack with hay. Upon this Rubezahl exclaimed—

"I don't eat hay. I eat nothing but roasted and boiled, and that of the best."

The boy's hair stood on end. He flew to his master, and related to him this wondrous tale, and he no sooner heard it than he hastened to the stable and there found nothing, for his ass and his nine dollars were alike vanished.

But the miller was rightly served, for he had cheated in his time many poor people, therefore Rubezahl punished in this manner the injustice of which he had been guilty.

In the year 1512 a man of noble family, who was a very tyrant and oppressor, had commanded one of his vassals or peasants to carry home with his horses and cart an oak of extraordinary magnitude, and threatened to visit him with the heaviest disgrace and punishment if he neglected to fulfil his desires. The peasant saw that it was impossible for him to execute the command of his lord, and fled to the woods with great sorrow and lamentation.

There he was accosted by Rubezahl, who appeared to him like a man, and inquired of him the cause of his so great sorrow and affliction. Upon this the peasant related to him all the circumstances of the case. When Rubezahl heard it he bade him be of good cheer and care not, but go home to his house again, as he himself would soon transport the oak, as his lord required, into his courtyard.

Scarcely had the peasant got well home again before Rubezahl took the monstrous oak-tree, with its thick and sturdy boughs, and hurled it into the courtyard of the nobleman, and with its huge stem, and its many thick branches, so choked and blocked up the entrance that no one could get either in or out.   And because the oak proved harder than their iron tools, and could in no manner or wise, and with no power which they could apply to it, be hewn or cut in pieces, the nobleman was compelled to break through the walls in another part of the courtyard, and have a new doorway made, which was only done with great labour and expense.

Once upon a time Rubezahl made, from what materials is not known, a quantity of pigs, which he drove to the neighbouring market and sold to a peasant, with a caution that the purchaser should not drive them through any water.

Now, what happened?   Why these same swine having chanced to get sadly covered with mire, what must the peasant do, but drive them to the river, which they had no sooner entered than the pigs suddenly became wisps of straw, and were carried away by the stream.   The purchaser was, moreover, obliged to put up with the loss, for he could neither find his pigs again, nor could he discover the person from whom he had bought them.

Rubezahl once betook himself to the Hirschberg, which is in the neighbourhood of his forest haunts, and there offered his services as a woodcutter to one of the townsmen, asking for his remuneration nothing more than a bundle of wood. This the man promised him, accepting his offer, and pointed out some cart-loads, intending to give him some assistance. To this offer of help in his labours Rubezahl replied—

"No. It is quite unnecessary. All that is to be done I can very well accomplish by myself."

Upon this his new master made a few further inquiries, asking him what sort of a hatchet he had got, for he had noticed that his supposed servant was without one.

"Oh," said Rubezahl, "I'll soon get a hatchet."

Accordingly he laid hands upon his left leg, and pulled that and his foot and all off at the thigh, and with it cut, as if he had been raving mad, all the wood into small pieces of proper lengths and sizes in about a quarter of an hour, thus proving that a dismembered foot is a thousand times more effectual for such purposes than the sharpest axe.

In the meanwhile the owner (who saw plainly that mischief was intended) kept calling upon the wondrous woodcutter to desist and go about his business. Rubezahl, however, kept incessantly answering—

"No, I won't stir from this spot until I have hewn the wood as small as I agreed to, and have got my wages for so doing."

In the midst of such quarrelling Rubezahl finished his job, and screwed his leg on again, for while at work he had been standing on one leg, after the fashion of a stork. Then he gathered together into one bundle all he had cut, placed it on his shoulder, and started off with it towards his favourite retreat, heedless of the tears and lamentations of his master.

On this occasion Rubezahl did not appear in the character of a sportive or mischievous spirit, but as an avenger of injustice, for his employer had induced a number of poor men to bring wood to his home upon the promise of paying them wages, which, however, he had never paid them. Rubezahl laid at the door of each of these poor men as much of the wood he carried away as would repay them, and so the business was brought to a proper termination.

It once happened that a messenger vexed or played some trick upon Rubezahl, who thereupon revenged himself in the following manner, and so wiped out the score.

The messenger, in one of his journeys over the mountains, entered an hotel to refresh himself, and placed his spear as usual behind the door. No sooner had he done so than Rubezahl carried off the spear, transformed himself into a similar one, and took its place.

When the messenger, after taking his rest, set forth again with the spear, and had got some little way on his journey, it began slipping about every now and then in such a manner that the messenger began pitching forward into the most intolerable mire, and got himself sadly bespattered. It did this so often that at last he could not tell for the soul of him what had come to the spear, or why he kept slipping forward with it instead of seizing fast hold of the ground.

He looked at it longways and sideways, from above, from underneath, but in spite of all his attempts, no change could he discover.

After this inspection he went forward a little way, when suddenly he was once more plunged into the morass, and commenced crying—

"Woe is me! woe is me!" at his spear, which led him into such scrapes, and did nothing to release him from them. At length he got himself once more to rights, and then he turned the spear the wrong way upwards. No sooner had he done so than he was driven backwards instead of forwards, and so got into a worse plight than ever.

After this he laid the spear across his shoulder like a pikeman, since it was no use to trail it upon the earth, and in this fashion he started on. But Rubezahl continued his tricks by pressing on the messenger as though he had got a yoke on his back. He changed the spear from one shoulder to the other, until at last, from very weariness, he threw away the bewitched weapon, imagining that the Evil One must possess it, and went his way without it.

He had not proceeded above a quarter of a mile, when, looking carelessly about him, he was astounded to find his spear by his side. He was sadly frightened, and little knew what to make of it. At last he boldly ventured to lay hands upon it. He did so, and lifted it up, but he could not conceive how he should carry it. He had no desire to trail it any more on the ground, and the thought of carrying it on his shoulder made him shudder. He decided, however, to give it another trial, carrying it in his hand. Fresh troubles now arose. The spear weighed so heavy that he could not stir it a foot from the spot, and though he tried first one hand and then another, all his efforts were in vain.

At last he bethought him of riding upon the spear, as a child bestrides a stick. A wonderful change now came over the weapon. It ran on as though it had been a fleet horse, and thus mounted the messenger rode on without ceasing until he descended the mountain and came into the city, where he excited the wonder, delight, and laughter of the worthy burghers.

Although he had endured some trouble in the

early part of his journey, the messenger thought he had been amply compensated at the close, and he comforted himself by making up his mind that in all future journeys he was destined to perform he would bestride his nimble spear. His good intentions were, however, frustrated. Rubezahl had played his game, and had had all the amusement he desired with the poor knave. Accordingly he scampered away, leaving in his place the real spear, which never played any more tricks, but, after the old fashion of other spears, accompanied its master in a becoming and orderly style.

A poor woman, who got her living by gathering herbs, once went, accompanied by her two children, to the mountains, carrying with her a basket in which to gather the plants, which she was in the habit of disposing of to the apothecaries. Having chanced to discover a large tract of land covered with such plants as were most esteemed, she busied herself so in filling her basket that she lost her way, and was troubled to find out how to get back to the path from which she had wandered. On a sudden a man dressed like a peasant appeared before her, and said—

"Well, good woman, what is it you are looking for so anxiously? and where do you want to go?"

"Alas!" replied she, "I am a poor woman who has neither bit nor sup, for which reason I am obliged to wander to gather herbs, so that I may buy bread for myself and my hungry children. I have lost my way, and cannot find it. I pray you, good man, take pity on me, and lead me out of the thicket into the right path, so that I may make the best of my way home."

"Well, my good woman," replied Rubezahl, for it was he, "make yourself happy. I will show you the way. But what good are those roots to you? They will be of little benefit. Throw away this rubbish, and gather from this tree as many leaves as will fill your basket; you will find them answer your purpose much better."

"Alas!" said the woman, "who would give a penny for them? They are but common leaves, and good for nothing."

"Be advised, my good woman," said Rubezahl; "throw away those you have got, and follow me."

He repeated his injunction over and over again in vain, until he got tired, for the woman would not be persuaded. At last, he fairly laid hold of the basket, threw the herbs out by main force, and supplied their place with leaves from the surround‑ing bushes. When he had finished, he told the woman to go home, and led her into the right path.

The woman, with her children and her basket, journeyed on some distance; but they had not gone far before she saw some valuable herbs growing by the wayside. No sooner did she perceive them

I

than she longed to gather them, for she hoped that she should obtain something for them, while the leaves with which her basket was crammed were, she thought, good for nothing. She accordingly emptied her basket, throwing away the rubbish, as she esteemed it, and having filled it once more with roots, journeyed on to her dwelling at Kirschdorf.

As soon as she arrived at her home she cleansed the roots she had gathered from the earth which clung around them, tied them neatly together, and emptied everything out of the basket. Upon doing this, something glittering caught her eye, and she commenced to make a careful examination of the basket. She was surprised to discover several ducats sticking to the wickerwork, and these were clearly such of the leaves as remained of those which she had so thoughtlessly thrown away on the mountains.

She rejoiced at having preserved what she had, but she was again sorely vexed that she had not taken care of all that the mountain spirit had gathered for her. She hastened back to the spot where she had emptied the basket, in hopes of finding some of the leaves there; but her search was in vain—they had all vanished.

THE HUNTER HACKELNBERG AND THE TUT-OSEL.

THE Wild Huntsman, Hackelnberg, traverses the Hartz mountains and the Thuringian forest, but he seems mostly to prefer the Hakel, from which place he derives his name, and especially the neighbourhood of Dummburg. Ofttimes is he heard at night, in rain and storm, when the moonlight is breaking by fits and starts through the troubled sky, following with his hounds the shadows of the wild beasts he slew in days of yore. His retinue generally proceed from the Dummburg, straight over the Hakel to the now desolate village of Ammendorf.

He has only been seen by a few children, who, having been born on a Sunday, had the power of seeing spirits. Sometimes he met them as a lonely huntsman, accompanied by one solitary hound. Sometimes he was seen in a carriage drawn by four horses, and followed by six dogs of the chase. But many have heard the low bellowing of his hounds, and the splashing of his horse's feet in the swamps of the moor; many have heard his cry of "Hu!

hu!" and seen his associate and forerunner—the Tut-Osel, or Tooting Ursula.

Once upon a time three wanderers seated themselves in the neighbourhood of the Dummburg. The night was already far advanced. The moon gleamed faintly through the chasing clouds. All around was still. Suddenly they heard something rush along over their heads. They looked up, and an immense screech-owl flew before them.

"Ha!" cried one of them, "there is the Tut-Osel! Hackelnberg, the Wild Huntsman, is not far off."

"Let us fly," exclaimed the second, "before the spirits overtake us."

"We cannot fly," said the third; "but you have nothing to fear if you do not irritate him. Lay yourselves down upon your faces when he passes over us. But, remember, you must not think of addressing Hackelnberg, lest he treat you as he treated the shepherd."

The wanderers laid themselves under the bushes. Presently they heard around them the rushing by, as it were, of a whole pack of hounds, and high in the air above them they heard a hollow sound like that of a hunted beast of the forest, and ever and anon they trembled at hearing the fearful-toned voice of the Wild Huntsman uttering his well-known "Hu! hu!" Two of the wanderers pressed close to the earth, but the third could not resist his inclination to have a peep at what was going on.   He looked up slantingly through the branches, and saw the shadow of a huntsman pass directly over him.

Suddenly all around was hushed. The wanderers rose slowly and timidly, and looked after Hackeln-berg; but he had vanished, and did not return.

"But who is the Tut-Osel?" inquired the second wanderer, after a long pause.

"In a distant nunnery in Thuringia," replied the first, "there once lived a nun named Ursula, who, even during her lifetime, tormented all the sisterhood by her discordant voice, and oftentimes interrupted the service of the church, for which reason they called her Tut-Osel, or Tooting Ursula. If matters were bad while she lived, they became far worse when she died.   At eleven o'clock every night she now thrust her head through a hole in the convent tower and tooted most miserably, and every morning at about four o'clock she joined unasked in the matin song.

"For a few days the sisterhood endured this with a beating heart, and on bended knees; but on the fourth morning, when she joined in the service, and one of the nuns whispered tremblingly to her neighbour—

"'Ha! it is surely our Tut-Osel!' the song ceased, the hair of the nuns stood on end, and they all rushed from the church, exclaiming—

"'Ha! Tut-Osel! Tut-Osel!'

"Despite the penances and chastisements with which they were threatened, not one of the nuns would enter the church again until the Tut-Osel was banished from the walls of the nunnery. To effect this, one of the most celebrated exorcists of the day, a Capuchin friar, from a cloister on the banks of the Danube, was sent for; and he succeeded, by prayer and fasting, in banishing Ursel in the shape of a screech-owl to the far-distant Dummburg.

"Here she met Hackelnberg, the Wild Huntsman, and found in his wood-cry, 'Hu! hu!' as great delight as he did in her 'U! hu!' So they now always hunt together; he glad to have a spirit after his own kind, and she rejoiced in the extreme to be no longer compelled to reside within the walls of a cloister, and there listen to the echo of her own song."

"So much for the Tut-Osel. Now tell us how it fared with the shepherd who spoke to Hackelnberg."

"Listen to the marvellous adventure," said the third wanderer. "A shepherd once hearing the Wild Huntsman journeying through the forest, encouraged the spirit hounds, and called out—

"'Good sport to you, Hackelnberg.'

"Hackelnberg instantly turned round and roared out to him, in a voice like thunder—

"'Since you have helped me to set on the hounds, you shall have part of the spoil.'

"The trembling shepherd tried to hide himself, but Hackelnberg hurled the half-consumed haunch of a horse into the shepherd's cart with such violence that it could scarcely be removed."

THE ALRAUN.

IT is a well-known tradition near Magdeburg, that
when a man who is a thief by inheritance,—that is
to say, whose father and grandfather and great-
grandfather before him, three generations of his
family, have been thieves; or whose mother has
committed a theft, or been possessed with an
intense longing to steal something at the time
immediately preceding his birth; it is the tradition that if such a man should be hanged, at the
foot of the gallows whereon his last breath was
exhaled will spring up a plant of hideous form
known as the Alraun or Gallows Mannikin. It is
an unsightly object to look at, and has broad, dark
green leaves, with a single yellow flower. The
plant, however, has great power, and whosoever is
its possessor never more knows what it is to want
money.

It is a feat full of the greatest danger to obtain
it. If not taken up from the root, clean out of the
soil, it is altogether valueless, and he who makes the
experiment wantonly risks his life. The moment

the earth is struck with the spade, the bitterest
cries and shrieks burst forth from it, and while the
roots are being laid bare demons are heard to howl
in horrid concert. When the preparatory work is
done, and when the hand of the daring man is laid
on the stem to pluck forth his prize, then is it as if
all the fiends of hell were let loose upon him, such
shrieking, such howling, such clanging of chains,
such crashing of thunder, and such flashing of forked
lightning assail him on every side. If his heart
fail him but for one moment his life is forfeit.
Many a bold heart engaged in this trial has ceased
to beat under the fatal tree; many a brave man's
body has been found mangled and torn to pieces on
that accursed spot.

There is, however, happily, only one day in the
month, the first Friday, on which this plant appears,
and on the night of that day only may it be plucked
from its hiding-place. The way it is done is this.
Whoso seeks to win it fasts all day. At sundown
he sets forth on his fearful adventure, taking with
him a coal-black hound, which has not a single fleck
of white on its whole body, and which he has compelled likewise to fast for four-and-twenty hours
previously. At midnight he takes his stand under
the gallows, and there stuffs his ears with wool or
wax, so that he may hear nothing. As the dread
hour arrives, he stoops down and makes three
crosses over the Alraun, and then commences to

dig for the roots in a perfect circle around it. When he has laid it entirely bare, so that it only holds to the ground by the points of its roots, he calls the hound to him, and ties the plant to its tail. He then shows the dog some meat, which he flings to a short distance from the spot. Ravenous with hunger, the hound springs after it, dragging the plant up by the root, but before he can reach the tempting morsel he is struck dead as by some invisible hand.

The adventurer, who all the while stood by the plant to aid in its uprooting should the strength of the animal prove insufficient, then rushes forward, and, detaching it from the body of the dead hound, grasps it firmly in both hands. He then wraps it up carefully in a silken cloth, first, however, washing it well in red wine, and then bears it homeward. The hound is buried in the spot whence the Alraun has been extracted.

On reaching home the man deposits his treasure in a strong chest, with three locks, and only visits it every first Friday in the month, or, rather, after the new moon. On these occasions he again washes it with red wine, and enfolds it afresh in a clean silken cloth of white and red colours.

If he has any question to ask, or any request to make, he then puts the one or proffers the other. If he wish to know of things in the future, the Alraun will tell him truly, but he will only get one answer in the moon, and nothing else will be done for him by the plant. If he desire to obtain some substantial favour, he has it performed for him on making his request, but then the Alraun will answer no inquiries as to the future until the next day of visitation shall arrive.

Whoso has this wonder of the world in his possession can never take harm from his foes, and never sustain any loss. If he be poor, he at once becomes rich. If his marriage be unblest by offspring, he at once has children.

If a piece of gold be laid beside the Alraun at night, it is found to be doubled in the morning, and so on for any sum whatsoever, but never has it been known to be increased more than two pieces for each one.

On the demise of the owner only a youngest son can inherit the Alraun. To inherit it effectually he must place a loaf of white bread and a piece of money in the coffin of his father, to be buried along with his corpse. If he fail to do so, then is the possession, like many others of great name in the world, of no value to him. Should, however, the youngest son fail before the father, then the Alraun rightfully belongs to the eldest, but he must also place bread and money in the coffin of his brother, as well as in that of his father, to inherit it to any purpose.

THE king of a great land died, and left his queen to take care of their only child. This child was a daughter, who was very beautiful, and her mother loved her dearly and was very kind to her. When she grew up, she was betrothed to a prince who lived a great way off; and as the time drew near for her to be married, she got ready to set off on her journey to his country. The queen, her mother, packed up a great many costly things—jewels, gold and silver trinkets, fine dresses, and, in short, everything that became a royal bride. She gave her a waiting-maid to ride with her and give her into the bridegroom's hands, and each had a horse for the journey. The princess' horse was called Falada, and could speak.

When the time came for them to set out, the aged mother went into the princess's bedchamber, took a knife, and having cut her finger till it bled, let three drops of the blood fall upon a handkerchief, and gave it to the princess, saying—

"Take care of it, dear child, for it is a charm that may be of use to you on the road."

They all took a sorrowful leave of the princess, and she put the handkerchief into her bosom, got upon her horse, and set off on her journey to her bridegroom's kingdom.

One day as they were riding along by a brook, the princess began to feel very thirsty, and said to her maid—

"Pray get down, and fetch me some water in my golden cup out of yonder brook, for I want to drink."

"Nay," said the maid, "if you are thirsty, get off yourself and stoop down by the water and drink. I shall not be your waiting-maid any longer."

The princess got down, and knelt over the brook and drank, for she was frightened, and dared not bring out her cup; and she wept, and said—

"Alas! what will become of me?"

The three drops of blood answered her, and said—

> "Alas, alas! if thy mother knew it,
> Sadly, sadly, would she rue it."

The princess was very gentle and meek, so she said nothing to her maid's ill-behaviour, but got upon her horse again.

They all rode further on their journey, till the day grew so warm and the sun so scorching that the bride began to feel very thirsty again; and at last, when they came to a river, she forgot her maid's rude speech, and said—

"Pray get down, and fetch me some water to drink in my cup."

But the maid answered her, and even spoke more haughtily than before—

"Drink if you will, but I shall not be your waiting-maid."

Then the princess got off her horse, and lay down, and held her head over the running stream, and cried and said—

"What will become of me?"

And the drops of blood answered her again as before. As the princess leaned down to drink, the handkerchief on which was the blood fell from her bosom and floated away on the water, but the princess was so frightened that she did not notice it. Her maid, however, saw it, and was very glad, for she knew the charm, and she saw that the poor bride would be in her power now that she had lost the drops of blood. So when the bride had done drinking, and would have got upon Falada again, the maid said—

"I will ride upon Falada, and you may have my horse instead;" so the princess was forced to give up her horse, and soon afterwards to take off her royal clothes and put on her maid's shabby ones.

At last, as they drew near the end of their journey, this treacherous servant threatened to kill her mistress if she ever told any one what had happened; but Falada saw it all, and marked it well.

Then the waiting-maid got upon Falada, while the real bride rode upon the other horse, and they went on in this way until they came at last to the royal court. There was great joy at their coming, and the prince flew to meet them, and lifted the maid from her horse, thinking she was the one who was to be his wife. She was led upstairs to the royal chamber, but the true princess was told to stay in the court below.

Now the old king happened just then to have nothing else to do, so he was amusing himself by sitting at his window looking at what was going on, and he saw her in the courtyard. As she looked very pretty, and too delicate for a waiting-maid, he went up into the royal chamber to ask the bride who it was she had brought with her that was thus left standing in the court below.

"I brought her with me for the sake of her company on the road," replied she. "Pray give the girl some work to do, that she may not be idle."

The king could not for some time think of any work for her to do, but at last he said—

"I have a lad who takes care of my geese, she may go and help him."

Now the name of this lad, whom the princess was to help in watching the king's geese, was Conrad.

The false bride said to the prince—

"Dear husband, pray do me one piece of kindness."

"That I will," said the prince.

"Then tell one of your knackers to cut off the head of the horse I rode upon, for it was very unruly, and plagued me sadly on the road."

In reality she was very much afraid lest Falada should some day or other speak, and tell all that she had done to the princess. She carried her point, and the faithful Falada was killed. When the true princess heard of it she wept, and begged the man to nail up Falada's head over a large dark gate of the city, through which she had to pass every morning and evening, that there she might see him sometimes. The slaughterer said he would do as she wished, and he cut off the head, and nailed it up under the dark gate.

Early the next morning, as the princess and Conrad went through the gate, she said sorrowfully—

"Falada, Falada, there thou hangest!"

The head answered—

"Bride, bride, there thou goest!
Alas, alas! if thy mother knew it,
Sadly, sadly would she rue it."

Then they went out of the city, and drove the geese on. When they were come to a meadow she sat down upon a bank there, and let down her waving locks of hair, which were like pure gold; and when Conrad saw it he ran up, and would have pulled some of the locks out, but the princess cried—

> " Blow, breezes, blow !
> Let Conrad's hat go !
> Blow, breezes, blow !
> Let him after it go !
> O'er hills, dales, and rocks,
> Away be it whirled,
> Till my golden locks
> Are all combed and curled."

Then there came a wind so strong that it blew off Conrad's hat. Away it flew over the hills, and he was forced to turn and run after it, so that when he came back she had done combing and curling her hair, and had put it up again safely, and he could not get any of it. He was very angry and sulky, and would not speak to her; but they watched the geese until it grew dark, and then drove them homewards.

The next morning, as they were going through the dark gate, the poor girl looked up at Falada's head, and cried—

> " Falada, Falada, there thou hangest !"

It answered—

> " Bride, bride, there thou goest !
> Alas, alas ! if thy mother knew it,
> Sadly, sadly would she rue it."

Then she drove on the geese, and sat down again in the meadow, and began to comb out her hair as before, and Conrad ran up to her, and wanted to take hold of it. The princess repeated the words she had used the day before, when the wind came and blew away his hat, and off it flew a great way, over the hills and far away, so that he had to run after it. When he returned, she had bound up her hair again, and all was safe. So they watched the geese until it grew dark.

In the evening, after they came home, Conrad went to the old king and said—

"I won't have that strange girl to help me to keep the geese any longer."

"Why?" said the king.

"Because instead of doing any good she does nothing but tease me all day long."

Then the king made him tell what had happened, and Conrad said—

"When we go in the morning through the dark gate with our flock of geese, she cries and talks with the head of a horse that hangs upon the wall, and the head answers her."

And Conrad went on telling the king what had happened in the meadow where the geese fed; how his hat was blown away, and how he was forced to run after it and leave his flock of geese to themselves. The old king told the boy to go out again the next day, and when morning came he placed himself behind the dark gate, and heard how the princess spoke to Falada, and how Falada answered. Then he went into the field and hid himself in a bush by the meadow's side, and he soon saw with his own eyes how they drove the flock of geese, and how, after a little time, she let down her hair that glittered in the sun. Then he heard her call the wind, and soon there came a gust that carried away Conrad's hat, and away he went after it, while the girl went on combing and curling her hair. All this the old king saw; so he went home without having been observed, and when the goose-girl came back in the evening, he called her aside and asked her why she did so. She burst into tears, and said—

" That I must not tell you nor any man, or I shall lose my life."

The old king begged hard, but she would tell him nothing. Then he said—

"If you will not tell me thy story, tell thy grief to the iron stove there," and then he went away.

Then the princess crept into the stove, and, weeping and lamenting, she poured forth her whole heart, saying—

" I am alone in the whole world, though I am a king's daughter. A treacherous waiting-maid has taken my place and compelled me to put off my royal dress, and even taken my place with my bridegroom, while I have to work as a goose-girl. If my mother knew it, it would break her heart."

The old king, however, was standing by the stove, listening to what the princess said, and overheard it all. He ordered royal clothes to be put upon her, and gazed at her in wonder, she was so beautiful. Then he called his son, and told him that he had only a false bride, for that she was merely the waiting-maid, while the true bride stood by. The young prince rejoiced when he saw the princess's beauty, and heard how meek and patient she had been, and the king ordered a great feast to be got ready for all his court. The bridegroom sat at the top of the table, with the false princess on one side and the true one on the other; but the waiting-maid did not recognise the princess, for her beauty was quite dazzling.

When they had eaten and drunk, and were very merry, the old king said he would tell them a tale. So he began, and told all the story of the princess, as if it were a tale he had heard, and he asked the waiting-woman what she thought ought to be done to any one who behaved so badly as the servant in the story.

" Nothing better," said the false bride, " than that she should be thrown into a cask stuck round with sharp nails, and that two white horses should be put to it, and should drag it from street to street till she were dead."

" Thou art she," said the old king, " and as thou hast judged thyself, so it shall be done to thee."

Then the young prince was married to his true wife, and they reigned over the kingdom in peace and happiness all their lives.

HANS JAGENTEUFEL.

IT is commonly believed that if any person is guilty of a crime for which he deserves to lose his head, he will, if he escape punishment during his lifetime, be condemned after his death to wander about with his head under his arm.

In the year 1644 a woman of Dresden went out early one Sunday morning into a neighbouring wood for the purpose of collecting acorns. In an open space, at a spot not very far from the place which is called the Lost Water, she heard somebody blow a very strong blast upon a hunting-horn, and immediately afterwards a heavy fall succeeded, as though a large tree had fallen to the ground. The woman was greatly alarmed, and concealed her little bag of acorns among the grass. Shortly afterwards the horn was blown a second time, and on looking round she saw a man without a head, dressed in a long grey cloak, and riding upon a grey horse. He was booted and spurred, and had a bugle-horn hanging at his back.

As he rode past her very quietly she regained her courage, went on gathering the acorns, and when evening came returned home undisturbed.

Nine days afterwards, the woman returned to that spot for the purpose of again collecting the acorns, and as she sat down by the Forsterberg, peeling an apple, she heard behind her a voice calling out to her—

"Have you taken a whole sack of acorns and nobody tried to punish you for doing so ?"

"No," said she. "The foresters are very kind to the poor, and they have done nothing to me— the Lord have mercy on my sins ! "

With these words she turned about, and there stood he of the grey cloak, but this time he was without his horse, and carried his head, which was covered with curling brown hair, under his arm.

The woman shrank from him in alarm, but the spirit said—

" Ye do well to pray to God to forgive you your sins, it was never my good lot to do so."

Thereupon he related to her how that he had lived about one hundred and thirty years before, and was called Hans Jagenteufel, as his father had been before him, and how his father had often besought him not to be too hard upon poor people, how he had paid no regard to the advice his father had given him, but had passed his time in drinking and carousing, and in all manner of wickedness, for which he was now condemned to wander about the world as an evil spirit.

THE WAITS OF BREMEN.

AN honest farmer had once an ass that had been a
faithful hard-working slave to him for a great many
years, but was now growing old, and every day
more and more unfit for work. His master therefore was tired of keeping him to live at ease like a
gentleman, and so began to think of putting an end
to him. The ass, who was a shrewd hand, saw that
some mischief was in the wind, so he took himself
slily off, and began his journey towards Bremen.

"There," thought he to himself, "as I have a
good voice, I may chance to be chosen town
musician."

After he had travelled a little way, he spied a dog
lying by the roadside, and panting as if very tired.

"What makes you pant so, my friend?" said the
ass.

"Alas!" said the dog, "my master was going to
knock me on the head, because I am old and weak,
and can no longer make myself useful to him in
hunting, so I ran away. But what can I do to
earn my livelihood?"

152

"Hark ye," said the ass, "I am going to Bremen to turn musician. Come with me, and try what you can do in the same way."

The dog said he was willing, and on they went.

They had not gone far before they saw a cat sitting in the middle of the road, with tears in her eyes, and making a most rueful face.

"Pray, my good lady," said the ass, "what's the matter with you? You look quite out of spirits."

"Ah, me!" said the cat. "How can a body be in good spirits when one's life is in danger? Because I am beginning to grow old, and had rather lie at my ease before the fire than run about the house after the mice, my mistress laid hold of me, and was going to drown me, and though I have been lucky enough to get away from her, I know not how I am to live."

"Oh!" said the ass, "by all means go with us to Bremen. You are a good night-singer, and may make your fortune as one of the waits."

The cat was pleased with the thought, and joined the party. Soon afterwards, as they were passing by a farmyard, they saw a cock perched upon a gate, screaming out with all his might and main.

"Bravo!" said the ass. "Upon my word, you make a famous noise. Pray, what is all this about?"

"Why," said the cock, "I was just now telling all our neighbours that we were to have fine weather for our washing-day; and yet my mistress and the cook don't thank me for my pains, but threaten to cut my head off to-morrow, and make broth of me for the guests that are coming on Sunday."

"Heaven forbid!" said the ass. "Come with us. Anything will be better than staying here. Besides, who knows, if we take care to sing in tune, we may get up a concert of our own, so come along with us."

"With all my heart," replied the cock; so they all four went on jollily together towards Bremen.

They could not, however, reach the town the first day, so when night came on they turned off the high-road into a wood to sleep. The ass and the dog laid themselves down under a great tree, and the cat climbed up into the branches; while the cock, thinking that the higher he sat the safer he should be, flew up to the very top of the tree, and then, according to his custom, before he sounded his trumpet and went to sleep, looked out on all sides to see that everything was well. In doing this he saw afar off something bright, and calling to his companions, said—

"There must be a house no great way off, for I see a light."

"If that be the case," replied the ass, "we had better change our quarters, for our lodging here is not the best in the world."

"Besides," said the dog, "I should not be the worse for a bone or two."

"And may be," remarked the cat, "a stray mouse will be found somewhere about the premises."

So they walked off together towards the spot where the cock had seen the light; and as they drew near, it became larger and brighter, till they came at last to a lonely house, in which was a gang of robbers.

The ass, being the tallest of the company, marched up to the window and peeped in.

"Well," said the cock, "what do you see?"

"What do I see?" replied the ass. "Why, I see a table spread with all kinds of good things, and robbers sitting round it making merry."

"That would be a noble lodging for us," said the cock.

"Yes," rejoined the ass, "if we could only get in."

They laid their heads together to see how they could get the robbers out, and at last they hit upon a plan. The ass set himself upright on his hind-legs, with his fore-feet resting on the window; the dog got upon his back; the cat scrambled up to the dog's shoulders, and the cock flew up and sat upon the cat. When all were ready the cock gave the signal, and up struck the whole band of music. The ass brayed, the dog barked, the cat mewed, and the cock crew. Then they all broke through the window at once, and came tumbling into the room amongst the broken glass, with a hideous clatter. The robbers, who had been not a little frightened by the opening concert, had now no doubt that some frightful hobgoblins had broken in upon them, and scampered away as fast as they could.

The coast once clear, the travellers soon sat down and despatched what the robbers had left, with as much eagerness as if they had not hoped to eat again for a month. As soon as they had had enough they put out the lights, and each once more sought out a resting-place to his liking. The donkey laid himself down upon a heap of straw in the yard; the dog stretched himself upon a mat behind the door; the cat rolled herself up on the hearth before the warm ashes; the cock perched upon a beam on the top of the house; and as all were rather tired with their journey, they soon fell fast asleep.

About midnight, however, when the robbers saw from afar that the lights were out and that all was quiet, they began to think that they had been in too great a hurry to run away; and one of them, who was bolder than the rest, went to see what was going on. Finding everything still, he marched into the kitchen, and groped about till he found a match in order to light a candle. Espying the glittering fiery eyes of the cat, he mistook them for live coals, and held the match to them to light it. The cat, however, not understanding such a joke, sprang at his face, and spat, and scratched him.

This frightened him dreadfully, and away he ran to the back door, where the dog jumped up and bit him in the leg. As he was crossing over the yard the ass kicked him; and the cock, who had been awakened by the noise, crew with all his might.

At this the robber ran back as fast as he could to his comrades, and told the captain that a horrid witch had got into the house, and had scratched his face with her long bony fingers—that a man with a knife in his hand had hidden himself behind the door, and stabbed him in the leg—that a black monster stood in the yard and struck him with a club—and that the devil sat upon the top of the house, and cried out—

"Throw the rascal up here!"

After this the robbers never dared to go back to the house; but the musicians were so pleased with their quarters, that they never found their way to Bremen, but took up their abode in the wood. And there they live, I dare say, to this very day.

THE FLAMING CASTLE.

Upon a high mountain in the Tyrol there stands an
old castle, in which there burns a fire every night,
and the flashes of that fire are so large that they rise
up over the walls, and may be seen far and wide.

It happened once that an old woman in want of
firewood was gathering the fallen twigs and branches
upon this castle-crowned mountain, and at length
arrived at the castle door. To indulge her curiosity
she began peering about her, and at last entered, not
without difficulty, for it was all in ruins and not easily
accessible. When she reached the courtyard, there
she beheld a goodly company of nobles and ladies
seated and feasting at a huge table. There were,
likewise, plenty of servants, who waited upon them,
changing their plates, handing round the viands, and
pouring out wine for the party.

As she thus stood gazing upon them, there came
one of the servants, who drew her on one side, and
placed a piece of gold in the pocket of her apron,
upon which the whole scene vanished in an instant,
and the poor frightened old woman was left to find

her way back as well as she could. However, she got outside the courtyard, and there stood before her a soldier with a lighted match, whose head was not placed upon his neck, but held by him under his arm. He immediately addressed the old woman, and commanded her not to tell any one what she had seen and heard upon peril of evil befalling her.

At length the woman reached home, full of anguish, still keeping possession of the gold, but telling no one whence she had obtained it. When the magistrates, however, got wind of the affair, she was summoned before them, but she would not speak one word upon the subject, excusing herself by saying that if she uttered one word respecting it great evil would ensue to her. When, however, they pressed her more strictly, she discovered to them all that had happened to her in the Fiery Castle, even to the smallest particular. In an instant, almost before her relation was fully ended, she was carried away, and no one could ever learn whither she fled.

A year or two afterwards, a young nobleman, a knight, and one well experienced in all things, took up his abode in those parts. In order that he might ascertain the issue of this affair, he set out on foot with his servant in the middle of the night on the road to the mountain. With great difficulty they made the ascent, and were on their way warned six times by an unknown voice to desist from their attempt.

They kept on, however, heedless of this caution, and at length reached the door of the castle. There again stood the soldier as a sentinel, and he called out as usual—

"Who goes there?"

The nobleman, who was bold of heart, gave for answer—

"It is I."

Upon this the spirit inquired further—

"Who art thou?"

This time the nobleman made no answer, but desired his servant to hand him his sword. When this was done, a black horseman came riding out of the castle, against whom the nobleman would have waged battle. The horseman, however, dragged him up upon his horse and rode with him into the courtyard, while the soldier chased the servant down the mountain. The nobleman was never more seen.

THE MONKS AT THE FERRY.

From time immemorial a ferry has existed from Andernach to the opposite side of the Rhine. Formerly it was more in use than at present, there being then a greater intercourse between the two shores of the river, much of which might be traced to the Convent of St. Thomas, once the most important and flourishing nunnery on the river.

Close by this ferry, on the margin of the Rhine, but elevated somewhat above the level of the water, stands a long, roofless, ruinous building, the remains of the castle of Friedrichstein, better known, however, to the peasantry, and to all passengers on the river, as the Devil's House. How it came by this suspicious appellative there are many traditions to explain. Some say that the Prince of Neuwied, who erected it, so ground down his subjects for its construction, that they unanimously gave it that name. Others derive its popular *sobriquet* from the godless revelries of the same prince within its walls, and the wild deeds of his companions in wickedness; while a third class of local historians insist upon it

L

that the ruin takes its name from the congregation of fiendish shapes which resort there on special occasions, and the riot and rout which they create in the roofless chambers, reeking vaults, and crumbling corridors of the desolate edifice. It is to this ruin, and of the adjacent ferry, that the following legend belongs.

It was in the time when the celebrated Convent of St. Thomas over Andernach existed in its pristine magnificence, that late on an autumnal night the ferryman from that city to the Devil's House on the other side of the river, who lived on the edge of the bank below the ruins of the ancient palace of the kings of Austrasia, was accosted by a stranger, who desired to be put across just as the man was about to haul up his boat for the day. The stranger seemed to be a monk, for he was closely cowled, and gowned from head to foot in the long, dark, flowing garb of some ascetic order.

" Hilloa! ferry," he shouted aloud as he approached the shore of the river, " hilloa! "

" Here, ahoy! here, most reverend father! " answered the poor ferryman. " What would ye have with me? "

" I would that you ferry me across the Rhine to yonder shore of the river," replied the monk. " I come from the Convent of St. Thomas, and I go afar on a weighty mission. Now, be ye quick, my good friend, and run me over."

"Most willingly, reverend father," said the ferry-man. "Most willingly. Step into my boat, and I'll put you across the current in a twinkling."

The dark-looking monk entered the boat, and the ferryman shoved off from the bank. They soon reached the opposite shore. The ferryman, however, had scarce time to give his fare a good-evening ere he disappeared from his sight, in the direction of the Devil's House. Pondering a little on this strange circumstance, and inwardly thinking that the dark monk might as well have paid him his fare, or, at least, bade him good-night before he took such unceremonious leave, he rowed slowly back across the stream to his abode at Andernach.

"Hilloa! ferry," once more resounded from the margin of the river as he approached, "hilloa!"

"Here, ahoy!" responded the ferryman, but with some strange sensation of fear. "What would ye?"

He rowed to the shore, but he could see no one for a while, for it was now dark. As he neared the landing-place, however, he became aware of the presence of two monks, garbed exactly like his late passenger, standing together, concealed by the shadow of the massive ruins.

"Here! here!" they cried.

"We would ye would ferry us over to yonder shore of the river," said the foremost of the twain. "We go afar on a weighty errand from the Convent of St. Thomas, and we must onwards this night. So be up quick, friend, and run us over soon."

"Step in, then," said the ferryman, not over courteously, for he remembered the trick played on him by their predecessor.

They entered the boat, and the ferryman put off. Just as the prow of the boat touched the opposite bank of the river, both sprang ashore, and disappeared at once from his view, like him who had gone before them.

"Ah!" said the ferryman, "if they call that doing good, or acting honestly, to cheat a hard-working poor fellow out of the reward of his labour, I do not know what bad means, or what it is to act knavishly."

He waited a little while to see if they would return to pay him, but finding that they failed to do so, he put across once more to his home at Andernach.

"Hilloa! ferry," again hailed a voice from the shore to which he was making, "hilloa!"

The ferryman made no reply to this suspicious hail, but pushed off his boat from the landing-place, fully resolved in his own mind to have nothing to do with any more such black cattle that night.

"Hilloa! ferry," was again repeated in a sterner voice. "Art dead or asleep?"

"Here, ahoy!" cried the ferryman. "What would ye?"

He had thought of passing downwards to the other extremity of the town, and there mooring his barque below the place she usually lay in, lest any other monks might feel disposed to make him their slave without offering any recompense. He had, however, scarcely entertained the idea, when three black-robed men, clothed as the former, in long, flowing garments, but more closely cowled, if possible, than they, stood on the very edge of the stream, and beckoned him to them. It was in vain for him to try to evade them, and as if to render any effort to that effect more nugatory, the moon broke forth from the thick clouds, and lit up the scene all around with a radiance like day.

"Step in, holy fathers! step in! quick!" said he, in a gruff voice, after they had told him the same tale in the very same words as the three others had used who had passed previously.

They entered the boat, and again the ferryman pushed off. They had reached the centre of the stream, when he bethought him that it was then a good time to talk of his fee, and he resolved to have it, if possible, ere they could escape him.

"But what do you mean to give me for my trouble, holy fathers?" he inquired. "Nothing for nothing, ye know."

"We shall give you all that we have to bestow," replied one of the monks. "Won't that suffice?"

"What is that?" asked the ferryman.

"Nothing," said the monk who had answered him first.

"But our blessing," interposed the second monk.

"Blessing ! bah ! That won't do. I can't eat blessings !" responded the grumbling ferryman.

"Heaven will pay you," said the third monk.

"That won't do either," answered the enraged ferryman. "I'll put back again to Andernach !"

"Be it so," said the monks.

The ferryman put about the head of his boat, and began to row back towards Andernach, as he had threatened. He had, however, scarcely made three strokes of his oars, when a high wind sprang up and the waters began to rise and rage and foam, like the billows of a storm-vexed sea. Soon a hurricane of the most fearful kind followed, and swept over the chafing face of the stream. In his forty years' experience of the river, the ferryman had never before beheld such a tempest—so dreadful and so sudden. He gave himself up for lost, threw down his oars, and flung himself on his knees, praying to Heaven for mercy. At that moment two of the dark-robed monks seized the oars which he had abandoned, while the third wrenched one of the thwarts of the boat from its place in the centre. All three then began to belabour the wretched man with all their might and main, until at length he lay senseless and without motion at the bottom of the boat. The barque, which was now veered about, bore them rapidly towards their original destination. The only words that passed on the occasion were an exclamation of the first monk who struck the ferryman down.

"Steer your boat aright, friend," he cried, "if you value your life, and leave off your prating. What have you to do with Heaven, or Heaven with you?"

When the poor ferryman recovered his senses, day had long dawned, and he was lying alone at the bottom of his boat. He found that he had drifted below Hammerstein, close to the shore of the right bank of the river. He could discover no trace of his companions. With much difficulty he rowed up the river, and reached the shore.

He learned afterwards from a gossiping neighbour, that, as the man returned from Neuwied late that night, or rather early the next morning, he met, just emerging from the Devil's House, a large black chariot running on three huge wheels, drawn by four horses without heads. In that vehicle he saw six monks seated *vis-à-vis*, apparently enjoying their morning ride. The driver, a curious-looking carl, with a singularly long nose, took, he said, the road along the edge of the river, and continued lashing his three coal-black, headless steeds at a tremendous rate, until a sharp turn hid them from the man's view.

DOCTOR ALL-WISE.

THERE was a poor peasant, named Crab, who once drove two oxen, with a load of wood, into the city, and there sold it for two dollars to a doctor. The doctor counted out the money to him as he sat at dinner, and the peasant, seeing how well he fared, yearned to live like him, and would needs be a doctor too. He stood a little while in thought, and at last asked if he could not become a doctor.

"Oh yes," said the doctor, "that may be easily managed. In the first place you must purchase an A, B, C book, only taking care that it is one that has got in the front of it a picture of a cock crowing. Then sell your cart and oxen, and buy with the money clothes, and all the other things needful. Thirdly, and lastly, have a sign painted with the words, 'I am Doctor All-Wise,' and have it nailed up before the door of your house."

The peasant did exactly as he had been told; and after he had doctored a little while, it chanced that a certain nobleman was robbed of a large sum of money. Some one told him that there lived in the village hard by a Doctor All-Wise, who was sure to be able to tell him where his money had gone. The nobleman at once ordered his carriage to be got ready and rode into the city, and having come to the doctor, asked him if he was Dr. All-Wise.

"Oh yes," answered he, "I am Doctor All-Wise, sure enough."

"Will you go with me, then," said the nobleman, "and get me back my money?"

"To be sure I will," said the doctor; "but my wife Grethel must go with me."

The nobleman was pleased to hear this, made them both get into the carriage with him, and away they all rode together. When they arrived at the nobleman's house dinner was already prepared, and he desired the doctor to sit down with him.

"My wife Grethel, too," said the doctor.

As soon as the first servant brought in the first dish, which was some great delicacy, the doctor nudged his wife, and said—

"Grethel, that is the first," meaning the first dish.

The servant overheard his remark, and thought he meant to say he was the first thief, which was actually the case, so he was sore troubled, and said to his comrades—

"The doctor knows everything. Things will certainly fall out ill, for he said I was the first thief."

The second servant would not believe what he said, but at last he was obliged, for when he carried the second dish into the room, the doctor remarked to his wife—

"Grethel, that is the second."

The second servant was now as much frightened as the first, and was pleased to leave the apartment. The third served no better, for the doctor said—

"Grethel, that is the third."

Now the fourth carried in a dish which had a cover on it, and the nobleman desired the doctor to show his skill by guessing what was under the cover. Now it was a crab. The doctor looked at the dish, and then at the cover, and could not at all divine what they contained, nor how to get out of the scrape. At length he said, half to himself and half aloud—

"Alas! poor crab!"

When the nobleman heard this, he cried out—

"You have guessed it, and now I am sure you will know where my money is."

The servant was greatly troubled at this, and he winked to the doctor to follow him out of the room, and no sooner did he do so than the whole four who had stolen the gold stood before him, and said that they would give it up instantly, and give him a good sum to boot, provided he would not betray them, for if he did their necks would pay for it. The doctor promised, and they conducted him to the place where the gold lay concealed. The doctor was well pleased to see it, and went back to the nobleman, and said—

"My lord, I will now search in my book and discover where the money is."

Now the fifth servant had crept into an oven to hear what the doctor said. He sat for some time turning over the leaves of his A, B, C book, looking for the picture of the crowing cock, and as he did not find it readily, he exclaimed—

"I know you are in here, and you must come out."

Then the man in the oven, thinking the doctor spoke of him, jumped out in a great fright, saying—

"The man knows everything."

Then Doctor All-Wise showed the nobleman where the gold was hidden, but he said nothing as to who stole it. So he received a great reward from all parties, and became a very famous man.

THE WHITE MAIDEN.

It is now centuries since a young noble of the
neighbourhood was hunting in the valleys which
lie behind the hills that skirt the Rhine opposite
the ancient town of St. Goar. In the heat of the
pursuit he followed the game to the foot of the
acclivity on which are seated the ruins of Thurnberg,
and there it disappeared all at once from his view. It
was the noon of a midsummer day, and the sun
shone down on him with all its strength. Despair-
ing of being able to find the object of his pursuit,
he determined to clamber up the steep hillside, and
seek shelter and repose in the shadow of the old
castle, or, mayhap, in one of its many crumbling chambers. With much labour he succeeded in reaching
the summit, and there, fatigued with his toil, and
parched with a burning thirst, he flung himself on
the ground beneath one of the huge towers, some
of whose remains still rear their heads on high, and
stretched out his tired limbs in the full enjoyment
of rest.

"Now," said he, as he wiped the perspiration

from his brow,—" now could I be happy indeed, if some kind being would bring me a beaker of the cool wine, which, they say, is ages old, down there in the cellars of this castle."

He had scarce spoken the words when a most beautiful maiden stepped forth from a cleft in the ivy-covered ruin, bearing in one hand a huge silver beaker of an antique form, full to the very brim of foaming wine. In her other hand she held a large bunch of keys of all sizes. She was clad in white from head to foot, her hair was flaxen, her skin was like a lily, and she had such loving eyes that they at once won the heart of the young noble.

" Here," said she, handing him the beaker, " thy wish is granted. Drink and be satisfied."

His heart leaped within him with joy at her condescension, and he emptied the contents of the goblet at a single draught. All the while she looked at him in such a manner as to intoxicate his very soul, so kindly and confidential were her glances. The wine coursed through his veins like liquid fire, his heart soon burned with love for the maiden, and the fever of his blood was by no means appeased by the furtive looks which ever and anon she cast upon him. She apparently read his state of mind, and when his passion was at its highest pitch, and all restraint seemed put an end to by the potent effects of love and wine, she disappeared in a moment by the way she came. The noble rushed after her in the hope of detaining the fugitive, or, at least, of catching a parting glimpse of her retreating form, but the ivy-encircled cleft, through which she seemed to have flitted, looked as though it had not been disturbed for centuries, and as he tried to force his way to the gloomy cavern below, a crowd of bats and owls and other foul birds of evil omen, aroused from their repose, rose upwards, and, amidst dismal hootings and fearful cries, almost flung him backward with the violence of their flight. He spent the remainder of the afternoon in search of the lost one, but without success. At the coming of night he wended his way homeward, weary, heart-sick, and overwhelmed with an indefinable sensation of sadness.

From that day forth he was an altered man— altered in appearance as well as in mind and in manners. Pleasure was a stranger to his soul, and he knew no longer what it was to enjoy peace. Wherever he went, whatever pursuit he was engaged in, whether in the chase, in the hall, in lady's bower, or in chapel, his eye only saw one object— the White Maiden. At the board she stood in imagination always before him, offering to his fevered lips the cool, brimming beaker ; and in the long-drawn aisles of the chapel she was ever present, beckoning him from his devotions to partake of the generous beverage which she still bore in her right hand. Every matron or maiden he met seemed by some wondrous process to take her shape, and even the very trees of the forest all looked to his thought like her.

Thenceforward he commenced to haunt the ruins in which she had appeared to him, still hoping to see, once again, her for whom he felt he was dying, and living alone in that hope. The sun scorched him, but it was nothing to the fever that burned within him. The rain drenched him, but he cared not for it. Time and change and circumstance seemed all forgotten by him, everything passed by him unheeded. His whole existence was completely swallowed up in one thought—the White Maiden of the ruined castle, and that, alas! was only vexation of spirit. A deadly fever seized him. It was a mortal disease. Still he raved, in his delirium, but of her. One morn a woodman, who occasionally provided him with food, found him a corpse at the entrance of the crevice in the wall whence the maiden had seemed to come, and where she had disappeared. It was long rumoured that he had struggled bravely with death—or rather that he could not die, because the curse was upon him—until the maiden, garbed in white as usual, appeared to him once more. That then he stretched forth his hands—she stooped over him. He raised his head—she kissed his lips—and he died.

The White Maiden, tradition says, has not since been seen in the ruins of Thurnberg.

THE STURGEON.

The Convent of Schwartz-Rheindorf was founded in the year of our Lord 1152 by the Bishop of Cologne, Arnold Graf von Wied, for the reception of noble ladies alone, and was placed by him under the strict rule of St. Benedict. The prelate, who died in the year 1159, lies buried beneath the high altar of the church.

Among the many other rights and privileges conferred on the convent by the Bishop was the right of fishing in the river, within certain limits above and below the convent's territorial boundaries. This was a most valuable right for a long period.

The certainty of a profitable fishing was always heralded by the appearance of two immense sturgeon. They came at the commencement of each year, harbingers of good luck, and they were ever succeeded by shoals of river fish, in such numbers as to be absolutely inexhaustible until the expiration of the season. Of these sturgeon the one, a huge male, always allowed himself to be taken by the fishermen, but the female was never captured. It was understood by those who knew all about these matters that on her freedom depended the fisher's success. This good fortune lasted for centuries.

It was, however, remarked that as the discipline of the convent became more and more relaxed, and grace grew to be less and less among its inmates, the fishing became more and more unprofitable. The sturgeon, it is true, still made their appearance, but they were spent and thin, and altogether unlike those which had been wont of yore to visit the fishing-ground of the sisterhood. The abbess and the nuns, however, either could not or they would not perceive the cause of the falling off in the take, or the change in the appearance of the sturgeon, but the common people who dwelt in the vicinity of the convent, and especially those poor persons to whom the river had been heretofore a source of support, were neither slow in seeing the cause nor in publishing the consequences to the world. Thus stood matters: dissoluteness of life on the one hand, distress on the other; profligacy and poverty, extravagance and starvation, linked inseparably together.

It was midwinter. On the bank of the river stood the purveyor of the convent, accompanied by the lady abbess herself and a great number of the nuns. They waited to watch the first haul made by the fishermen on the New Year's morning, according to the custom which had prevailed in the convent for centuries. It was not usual for the river to be open at that time, but this year there was not a piece of ice on its surface. The fishermen put out in their boats, and cast their nets into the current ; then, making the circuit of the spot, they returned to the bank and commenced to haul them in. Little difficulty was at first experienced by them in this operation. For several years preceding the supply of fish had scarcely sufficed to defray the expense of catching. It would seem, however, as if fortune were inclined to smile on the sisterhood once more. The nets had not been more than half drawn in when the fishermen began to perceive that they contained something heavier than usual. The lady abbess and the nuns were made acquainted with the circumstance, and they watched, in eager expectancy, the landing of the fish. The nets were at length with much trouble hauled on shore.

"Hilloa!" said the principal fisherman, an aged man, to the purveyor of the convent, "hast thou ever seen such monsters before? My soul! but this will glad the hearts of the whole convent, and make many poor folk happy, an it be but the harbinger of a return to the old times."

While he spoke two immense sturgeon were landed. The abbess and her train approached the landing-place, and admired the strength and superior size of the fish.

"It would be but folly to set one of them free," she partially soliloquised and partially spoke to the purveyor. "The convent has not had such a treat for years past, and we absolutely require some change. I 'll warrant me they will eat delightfully."

The purveyor, a wily Jewish-looking fellow, who passed for an Italian, at once assented to the observations of his mistress, and added a few remarks of his own in support of them. Not so, however, the old fisherman, who overheard the conversation, having approached the abbess with the purveyor to learn her will and pleasure as to the disposal of the fish.

"Nay, nay, master," he interposed, in his rough way, "not so fast, not so fast. My father fished on this river for full fifty years, and my father's father did the same; and fifty years have I drawn net here too, all in the service of the noble ladies of Schwartz-Rheindorf. Never, in that time, knew I other than this done with these fish—the one to be let free, the other to be given away among the poor. I 'll do nought else with them."

The abbess and the purveyor were but ill-pleased to hear what the old man said.

"You must do as I bid you, Herman," said the former.

"You must obey my lady, your mistress," echoed the latter. "She is too good and gracious to ye."

"Not I," said the old man bluntly,—"not I. For all the broad lands on the Rhine I would not have hand, act, nor part in such a matter. Do as ye list, but I 'll be none your servant in the matter."

The old man walked away as he said these words, and neither the entreaties of the abbess, the threats of the purveyor, nor the interposition of some of the nuns present could bring him back.

Others, however, were soon found among his companions who were less scrupulous; and the two fish were accordingly removed to the convent, and consigned to the care of the cook, to be served up for dinner that day.

The dinner-hour arrived—the sisterhood were all seated at table—the servitors, marshalled by the supple purveyor, made their appearance, bearing the expected banquet in large covered dishes. A hasty grace was muttered, and then every eye was turned to the covers. The abbess had ordered the sturgeon to be served up first.

"And now, sisters," she said, with a complacent look of benignant condescension, "I hope soon to know how you approve of our dinner. It is my constant study to make you happy, and my efforts are unceasing to afford you every gratification in my power. Let us begin."

The covers were removed in a twinkling by the servitors, the carvers clattered their knives and forks impatiently; but what was the surprise of all, when every dish as it was uncovered was found to be empty. The wrath of the abbess rose at the sight, and the zeal of the nuns knew no bounds in seconding her indignation. The cook was hurriedly sent for. He stood before the excited sisterhood an abject, trembling wretch, far more like one who expected to be made a victim of himself, than one who would voluntarily make victims of others.

"How is this, villain?" exclaimed the abbess, her face reddening with rage.

"How's this, villain?" echoed threescore female voices, some of them not musical.

"Ay, how is this, hound?" growled the purveyor.

"Do you mock us?" continued the abbess, as the cook stood trembling and silent.

"Do you mock us?" echoed the purveyor, with as much dignity as he could impart into his thin, meagre figure.

"Speak!" said the abbess in a loud voice, while the cook cast his eyes around as if seeking aid against the excited throng the room contained,—"speak!"

Thus urged, the cook proceeded to explain—as far, at least, as he was able. He declared that he had cut up and cooked the sturgeon, according to the directions he had received from the purveyor, and that, when dinner was served up, he had sent them up dressed in the manner that official had directed.

The abbess and her nuns were much puzzled how to explain this extraordinary occurrence, and each busied herself in conjectures which, as usual in such cases, never approached the fact.   At this juncture the aged fisherman entered the room.

"My lady," he said to the abbess, when he learnt what had occurred, "it is the judgment of Heaven. Even now I saw the fish in the river. I knew them well, and I'll swear to them if necessary. They floated away, swimming down the stream, and I am a much mistaken man if ever ye see them any more."

The pleasurable anticipations of the day that the sisters had entertained were completely annihilated; but it would have been well for them if the consequences of their avarice and gluttony had ended with that hour. Never more did the sturgeon make their appearance, and the part of the stream which pertained to the convent thenceforth ceased to produce fish of any kind whatsoever.

People say that the Reformation had the effect of wooing the finny tribe back to their old haunts. At all events, whatever may have been the cause, it is the fact that there is not at present a less plentiful supply in this spot than there is in any other part of that rich river.

SAINT ANDREW'S NIGHT.

IT is commonly believed in Germany that on St. Andrew's night, St. Thomas' night, and Christmas and New Year's nights, a girl has the power of inviting and seeing her future lover. A table is to be laid for two persons, taking care, however, that there are no forks upon it. Whatever the lover leaves behind him must be carefully preserved, for he then returns to her who has it, and loves her passionately. The article must, however, be kept carefully concealed from his sight, for he would otherwise remember the torture of superhuman power exercised over him which he that night endured, become conscious of the charms employed, and this would lead to fatal consequences.

A fair maiden in Austria once sought at midnight, after performing the necessary ceremonies, to obtain a sight of her lover, whereupon a shoemaker appeared having a dagger in his hand, which he threw at her and then disappeared. She picked up the dagger which he had thrown at her and concealed it in a trunk.

Not long afterwards the shoemaker visited, courted, and married her. Some years after her marriage she chanced to go one Sunday about the hour of vespers to the trunk in search of something that she required for her work the next day. As she opened the trunk her husband came to her, and would insist on looking into it. She kept him off, until at last he pushed her away, and there saw his long-lost dagger. He immediately seized it, and demanded how she obtained it, because he had lost it at a very particular time. In her fear and alarm she had not the power to invent any excuse, so declared the truth, that it was the same dagger he had left behind him the night when she had obliged him to appear to her. Her husband hereupon grew enraged, and said, with a terrible voice—

"'Twas you, then, that caused me that night of dreadful misery?"

With that he thrust the dagger into her heart.

Printed by T. and A. Constable, Printers to Her Majesty,
at the Edinburgh University Press.

FOLK-LORE

AND

LEGENDS

ORIENTAL

J. B. LIPPINCOTT COMPANY

PHILADELPHIA

1892

PREFATORY NOTE

THE East is rich in Folklore, and the lorist is
not troubled to discover material, but to select
only that which it is best worth his while to
preserve. The conditions under which the people
live are most favourable to the preservation
of the ancient legends, and the cultivation of
the powers of narration fits the Oriental to
present his stories in a more polished style than
is usual in the Western countries. The reader
of these tales will observe many points of similarity between them and the popular fictions
of the West—similarity of thought and incident
—and nothing, perhaps, speaks more eloquently
the universal brotherhood of man than this

oneness of folk-fiction. At the same time, the Tales of the East are unique, lighted up as they are by a gorgeous extravagance of imagination which never fails to attract and delight.

C. J. T.

CONTENTS

CONTENTS.

THE COBBLER ASTROLOGER.

In the great city of Isfahan lived Ahmed the obbler, an honest and industrious man, whose wish was to pass through life quietly; and he might have done so, had he not married a handsome wife, who, although she had condescended to accept of him as a husband, was far from being contented with his humble sphere of life.

Sittâra, such was the name of Ahmed's wife, was ever forming foolish schemes of riches and grandeur; and though Ahmed never encouraged them, he was too fond a husband to quarrel with what gave her pleasure. An incredulous smile or a shake of the head was his only answer to her often-told day-dreams; and she continued to persuade herself that she was certainly destined to great fortune.

It happened one evening, while in this temper of mind, that she went to the Hemmâm, where she saw a lady retiring dressed in a magnificent robe, covered with jewels, and surrounded by slaves. This was the very condition Sittâra had always longed for, and she eagerly inquired the name of the happy person who had so many attendants and such fine jewels. She learned it was the wife of the chief astrologer to the king. With this information she returned home. Her husband met her at the door, but was received with a frown, nor could all his caresses obtain a smile or a word; for several hours she continued silent, and in apparent misery. At length she said—

"Cease your caresses, unless you are ready to give me a proof that you do really and sincerely love me."

"What proof of love," exclaimed poor Ahmed, "can you desire which I will not give?"

"Give over cobbling; it is a vile, low trade, and never yields more than ten or twelve dinars a day. Turn astrologer! your fortune will be made, and I shall have all I wish, and be happy."

"Astrologer!" cried Ahmed,—"astrologer! Have you forgotten who I am—a cobbler, without any learning—that you want me to engage in a profession which requires so much skill and knowledge?"

"I neither think nor care about your qualifications," said the enraged wife; "all I know is, that if you do not turn astrologer immediately I will be divorced from you to-morrow."

The cobbler remonstrated, but in vain. The figure of the astrologer's wife, with her jewels and her slaves, had taken complete possession of Sittâra's imagination. All night it haunted her; she dreamt of nothing else, and on awaking declared she would leave the house if her husband did not comply with her wishes. What could poor Ahmed do? He was no astrologer, but he was dotingly fond of his wife, and he could not bear the idea of losing her. He promised to obey, and, having sold his little stock, bought an astrolabe, an astronomical almanac, and a table of the twelve signs of the zodiac. Furnished with these he went to the market-place, crying, "I am an astrologer! I know the sun, and the moon, and the stars, and the twelve signs of the zodiac; I can calculate nativities; I can foretell everything that is to happen!"

No man was better known than Ahmed the cobbler. A crowd soon gathered round him. "What! friend Ahmed," said one, "have you worked till your head is turned?" "Are you tired of looking down at your last," cried another, "that you are now looking up at the planets?" These and a thousand other jokes assailed the ears of the poor cobbler, who, notwithstanding, continued to exclaim that he was an astrologer, having resolved on doing what he could to please his beautiful wife.

It so happened that the king's jeweller was passing by. He was in great distress, having lost the richest ruby belonging to the crown. Every search had been made to recover this inestimable jewel, but to no purpose; and as the jeweller knew he could no longer conceal its loss from the king, he looked forward to death as inevitable. In this hopeless state, while wandering about the town, he reached the crowd around Ahmed and asked what was the matter. "Don't you know Ahmed the cobbler?" said one of the bystanders, laughing; "he has been inspired, and is become an astrologer."

A drowning man will catch at a broken reed: the jeweller no sooner heard the sound of the word astrologer, than he went up to Ahmed, told him what had happened, and said, "If you understand your art, you must be able to discover the king's ruby. Do so, and I will give you two hundred pieces of gold. But if you do not succeed within six hours, I will use all my influence at court to have you put to death as an impostor."

Poor Ahmed was thunderstruck. He stood long without being able to move or speak, reflecting on his misfortunes, and grieving, above all, that his wife, whom he so loved, had, by her envy and selfishness, brought him to such a fearful alternative. Full of these sad thoughts, he exclaimed aloud, "O woman, woman! thou art more baneful to the happiness of man than the poisonous dragon of the desert!"

The lost ruby had been secreted by the jeweller's wife, who, disquieted by those alarms which ever attend guilt, sent one of her female slaves to watch her husband. This slave, on seeing her master speak to the astrologer, drew near; and when she heard Ahmed, after some moments of apparent abstraction, compare a woman to a poisonous dragon, she was satisfied that he must know everything. She ran to her mistress, and, breathless with fear, cried, "You are discovered, my dear mistress, you are discovered by a vile astrologer. Before six hours are past the whole story will be known, and you will become infamous, if you are even so fortunate as to escape with life, unless you can find some way of prevailing on him to be merciful." She then related what she had seen and heard; and Ahmed's exclamation carried as complete conviction to the mind of the terrified mistress as it had done to that of her slave.

The jeweller's wife, hastily throwing on her veil, went in search of the dreaded astrologer. When she found him, she threw herself at his feet, crying, "Spare my honour and my life, and I will confess everything!"

"What can you have to confess to me?" exclaimed Ahmed in amazement.

"Oh, nothing! nothing with which you are not already acquainted. You know too well that I stole the ruby from the king's crown. I did so to punish my husband, who uses me most cruelly; and I thought by this means to obtain riches for myself, and to have him put to death. But you, most wonderful man, from whom nothing is hidden, have discovered and defeated my wicked plan. I beg only for mercy, and will do whatever you command me."

An angel from heaven could not have brought more consolation to Ahmed than did the jeweller's wife. He assumed all the dignified solemnity that became his new character, and said, "Woman! I know all thou hast done, and it is fortunate for thee that thou hast come to confess thy sin and beg for mercy before it was too late. Return to thy house, put the ruby under the pillow of the couch on which thy husband sleeps; let it be laid on the side furthest from the door; and be satisfied thy guilt shall never be even suspected."

The jeweller's wife returned home, and did as she was desired. In an hour Ahmed followed her, and told the jeweller he had made his calculations, and found by the aspect of the sun and moon, and by the configuration of the stars, that the ruby was at that moment lying under the pillow of his couch, on the side furthest from the door. The jeweller thought Ahmed must be crazy; but as a ray of hope is like a ray from heaven to the wretched, he ran to his couch, and there, to his joy and wonder, found the ruby in the very place described. He came back to Ahmed, embraced him, called him his dearest friend and the preserver of his life, and gave him the two hundred pieces of gold, declaring that he was the first astrologer of the age.

These praises conveyed no joy to the poor cobbler, who returned home more thankful to God for his preservation than elated by his good fortune. The moment he entered the door his wife ran up to him and exclaimed, "Well, my dear astrologer! what success?"

"There!" said Ahmed, very gravely,—"there are two hundred pieces of gold. I hope you will be satisfied now, and not ask me again to hazard my life, as I have done this morning." He then related all that had passed. But the recital made a very different impression on the lady from what these occurrences had made on Ahmed. Sittâra saw nothing but the gold, which would enable her to vie with the chief astrologer's wife at the Hemmâm. "Courage!" she said, "courage! my dearest husband. This is only your first labour in your new and noble profession. Go on and prosper, and we shall become rich and happy."

In vain Ahmed remonstrated and represented the danger; she burst into tears, and accused him of not loving her, ending with her usual threat of insisting upon a divorce.

Ahmed's heart melted, and he agreed to make another trial. Accordingly, next morning he sallied forth with his astrolabe, his twelve signs of the zodiac, and his almanac, exclaiming, as before, "I am an astrologer! I know the sun, and the moon, and the stars, and the twelve signs of the zodiac; I can calculate nativities; I can foretell everything that is to happen!" A crowd again gathered round him, but it was now with wonder, and not ridicule; for the story of the ruby had gone abroad, and the voice of fame had converted the poor cobbler Ahmed into the ablest and most learned astrologer that was ever seen at Isfahan.

While everybody was gazing at him, a lady passed by veiled. She was the wife of one of the richest merchants in the city, and had just been at the Hemmâm, where she had lost a valuable necklace and earrings. She was now returning home in great alarm lest her husband should suspect her of having given her jewels to a lover. Seeing the crowd around Ahmed, she asked the reason of their assembling, and was informed of the whole story of the famous astrologer: how he had been a cobbler, was inspired with supernatural knowledge, and could, with the help of his astrolabe, his twelve signs of the zodiac, and his almanac, discover all that ever did or ever would happen in the world. The story of the jeweller and the king's ruby was then told her, accompanied by a thousand wonderful circumstances which had never occurred. The lady, quite satisfied of his skill, went up to Ahmed and mentioned her loss, saying: "A man of your knowledge and penetration will easily discover my jewels; find them, and I will give you fifty pieces of gold."

The poor cobbler was quite confounded, and looked

down, thinking only how to escape without a public exposure of his ignorance. The lady, in pressing through the crowd, had torn the lower part of her veil. Ahmed's downcast eyes noticed this; and wishing to inform her of it in a delicate manner, before it was observed by others, he whispered to her, " Lady, look down at the rent." The lady's head was full of her loss, and she was at that moment endeavouring to recollect how it could have occurred. Ahmed's speech brought it at once to her mind, and she exclaimed in delighted surprise : " Stay here a few moments, thou great astrologer. I will return immediately with the reward thou so well deservest." Saying this, she left him, and soon returned, carrying in one hand the necklace and earrings, and in the other a purse with the fifty pieces of gold. " There is gold for thee," she said, " thou wonderful man, to whom all the secrets of Nature are revealed! I had quite forgotten where I laid the jewels, and without thee should never have found them. But when thou desiredst me to look at the rent below, I instantly recollected the rent near the bottom of the wall in the bathroom, where, before undressing, I had hid them. I can now go home in peace and comfort; and it is all owing to thee, thou wisest of men !"

After these words she walked away, and Ahmed returned to his home, thankful to Providence for his preservation, and fully resolved never again to tempt it. His handsome wife, however, could not yet rival the chief astrologer's lady in her appearance at the Hemmâm, so she renewed her entreaties and threats, to make her fond husband continue his career as an astrologer.

About this time it happened that the king's treasury was robbed of forty chests of gold and jewels, forming the greater part of the wealth of the kingdom. The high treasurer and other officers of state used all diligence to find the thieves, but in vain. The king sent for his astrologer, and declared that if the robbers were not detected by a stated time, he, as well as the principal ministers, should be put to death. Only one day of the short period given them remained. All their search had proved fruitless, and the chief astrologer, who had made his calculations and exhausted his art to no purpose, had quite resigned himself to his fate, when one of his friends advised him to send for the wonderful cobbler, who had become so famous for his extraordinary discoveries. Two slaves were immediately despatched for Ahmed, whom they commanded to go with them to their master. " You see the effects of your ambition," said the poor cobbler to his wife; " I am going to my death. The king's astrologer has heard of my presumption, and is determined to have me executed as an impostor."

On entering the palace of the chief astrologer, he was surprised to see that dignified person come forward to receive him, and lead him to the seat of honour, and not less so to hear himself thus addressed: "The ways of Heaven, most learned and excellent Ahmed, are unsearchable. The high are often cast down, and the low are lifted up. The whole world depends upon fate and fortune. It is my turn now to be depressed by fate; it is thine to be exalted by fortune."

His speech was here interrupted by a messenger from the king, who, having heard of the cobbler's fame, desired his attendance. Poor Ahmed now concluded that it was all over with him, and followed the king's messenger, praying to God that he would deliver him from this peril. When he came into the king's presence, he bent his body to the ground, and wished his majesty long life and prosperity. "Tell me, Ahmed," said the king, "who has stolen my treasure?"

"It was not one man," answered Ahmed, after some consideration; "there were forty thieves concerned in the robbery."

"Very well," said the king; "but who were they? and what have they done with my gold and jewels?"

"These questions," said Ahmed, "I cannot now answer; but I hope to satisfy your Majesty, if you will grant me forty days to make my calculations."

"I grant you forty days," said the king; "but when they are past, if my treasure is not found, your life shall pay the forfeit."

Ahmed returned to his house well pleased ; for he resolved to take advantage of the time allowed him to fly from a city where his fame was likely to be his ruin.

"Well, Ahmed," said his wife, as he entered, "what news at Court?"

"No news at all," said he, "except that I am to be put to death at the end of forty days, unless I find forty chests of gold and jewels which have been stolen from the royal treasury."

"But you will discover the thieves."

"How? By what means am I to find them?"

"By the same art which discovered the ruby and the lady's necklace."

"The same art!" replied Ahmed. "Foolish woman! thou knowest that I have no art, and that I have only pretended to it for the sake of pleasing thee. But I have had sufficient skill to gain forty days, during which time we may easily escape to some other city; and with the money I now possess, and the aid of my former occupation, we may still obtain an honest livelihood."

"An honest livelihood!" repeated his lady, with scorn. "Will thy cobbling, thou mean, spiritless wretch, ever enable me to go to the Hemmâm like the wife of the chief astrologer? Hear me, Ahmed! Think only of discovering the king's treasure. Thou hast just as good a chance of doing so as thou hadst of finding the ruby, and the necklace and earrings.

At all events, I am determined thou shalt not escape; and shouldst thou attempt to run away, I will inform the king's officers, and have thee taken up and put to death, even before the forty days are expired. Thou knowest me too well, Ahmed, to doubt my keeping my word. So take courage, and endeavour to make thy fortune, and to place me in that rank of life to which my beauty entitles me."

The poor cobbler was dismayed at this speech; but knowing there was no hope of changing his wife's resolution, he resigned himself to his fate. "Well," said he, "your will shall be obeyed. All I desire is to pass the few remaining days of my life as comfortably as I can. You know I am no scholar, and have little skill in reckoning; so there are forty dates: give me one of them every night after I have said my prayers, that I may put them in a jar, and, by counting them may always see how many of the few days I have to live are gone."

The lady, pleased at carrying her point, took the dates, and promised to be punctual in doing what her husband desired.

Meanwhile the thieves who had stolen the king's treasure, having been kept from leaving the city by fear of detection and pursuit, had received accurate information of every measure taken to discover them. One of them was among the crowd before the palace on the day the king sent for Ahmed;

and hearing that the cobbler had immediately declared their exact number, he ran in a fright to his comrades, and exclaimed, "We are all found out! Ahmed, the new astrologer, has told the king that there are forty of us."

"There needed no astrologer to tell that," said the captain of the gang. "This Ahmed, with all his simple good-nature, is a shrewd fellow. Forty chests having been stolen, he naturally guessed that there must be forty thieves, and he has made a good hit, that is all; still it is prudent to watch him, for he certainly has made some strange discoveries. One of us must go to-night, after dark, to the terrace of this cobbler's house, and listen to his conversation with his handsome wife; for he is said to be very fond of her, and will, no doubt, tell her what success he has had in his endeavours to detect us."

Everybody approved of this scheme; and soon after nightfall one of the thieves repaired to the terrace. He arrived there just as the cobbler had finished his evening prayers, and his wife was giving him the first date. "Ah!" said Ahmed, as he took it, "there is one of the forty."

The thief, hearing these words, hastened in consternation to the gang, and told them that the moment he took his post he had been perceived by the supernatural knowledge of Ahmed, who immediately told his wife that one of them was there.

The spy's tale was not believed by his hardened companions; something was imputed to his fears; he might have been mistaken;—in short, it was determined to send two men the next night at the same hour. They reached the house just as Ahmed, having finished his prayers, had received the second date, and heard him exclaim, " My dear wife, to-night there are two of them !"

The astonished thieves fled, and told their still incredulous comrades what they had heard. Three men were consequently sent the third night, four the fourth, and so on. Being afraid of venturing during the day, they always came as evening closed in, and just as Ahmed was receiving his date, hence they all in turn heard him say that which convinced them he was aware of their presence. On the last night they all went, and Ahmed exclaimed aloud, " The number is complete! To-night the whole forty are here !"

All doubts were now removed. It was impossible that Ahmed should have discovered them by any natural means. How could he ascertain their exact number? and night after night, without ever once being mistaken? He must have learnt it by his skill in astrology. Even the captain now yielded, in spite of his incredulity, and declared his opinion that it was hopeless to elude a man thus gifted; he therefore advised that they should make a friend of the cobbler, by confessing everything to him, and bribing him to secrecy by a share of the booty.

His advice was approved of, and an hour before dawn they knocked at Ahmed's door. The poor man jumped out of bed, and supposing the soldiers were come to lead him to execution, cried out, "Have patience! I know what you are come for. It is a very unjust and wicked deed."

"Most wonderful man!" said the captain, as the door was opened, "we are fully convinced that thou knowest why we are come, nor do we mean to justify the action of which thou speakest. Here are two thousand pieces of gold, which we will give thee, provided thou wilt swear to say nothing more about the matter."

"Say nothing about it!" said Ahmed. "Do you think it possible I can suffer such gross wrong and injustice without complaining, and making it known to all the world?"

"Have mercy upon us!" exclaimed the thieves, falling on their knees; "only spare our lives, and we will restore the royal treasure."

The cobbler started, rubbed his eyes to see if he were asleep or awake; and being satisfied that he was awake, and that the men before him were really the thieves, he assumed a solemn tone, and said: "Guilty men! ye are persuaded that ye cannot escape from my penetration, which reaches unto the sun and moon, and knows the position and aspect of

every star in the heavens. Your timely repentance
has saved you. But ye must immediately restore
all that ye have stolen. Go straightway, and carry
the forty chests exactly as ye found them, and bury
them a foot deep under the southern wall of the old
ruined Hemmâm, beyond the king's palace. If ye
do this punctually, your lives are spared ; but if ye
fail in the slightest degree, destruction will fall upon
you and your families."

The thieves promised obedience to his commands
and departed. Ahmed then fell on his knees, and
returned thanks to God for this signal mark of his
favour. About two hours after the royal guards
came, and desired Ahmed to follow them. He said
he would attend them as soon as he had taken leave
of his wife, to whom he determined not to impart
what had occurred until he saw the result. He bade
her farewell very affectionately ; she supported herself with great fortitude on this trying occasion,
exhorting her husband to be of good cheer, and said
a few words about the goodness of Providence. But
the fact was, Sittâra fancied that if God took the
worthy cobbler to himself, her beauty might attract
some rich lover, who would enable her to go to the
Hemmâm with as much splendour as the astrologer's
lady, whose image, adorned with jewels and fine
clothes, and surrounded by slaves, still haunted her
imagination.

The decrees of Heaven are just : a reward suited

to their merits awaited Ahmed and his wife. The good man stood with a cheerful countenance before the king, who was impatient for his arrival, and immediately said, "Ahmed, thy looks are promising; hast thou discovered my treasure?"

"Does your Majesty require the thieves or the treasure? The stars will only grant one or the other," said Ahmed, looking at his table of astrological calculations. "Your Majesty must make your choice. I can deliver up either, but not both."

"I should be sorry not to punish the thieves," answered the king; "but if it must be so, I choose the treasure."

"And you give the thieves a full and free pardon?"

"I do, provided I find my treasure untouched."

"Then," said Ahmed, "if your majesty will follow me, the treasure shall be restored to you."

The king and all his nobles followed the cobbler to the ruins of the old Hemmâm. There, casting his eyes towards heaven, Ahmed muttered some sounds, which were supposed by the spectators to be magical conjurations, but which were in reality the prayers and thanksgivings of a sincere and pious heart to God for his wonderful deliverance. When his prayer was finished, he pointed to the southern wall, and requested that his majesty would order his attendants to dig there. The work was hardly begun, when the whole forty chests were found in the same state as when stolen, with the treasurer's seal upon them still unbroken.

The king's joy knew no bounds; he embraced Ahmed, and immediately appointed him his chief astrologer, assigned to him an apartment in the palace, and declared that he should marry his only daughter, as it was his duty to promote the man whom God had so singularly favoured, and had made instrumental in restoring the treasures of his kingdom. The young princess, who was more beautiful than the moon, was not dissatisfied with her father's choice; for her mind was stored with religion and virtue, and she had learnt to value beyond all earthly qualities that piety and learning which she believed Ahmed to possess. The royal will was carried into execution as soon as formed. The wheel of fortune had taken a complete turn. The morning had found Ahmed in a wretched hovel, rising from a sorry bed, in the expectation of losing his life; in the evening he was the lord of a rich palace, and married to the only daughter of a powerful king. But this change did not alter his character. As he had been meek and humble in adversity, he was modest and gentle in prosperity. Conscious of his own ignorance, he continued to ascribe his good fortune solely to the favour of Providence. He became daily more attached to the beautiful and virtuous princess whom he had married; and he could not help contrasting her character with that of his former wife, whom he had ceased to love, and of whose unreasonable and unfeeling vanity he was now fully sensible.

THE LEGEND OF THE TERRESTRIAL PARADISE OF SHEDDÁD, THE SON OF 'A'D.

It is related that 'Abd Allah, the son of Aboo Kilábeh, went forth to seek a camel that had run away, and while he was proceeding over the deserts of El-Yeman and the district of Seba, he chanced to arrive at a vast city encompassed by enormous fortifications, around the circuit of which were pavilions rising high into the sky. So when he approached it, he imagined that there must be inhabitants within it, of whom he might inquire for his camel; and, accordingly, he advanced, but on coming to it he found that it was desolate, without any one to cheer its solitude.

"I alighted," says he, "from my she-camel, and tied up her foot; and then, composing my mind, entered the city. On approaching the fortifications, I found that they had two enormous gates, the lik of which, for size and height, have never been seen elsewhere in the world, set with a variety of jewels and jacinths, white and red, and yellow and green;

and when I beheld this, I was struck with the utmost wonder at it, and the sight astonished me. I entered the fortifications in a state of terror and with a wandering mind, and saw them to be of the same large extent as the city, and to comprise elevated pavilions, every one of these containing lofty chambers, and all of them constructed of gold and silver, and adorned with rubies and chrysolites and pearls and various-coloured jewels. The folding-doors of these pavilions were like those of the fortifications in beauty, and the floors were overlaid with large pearls, and with balls like hazel-nuts, composed of musk and ambergris and saffron. And when I came into the midst of the city, I saw not in it a created being of the sons of Adam; and I almost died of terror. I then looked down from the summits of the lofty chambers and pavilions, and saw rivers running beneath them; and in the great thoroughfare-streets of the city were fruit-bearing trees and tall palm-trees. And the construction of the city was of alternate bricks of gold and silver; so I said within myself, No doubt this is the paradise promised in the world to come.

"I carried away of the jewels which were as its gravel, and the musk that was as its dust, as much as I could bear, and returned to my district, where I acquainted the people with the occurrence. And the news reached Mo'áwiyeh, the son of Aboo Sufyán (who was then Caliph), in the Hejáz; so he wrote to his lieutenant in San'a of El-Yemen, saying, 'Summon that man, and inquire of him the truth of the matter!'   His lieutenant therefore caused me to be brought, and demanded of me an account of my adventure, and of what had befallen me; and I informed him of what I had seen.   He then sent me to Mo'áwiyeh, and I acquainted him also with that which I had seen, but he disbelieved it; so I produced to him some of those pearls and the little balls of ambergris and musk and saffron. The latter retained somewhat of their sweet scent; but the pearls had become yellow and discoloured.

"At the sight of these Mo'áwiyeh wondered, and he sent and caused Kaab el-Ahbár to be brought before him, and said to him, 'O Kaab el-Ahbár, I have called thee on account of a matter of which I desire to know the truth, and I hope that thou mayest be able to certify me of it.'   'And what is it, O Prince of the Faithful?' asked Kaab el-Ahbár. Mo'áwiyeh said, 'Hast thou any knowledge of the existence of a city constructed of gold and silver, the pillars whereof are of chrysolite and ruby, and the gravel of which is of pearls, and of balls like hazel-nuts, composed of musk and ambergris and saffron?'   He answered, 'Yes, O Prince of the Faithful!   It is Irem Zat - el - 'Emád, the like of which hath never been constructed in the regions of the earth; and Sheddád, the son of 'A'd the Greater, built it.'   'Relate to us,' said Mo'áwiyeh, 'somewhat of its history.' And Kaab el-Ahbár replied thus :—

" " 'A'd the Greater had two sons, Shedeed and Sheddád, and when their father perished they reigned conjointly over the countries after him, and there was no one of the kings of the earth who was not subject to them. And Shedeed the son of 'A'd died, so his brother Sheddád ruled alone over the earth after him. He was fond of reading the ancient books; and when he met with the description of the world to come, and of paradise, with its pavilions and lofty chambers, and its trees and fruits, and of the other things in paradise, his heart enticed him to construct its like on the earth, after this manner which hath been above mentioned. He had under his authority a hundred thousand kings, under each of whom were a hundred thousand valiant chieftains, and under each of these were a hundred thousand soldiers. And he summoned them all before him, and said to them, " I find in the ancient books and histories the description of the paradise that is in the other world, and I desire to make its like upon the earth. Depart ye therefore to the most pleasant and most spacious vacant tract in the earth, and build for me in it a city of gold and silver, and spread, as its gravel, chrysolites and rubies and pearls, and as the supports of the vaulted roofs of that city make columns of chrysolite, and fill it with pavilions, and over the pavilions construct lofty chambers, and beneath them plant, in the by-streets and great-thoroughfare streets, varieties of trees bearing different kinds of ripe fruits, and make rivers to run beneath them in channels of gold and silver." To this they all replied, "How can we accomplish that which thou hast described to us, and how can we procure the chrysolites and rubies and pearls that thou hast mentioned?" But he said, "Know ye not that the kings of the world are obedient to me, and under my authority, and that no one who is in it disobeyeth my command?" They answered, "Yes, we know that." "Depart then," said he, "to the mines of chrysolite and ruby, and to the places where pearls are found, and gold and silver, and take forth and collect their contents from the earth, and spare no exertions. Take also for me, from the hands of me, such of those things as ye find, and spare none, nor let any escape you; and beware of disobedience!"

" 'He then wrote a letter to each of the kings in the regions of the earth, commanding them to collect all the articles of the kinds above mentioned that their subjects possessed, and to repair to the mines in which these things were found, and extract the precious stones that they contained, even from the beds of the seas. And they collected the things that he required in the space of twenty years; after which he sent forth the geometricians and sages, and labourers and artificers, from all the countries and regions, and they dispersed themselves through the deserts and wastes, and tracts and districts, until they came to a desert wherein was a vast open plain, clear from hills and mountains, and in it were springs gushing forth, and rivers running. So they said, "This is the kind of place which the king commanded us to seek, and called us to find." They then busied themselves in building the city according to the direction of the King Sheddád, king of the whole earth, in its length and breadth; and they made through it the channels for the rivers, and laid the foundations conformably with the prescribed extent. The kings of the various districts of the earth sent thither the jewels and stones, and large and small pearls, and carnelian and pure gold, upon camels over the deserts and wastes, and sent great ships with them over the seas; and a quantity of those things, such as cannot be described nor calculated nor defined, was brought to the workmen, who laboured in the construction of this city three hundred years. And when they had finished it, they came to the king and acquainted him with the completion; and he said to them, " Depart, and make around it impregnable fortifications of great height, and construct around the circuit of the fortifications a thousand pavilions, each with a thousand pillars beneath it, in order that there may be in each pavilion a vizier." So they went immediately, and did this in twenty years; after which they presented themselves before Sheddád, and informed him of the accomplishment of his desire.

" ' He therefore ordered his viziers, who were a thousand in number, and his chief officers, and such of his troops and others as he confided in, to make themselves ready for departure, and to prepare themselves for removal to Irem Zat-el-'Emád, in attendance upon the king of the world, Sheddád, the son of 'A'd. He ordered also such as he chose of his women and his hareem, as his female slaves and his eunuchs, to fit themselves out. And they passed twenty years in equipping themselves. Then Sheddád proceeded with his troops, rejoiced at the accomplishment of his desire, until there remained between him and Irem Zat-el-'Emád one day's journey, when God sent down upon him and upon the obstinate infidels who accompanied him a loud cry from the heaven of His power, and it destroyed them all by the vehemence of its sound. Neither Sheddád nor any of those who were with him arrived at the city, or came in sight of it, and God obliterated the traces of the road that led to it, but the city remaineth as it was in its place until the hour of the judgment !'

" At this narrative, related by Kaab el-Ahbár, Mo'áwiyeh wondered, and he said to him, ' Can any one of mankind arrive at that city ?' ' Yes,' answered Kaab el-Ahbár; ' a man of the companions

of Mohammed (upon whom be blessing and peace !),
in appearance like this man who is sitting here,
without any doubt.' Esh-Shaabee also saith, ' It is
related, on the authority of the learned men of
Hemyer, in El-Yemen, that when Sheddád and those
who were with him were destroyed by the loud cry,
his son Sheddád the Less reigned after him; for his
father, Sheddád the Greater, had left him as successor
to his kingdom, in the land of Hadramót and Seba,
on his departure with the troops who accompanied
him to Irem Zat-el-'Emád. And as soon as the
news reached him of the death of his father, on the
way before his arrival at the city of Irem, he gave
orders to carry his father's body from those desert
tracts to Hadramót, and to excavate the sepulchre
for him in a cavern. And when they had done this,
he placed his body in it, upon a couch of gold, and
covered the corpse with seventy robes, interwoven
with gold and adorned with precious jewels; and he
placed at his head a tablet of gold, whereon were
inscribed these verses :—

" ' Be admonished, O thou who art deceived by a pro-
longed life !
I am Sheddád, the son of 'A'd, the lord of a strong
fortress,
The lord of power and might, and of excessive valour.
The inhabitants of the earth obeyed me, fearing my
severity and threats ;
And I held the east and west under a strong dominion.
And a preacher of the true religion invited us to the
right way ;

But we opposed him, and said, Is there no refuge from
it ?
And a loud cry assaulted us from a tract of the distant
horizon ;
Whereupon we fell down like corn in the midst of a
plain at harvest ;
And now, beneath the earth, we await the threatened
day.'

" Eth-Tha'álibee also saith, ' It happened that two
men entered this cavern, and found at its upper end
some steps, and having descended these, they found
an excavation, the length whereof was a hundred
cubits, and its breadth forty cubits, and its height a
hundred cubits.   And in the midst of this excavation was a couch of gold, upon which was a man of
enormous bulk, occupying its whole length and
breadth, covered with ornaments and with robes
interwoven with gold and silver; and at his head
was a tablet of gold, whereon was an inscription.
And they took that tablet, and carried away from
the place as much as they could of bars of gold and
silver and other things.' "

THE TOMB OF NOOSHEERWAN.

The caliph Hâroon-oor-Rasheed went to visit the tomb of the celebrated Noosheerwân, the most famous of all the monarchs who ever governed Persia. Before the tomb was a curtain of gold cloth, which, when Hâroon touched it, fell to pieces. The walls of the tomb were covered with gold and jewels, whose splendour illumined its darkness. The body was placed in a sitting posture on a throne enchased with jewels, and had so much the appearance of life that, on the first impulse, the Commander of the Faithful bent to the ground, and saluted the remains of the just Noosheerwân.

Though the face of the departed monarch was like that of a living man, and the whole of the body in a state of preservation, which showed the admirable skill of those who embalmed it, yet when the caliph touched the garments they mouldered into dust. Hâroon upon this took his own rich robes and threw them over the corpse; he also hung up a new curtain richer than that he had destroyed, and perfumed the whole tomb with camphor, and other sweet scents.

It was remarked that no change was perceptible in the body of Noosheerwân, except that the ears had become white. The whole scene affected the caliph greatly; he burst into tears, and repeated from the Koran—"What I have seen is a warning to those who have eyes." He observed some writing upon the throne, which he ordered the Moobids (priests), who were learned in the Pehlevee language, to read and explain. They did so: it was as follows:—

"This world remains not; the man who thinks least of it is the wisest.

"Enjoy this world before thou becomest its prey.

"Bestow the same favour on those below thee as thou desirest to receive from those above thee.

"If thou shouldst conquer the whole world, death will at last conquer thee.

"Be careful that thou art not the dupe of thine own fortune.

"Thou shalt be paid exactly for what thou hast done; no more, no less."

The caliph observed a dark ruby-ring on the finger of Noosheerwân, on which was written—

"Avoid cruelty, study good, and never be precipitate in action.

"If thou shouldst live for a hundred years, never for one moment forget death.

"Value above all things the society of the wise."

Around the right arm of Noosheerwân was a clasp of gold, on which was engraved—

"On a certain year, on the 10th day of the month Erdebehisht, a caliph of the race of Adean, professing the faith of Mahomed, accompanied by four good men, and one bad, shall visit my tomb."

Below this sentence were the names of the fore-fathers of the caliph. Another prophecy was added concerning Hâroon's pilgrimage to Noosheerwân's tomb.

"This prince will honour me, and do good unto me, though I have no claim upon him ; and he will clothe me in a new vest, and besprinkle my tomb with sweet-scented essences, and then depart unto his home. But the bad man who accompanies him shall act treacherously towards me. I pray that God may send one of my race to repay the great favours of the caliph, and to take vengeance on his un-worthy companion. There is, under my throne, an inscrip-tion which the caliph must read and contemplate. Its contents will remind him of me, and make him pardon my inability to give him more."

The caliph, on hearing this, put his hand under the throne, and found the inscription, which con-sisted of some lines, inscribed on a ruby as large as the palm of the hand. The Moobids read this also. It contained information where would be found con-cealed a treasure of gold and arms, with some caskets of rich jewels ; under this was written—

"These I give to the caliph in return for the good he has done me ; let him take them and be happy."

When Hâroon-oor-Rasheed was about to leave the tomb, Hoosein-ben-Sâhil, his vizier, said to him : "O Lord of the Faithful, what is the use of all these

precious gems which ornament the abode of the
dead, and are of no benefit to the living? Allow
me to take some of them." The caliph replied with
indignation, "Such a wish is more worthy of a thief
than of a great or wise man." Hoosein was ashamed
of his speech, and said to the servant who had been
placed at the entrance of the tomb, "Go thou, and
worship the holy shrine within." The man went
into the tomb; he was above a hundred years old,
but he had never seen such a blaze of wealth. He
felt inclined to plunder some of it, but was at first
afraid; at last, summoning all his courage, he took
a ring from the finger of Noosheerwân, and came
away.

Hâroon saw this man come out, and observing
him alarmed, he at once conjectured what he had
been doing. Addressing those around him, he said,
" Do not you now see the extent of the knowledge
of Noosheerwân? He prophesied that there should
be one unworthy man with me. It is this fellow.
What have you taken? " said he, in an angry tone.
"Nothing," said the man. "Search him," said the
caliph. It was done, and the ring of Noosheerwân
was found. This the caliph immediately took, and,
entering the tomb, replaced it on the cold finger of
the deceased monarch. When he returned, a
terrible sound like that of loud thunder was heard.

Hâroon came down from the mountain on which
the tomb stood, and ordered the road to be made

inaccessible to future curiosity. He searched for, and found, in the place described, the gold, the arms, and the jewels bequeathed to him by Noosheerwân, and sent them to Bagdad.

Among the rich articles found was a golden crown, which had five sides, and was richly ornamented with precious stones. On every side a number of admirable lessons were written. The most remarkable were as follows :—

First side.

"Give my regards to those who know themselves.

"Consider the end before you begin, and before you advance provide a retreat.

"Give not unnecessary pain to any man, but study the happiness of all.

"Ground not your dignity upon your power to hurt others."

Second side.

"Take counsel before you commence any measure, and never trust its execution to the inexperienced.

"Sacrifice your property for your life, and your life for your religion.

"Spend your time in establishing a good name; and if you desire fortune, learn contentment."

Third side.

"Grieve not for that which is broken, stolen, burnt, or lost.

"Never give orders in another man's house; and accustom yourself to eat your bread at your own table.

"Make not yourself the captive of women."

Fourth side.

"Take not a wife from a bad family, and seat not thyself with those who have no shame.

"Keep thyself at a distance from those who are incorrigible in bad habits, and hold no intercourse with that man who is insensible to kindness.

"Covet not the goods of others.

"Be guarded with monarchs, for they are like fire which blazeth but destroyeth.

"Be sensible to your own value; estimate justly the worth of others ; and war not with those who are far above thee in fortune."

Fifth side.

"Fear kings, women, and poets.

"Be envious of no man, and habituate not thyself to search after the faults of others.

"Make it a habit to be happy, and avoid being out of temper, or thy life will pass in misery.

"Respect and protect the females of thy family.

"Be not the slave of anger ; and in thy contests always leave open the door of conciliation.

"Never let your expenses exceed your income.

"Plant a young tree, or you cannot expect to cut down an old one.

"Stretch your legs no further than the size of your carpet."

The caliph Hâroon-oor-Rasheed was more pleased with the admirable maxims inscribed on this crown than with all the treasures he had found. "Write these precepts," he exclaimed, "in a book, that the faithful may eat of the fruit of wisdom." When he returned to Bagdad, he related to his favourite vizier, Jaffier Bermekee, and his other chief officers, all that had passed; and the shade of Noosheerwân was propitiated by the disgrace of Hoosein-ben-Sâhil (who had recommended despoiling his tomb), and the exemplary punishment of the servant who had committed the sacrilegious act of taking the ring from the finger of the departed monarch.

AMEEN AND THE GHOOL.

THERE is a dreadful place in Persia called the
"Valley of the Angel of Death." That terrific
minister of God's wrath, according to tradition, has
resting-places upon the earth and his favourite
abodes. He is surrounded by ghools, horrid beings
who, when he takes away life, feast upon the
carcasses.

The natural shape of these monsters is terrible;
but they can assume those of animals, such as cows
or camels, or whatever they choose, often appearing
to men as their relations or friends, and then they
do not only transform their shapes, but their voices
also are altered. The frightful screams and yells
which are often heard amid these dreaded ravines
are changed for the softest and most melodious
notes. Unwary travellers, deluded by the appearance
of friends, or captivated by the forms and charmed
by the music of these demons, are allured from their
path, and after feasting for a few hours on every
luxury, are consigned to destruction.

The number of these ghools has greatly decreased

since the birth of the Prophet, and they have no power to hurt those who pronounce his name in sincerity of faith. These creatures are the very lowest of the supernatural world, and, besides being timid, are extremely stupid, and consequently often imposed upon by artful men.

The natives of Isfahan, though not brave, are the most crafty and acute people upon earth, and often supply the want of courage by their address. An inhabitant of that city was once compelled to travel alone at night through this dreadful valley. He was a man of ready wit, and fond of adventures, and, though no lion, had great confidence in his cunning, which had brought him through a hundred scrapes and perils that would have embarrassed or destroyed your simple man of valour.

This man, whose name was Ameen Beg, had heard many stories of the ghools of the " Valley of the Angel of Death," and thought it likely he might meet one. He prepared accordingly, by putting an egg and a lump of salt in his pocket. He had not gone far amidst the rocks, when he heard a voice crying, " Holloa, Ameen Beg Isfahânee! you are going the wrong road, you will lose yourself; come this way. I am your friend Kerreem Beg; I know your father, old Kerbela Beg, and the street in which you were born." Ameen knew well the power the ghools had of assuming the shape of any person they choose; and he also knew their skill as genealogists, and their knowledge of towns as well as families; he had therefore little doubt this was one of those creatures alluring him to destruction. He, however, determined to encounter him, and trust to his art for his escape.

"Stop, my friend, till I come near you," was his reply. When Ameen came close to the ghool, he said, "You are not my friend Kerreem; you are a lying demon, but you are just the being I desired to meet. I have tried my strength against all the men and all the beasts which exist in the natural world, and I can find nothing that is a match for me. I came therefore to this valley in the hope of encountering a ghool, that I might prove my prowess upon him."

The ghool, astonished at being addressed in this manner, looked keenly at him, and said, "Son of Adam, you do not appear so strong." "Appearances are deceitful," replied Ameen, "but I will give you a proof of my strength. There," said he, picking up a stone from a rivulet, "this contains a fluid; try if you can so squeeze it that it will flow out." The ghool took the stone, but, after a short attempt, returned it, saying, "The thing is impossible." "Quite easy," said the Isfahânee, taking the stone and placing it in the hand in which he had before put the egg. "Look there!" And the astonished ghool, while he heard what he took for the breaking of the stone, saw the liquid run from between Ameen's fingers, and this apparently without any effort.

Ameen, aided by the darkness, placed the stone upon the ground while he picked up another of a darker hue. "This," said he, "I can see contains salt, as you will find if you can crumble it between your fingers;" but the ghool, looking at it, confessed he had neither knowledge to discover its qualities nor strength to break it. "Give it me," said his companion impatiently; and, having put it into the same hand with the piece of salt, he instantly gave the latter all crushed to the ghool, who, seeing it reduced to powder, tasted it, and remained in stupid astonishment at the skill and strength of this wonderful man. Neither was he without alarm lest his strength should be exerted against himself, and he saw no safety in resorting to the shape of a beast, for Ameen had warned him that if he commenced any such unfair dealing, he would instantly slay him; for ghools, though long-lived, are not immortal.

Under such circumstances he thought his best plan was to conciliate the friendship of his new companion till he found an opportunity of destroying him.

"Most wonderful man," he said, "will you honour my abode with your presence? it is quite at hand: there you will find every refreshment; and after a comfortable night's rest you can resume your journey."

"I have no objection, friend ghool, to accept your offer; but, mark me, I am, in the first place, very passionate, and must not be provoked by any expressions which are in the least disrespectful; and, in the second, I am full of penetration, and can see through your designs as clearly as I saw into that hard stone in which I discovered salt. So take care you entertain none that are wicked, or you shall suffer."

The ghool declared that the ear of his guest should be pained by no expression to which it did not befit his dignity to listen; and he swore by the head of his liege lord, the Angel of Death, that he would faithfully respect the rights of hospitality and friendship.

Thus satisfied, Ameen followed the ghool through a number of crooked paths, rugged cliffs, and deep ravines, till they came to a large cave, which was dimly lighted. "Here," said the ghool, "I dwell, and here my friend will find all he can want for refreshment and repose." So saying, he led him to various apartments, in which were hoarded every species of grain, and all kinds of merchandise, plundered from travellers who had been deluded to this den, and of whose fate Ameen was too well informed by the bones over which he now and then stumbled, and by the putrid smell produced by some half-consumed carcasses.

"This will be sufficient for your supper, I hope,"

said the ghool, taking up a large bag of rice; "a man of your prowess must have a tolerable appetite." "True," said Ameen, "but I ate a sheep and as much rice as you have there before I proceeded on my journey. I am, consequently, not hungry, but will take a little lest I offend your hospitality." "I must boil it for you," said the demon; "you do not eat grain and meat raw, as we do. Here is a kettle," said he, taking up one lying amongst the plundered property. "I will go and get wood for a fire, while you fetch water with that," pointing to a bag made of the hides of six oxen.

Ameen waited till he saw his host leave the cave for the wood, and then with great difficulty he dragged the enormous bag to the bank of a dark stream, which issued from the rocks at the other end of the cavern, and, after being visible for a few yards, disappeared underground.

"How shall I," thought Ameen, "prevent my weakness being discovered? This bag I could hardly manage when empty; when full, it would require twenty strong men to carry it; what shall I do? I shall certainly be eaten up by this cannibal ghool, who is now only kept in order by the impression of my great strength." After some minutes' reflection the Isfahânee thought of a scheme, and began digging a small channel from the stream towards the place where his supper was preparing.

"What are you doing?" vociferated the ghool, as

he advanced towards him; "I sent you for water to boil a little rice, and you have been an hour about it. Cannot you fill the bag and bring it away?" "Certainly I can," said Ameen; "if I were content, after all your kindness, to show my gratitude merely by feats of brute strength, I could lift your stream if you had a bag large enough to hold it. But here," said he, pointing to the channel he had begun,—" here is the commencement of a work in which the mind of a man is employed to lessen the labour of his body. This canal, small as it may appear, will carry a stream to the other end of the cave, in which I will construct a dam that you can open and shut at pleasure, and thereby save yourself infinite trouble in fetching water. But pray let me alone till it is finished," and he began to dig. "Nonsense!" said the ghool, seizing the bag and filling it; "I will carry the water myself, and I advise you to leave off your canal, as you call it, and follow me, that you may eat your supper and go to sleep; you may finish this fine work, if you like it, to-morrow morning."

Ameen congratulated himself on this escape, and was not slow in taking the advice of his host. After having ate heartily of the supper that was prepared, he went to repose on a bed made of the richest coverlets and pillows, which were taken from one of the store-rooms of plundered goods. The ghool, whose bed was also in the cave, had no sooner

laid down than he fell into a sound sleep. The
anxiety of Ameen's mind prevented him from
following his example; he rose gently, and having
stuffed a long pillow into the middle of his bed,
to make it appear as if he was still there, he retired
to a concealed place in the cavern to watch the
proceedings of the ghool. The latter awoke a short
time before daylight, and rising, went, without
making any noise, towards Ameen's bed, where, not
observing the least stir, he was satisfied that his
guest was in a deep sleep; so he took up one of his
walking-sticks, which was in size like the trunk of
a tree, and struck a terrible blow at what he supposed to be Ameen's head. He smiled not to hear
a groan, thinking he had deprived him of life; but
to make sure of his work, he repeated the blow
seven times. He then returned to rest, but had
hardly settled himself to sleep, when Ameen, who
had crept into the bed, raised his head above the
clothes and exclaimed, "Friend ghool, what insect
could it be that has disturbed me by its tapping?
I counted the flap of its little wings seven times on
the coverlet. These vermin are very annoying, for,
though they cannot hurt a man, they disturb his
rest!"

The ghool's dismay on hearing Ameen speak at
all was great, but that was increased to perfect fright
when he heard him describe seven blows, any one of
which would have felled an elephant, as seven flaps

of an insect's wing. There was no safety, he thought, near so wonderful a man, and he soon afterwards arose and fled from the cave, leaving the Isfahânee its sole master.

When Ameen found his host gone, he was at no loss to conjecture the cause, and immediately began to survey the treasures with which he was surrounded, and to contrive means for removing them to his home.

After examining the contents of the cave, and arming himself with a matchlock, which had belonged to some victim of the ghool, he proceeded to survey the road. He had, however, only gone a short distance when he saw the ghool returning with a large club in his hand, and accompanied by a fox. Ameen's knowledge of the cunning animal instantly led him to suspect that it had undeceived his enemy, but his presence of mind did not forsake him. "Take that," said he to the fox, aiming a ball at him from his matchlock, and shooting him through the head,—"Take that for your not performing my orders. That brute," said he, "promised to bring me seven ghools, that I might chain them, and carry them to Isfahan, and here he has only brought you, who are already my slave." So saying, he advanced towards the ghool; but the latter had already taken to flight, and by the aid of his club bounded so rapidly over rocks and precipices that he was soon out of sight.

Ameen having well marked the path from the cavern to the road, went to the nearest town and hired camels and mules to remove the property he had acquired. After making restitution to all who remained alive to prove their goods, he became, from what was unclaimed, a man of wealth, all of which was owing to that wit and art which ever overcome brute strength and courage.

THE RELATIONS OF SSIDI KUR.

GLORIFIED Nangasuna Garbi! thou art radiant within and without; the holy vessel of sublimity, the fathomer of concealed thoughts, the second of instructors, I bow before thee. What wonderful adventures fell to the lot of Nangasuna, and to the peaceful wandering Chan, and how instructive and learned the Ssidi will be found, all this is developed in thirteen pleasing narratives.

And I will first relate the origin of these tales :—

In the central kingdom of India there once lived seven brothers, who were magicians; and one berren (a measure of distance) further dwelt two brothers, who were sons of a Chan. Now the eldest of these sons of the Chan betook himself to the magicians, that he might learn their art; but although he studied under them for seven years, yet the magicians taught him not the true key to magic.

And once upon a time it happened that the youngest brother, going to bring food to the elder, peeped through the opening of the door, and obtained the key to magic. Thereupon, without delivering to the elder the food which he had brought for him, he returned home to the palace. Then said the younger son of the Chan to his brother, "That we have learned magic, let us keep to ourselves. We have in the stable a beautiful horse; take this horse, and ride not with him near the dwelling-place of the magicians, but sell the horse in their country, and bring back merchandise."

And when he had said thus, he changed himself into a horse. But the elder son of the Chan heeded not the words of his brother, but said unto himself: "Full seven years have I studied magic, and as yet have learned nothing. Where, then, has my young brother found so beautiful a horse? and how can I refuse to ride thereon?"

With these words he mounted, but the horse being impelled by the power of magic was not to be restrained, galloped away to the dwelling-place of the magicians, and could not be got from the door. "Well, then, I will sell the horse to the magicians." Thus thinking to himself, the elder called out to the magicians, "Saw ye ever a horse like unto this? My younger brother it was who found him." At these words the magicians communed with one another. "This is a magic horse; if magic grow at all common, there will be no wonderful art remaining. Let us, therefore, take this horse and slay him."

The magicians paid the price demanded for the horse, and tied him in a stall; and that he might not escape out of their hands, they fastened him, ready for slaughter, by the head, by the tail, and by the feet. "Ah!" thought the horse to himself, "my elder brother hearkened not unto me, and therefore am I fallen into such hands. What form shall I assume?" While the horse was thus considering, he saw a fish swim by him in the water, and immediately he changed himself into a fish.

But the seven magicians became seven herons, and pursued the fish, and were on the point of catching it, when it looked up and beheld a dove in the sky, and thereupon transformed itself into a dove. The seven magicians now became seven hawks, and followed the dove over mountains and rivers, and would certainly have seized upon it, but the dove, flying eastwards to the peaceful cave in the rock Gulumtschi, concealed itself in the bosom of Nangasuna Baktschi (the Instructor). Then the seven hawks became seven beggars, and drew nigh unto the rock Gulumtschi. "What may this import?" bethought the Baktschi to himself, "that this dove has fled hither pursued by seven hawks?" Thus thinking, the Baktschi said, "Wherefore, O dove, fliest thou hither in such alarm?" Then the dove related to him the cause of its flight, and spake afterwards as follows:—"At the entrance to the rock Gulumtschi stand seven beggars, and they will come to the Baktschi and say, ' We pray thee give us the rosary of the Baktschi ? ' Then will I transform myself into the Bumba of the rosary ; let the Baktschi then vouchsafe to take this Bumba into his mouth and to cast the rosary from him."

Hereupon the seven beggars drew nigh, and the Baktschi took the first bead into his mouth and the rest he cast from him. The beads which were cast away then became worms, and the seven beggars became fowls and ate up the worms. Then the Baktschi let the first bead fall from his mouth, and thereupon the first bead was transformed into a man with a sword in his hand. When the seven fowls were slain and become human corses, the Baktschi was troubled in his soul, and said these words, "Through my having preserved one single man have seven been slain. Of a verity this is not good."

To these words the other replied, " I am the Son of a Chan. Since, therefore, through the preservation of my life, several others have lost their lives, I will, to cleanse me from my sins, and also to reward the Baktschi, execute whatsoever he shall command me." The Baktschi replied thereto, " Now, then, in the cold Forest of Death there abides Ssidi Kur; the upper part of his body is decked with gold, the lower is of brass, his head is covered with silver. Seize him and hold him fast. Whosoever finds this wonderful Ssidi Kur, him will I make for a thousand years a man upon the earth."

Thus spake he, and the youth thereupon began these words: "The way which I must take, the food which I require, the means which I must employ, all these vouchsafe to make known unto me." To this the Baktschi replied, "It shall be as thou demandest. At the distance of a berren (a measure of distance) from this place you will come to a gloomy forest, through which you will find there runs only one narrow path. The place is full of spirits. When thou reachest the spirits, they will throng around you; then cry ye with a loud voice, 'Spirits, chu lu chu lu ssochi!' And when thou hast spoken these words, they will all be scattered like grain. When thou hast proceeded a little further, you will encounter a crowd of other spirits; then cry ye, 'Spirits, chu lu chu lu ssosi!' And a little further on you will behold a crowd of child-spirits: say unto these, 'Child-spirits, Ri ra pa dra!' In the middle of this wood sits Ssidi Kur, beside an amiri-tree. When he beholds you, he will climb up it, but you must take the moon-axe, with furious gestures draw nigh unto the tree, and bid Ssidi Kur descend. To bring him away you will require this sack, which would hold a hundred men. To bind him fast this hundred fathoms of checkered rope will serve you. This inexhaustible cake will furnish thee with provender for thy journey. When thou hast got thy load upon thy back, wander then on without speaking, until thou art returned home again. Thy name is Son of the Chan; and since thou hast reached the peaceful rock Gulumtschi, thou shalt be called the peaceful wandering Son of the Chan."

Thus spake the Baktschi, and showed him the way of expiation. When Ssidi Kur beheld his pursuer, he speedily climbed up the amiri-tree, but the Son of the Chan drew nigh unto the foot of the tree, and spake with threatening words: "My Baktschi is Nangasuna Garbi; mine axe is called the white moon; an inexhaustible cake is my provender. This sack, capable of holding a hundred men, will serve to carry thee away, this hundred fathoms of rope will serve to bind thee fast; I myself am the peaceful wandering Son of the Chan. Descend, or I will hew down the tree."

Then spake Ssidi Kur, "Do not hew down the tree; I will descend from it."

And when he had descended, the Son of the Chan thrust him into the sack, tied the sack fast with the rope, ate of the butter-cake, and wandered forth many days with his burden. At length Ssidi Kur said to the Son of the Chan, "Since our long journey is wearisome unto us, I will tell a story unto you, or do you relate one unto me."

The Son of the Chan kept on his way, however, without speaking a word, and Ssidi began afresh,

"If thou wilt tell a story, nod your head to me; if I shall relate one, then do you shake your head."

But because the Son of the Chan shook his head from side to side, without uttering a word, Ssidi began the following tale :—

THE ADVENTURES OF THE RICH YOUTH.

"In former times there lived, in a great kingdom, a rich youth, a calculator, a mechanic, a painter, a physician, and a smith, and they all departed from their parents and went forth into a foreign land. When they at length arrived at the mouth of a great river, they planted, every one of them, a tree of life; and each of them, following one of the sources of the river, set forth to seek their fortunes. 'Here,' said they to one another,—' here will we meet again. Should, however, any one of us be missing, and his tree of life be withered, we will search for him in the place whither he went to.'

"Thus they agreed, and separated one from another. And the rich youth found at the source of the stream, which he had followed, a pleasure-garden with a house, in the entrance to which were seated an old man and an old woman. 'Good youth,' exclaimed they both, 'whence comest thou— whither goest thou ?' The youth replied, 'I come from a distant country, and am going to seek my fortune.' And the old couple said unto him, 'It is well thou hast come hither. We have a daughter, slender of shape and pleasant of behaviour. Take her, and be a son unto us!'

"And when they had so spoken, the daughter made her appearance. And when the youth beheld her, he thought unto himself, 'It is well I left my father and my mother. This maiden is more beauteous than a daughter of the Tângâri (god-like spirits of the male and female sex). I will take the maiden and dwell here.' And the maiden said, 'Youth, it is well that thou camest here.' Thereupon they conversed together, went together into the house, and lived peacefully and happily.

"Now, over the same country there reigned a mighty Chan. And once in the spring-time, when his servants went forth together to bathe, they found, near the mouth of the river, in the water, a pair of costly earrings, which belonged to the wife of the rich youth. Because, therefore, these jewels were so wondrously beautiful, they carried them to the Chan, who, being greatly surprised thereat, said unto his servants, 'Dwells there at the source of the river a woman such as these belong to? Go, and bring her unto me.'

"The servants went accordingly, beheld the woman, and were amazed at the sight. 'This woman,' said they to one another, 'one would never tire of beholding.' But to the woman they said, 'Arise! and draw nigh with us unto the Chan.'

"Hereupon the rich youth conducted his wife to the presence of the Chan; but the Chan, when he beheld her, exclaimed, 'This maiden is a Tângâri, compared with her, my wives are but ugly.'

Thus spake he, and he was so smitten with love of her, that he would not let her depart from his house. But as she remained true and faithful to the rich youth, the Chan said unto his servants, 'Remove this rich youth instantly out of my sight.'

"At these commands the servants went forth, taking with them the rich youth, whom they led to the water, where they laid him in a pit by the side of the stream, covered him with a huge fragment of the rock, and thus slew him.

"At length it happened that the other wanderers returned from all sides, each to his tree of life; and when the rich youth was missed, and they saw that his tree of life was withered, they sought him up the source of the river which he had followed, but found him not. Hereupon the reckoner discovered, by his calculations, that the rich youth was lying dead under a piece of the rock; but as they could by no means remove the stone, the smith took his hammer, smote the stone, and drew out the body. Then the physician mixed a life-inspiring draught, gave the same to the dead youth, and so restored him to life.

"They now demanded of him whom they had recalled to life, 'In what manner wert thou slain?'

He accordingly related unto them the circumstances; and they communed one with another, saying, 'Let us snatch this extraordinary beautiful woman from the Chan!' Thereupon the mechanic constructed a wooden gerudin, or wonderful bird, which, when moved upwards from within, ascended into the air; when moved downwards, descended into the earth; when moved sideways, flew sideways accordingly. When this was done, they painted it with different colours, so that it was pleasant to behold.

"Then the rich youth seated himself within the wooden bird, flew through the air, and hovered over the roof of the royal mansion; and the Chan and his servants were astonished at the form of the bird, and said, 'A bird like unto this we never before saw or heard of.' And to his wife the Chan said, 'Go ye to the roof of the palace, and offer food of different kinds unto this strange bird.' When she went up to offer food, the bird descended, and the rich youth opened the door which was in the bird. Then said the wife of the Chan, full of joy, 'I had never hoped or thought to have seen thee again, yet now have I found thee once more. This has been accomplished by this wonderful bird.' After the youth had related to her all that had happened, he said unto her, 'Thou art now the wife of the Chan— but if your heart now yearns unto me, step thou into this wooden gerudin, and we will fly hence through the air, and for the future know care no more.'

"After these words the wife said, 'To the first husband to whom destiny united me am I inclined more than ever.' Having thus spoken they entered into the wooden gerudin, and ascended into the sky. The Chan beheld this, and said, 'Because I sent thee up that thou mightest feed this beautiful bird, thou hast betaken thyself to the skies.' Thus spake he full of anger, and threw himself weeping on the ground.

" The rich youth now turned the peg in the bird downwards, and descended upon the earth close to his companions. And when he stepped forth out of the bird, his companions asked him, 'Hast thou thoroughly accomplished all that thou didst desire?' Thereupon his wife also stepped forth, and all who beheld her became in love with her. 'You, my companions,' said the rich youth, 'have brought help unto me; you have awakened me from death; you have afforded me the means of once more finding my wife. Do not, I beseech you, rob me of my charmer once again.'

"Thus spake he; and the calculator began with these words :—'Had I not discovered by my calculation where thou wert lying, thou wouldst never have recovered thy wife.'

"'In vain,' said the smith, ' would the calculations have been, had I not drawn thee out of the rock. By means of the shattered rock it was that you obtained your wife. Then your wife belongs to me.'

"'A body,' said the physician, 'was drawn from out of the shattered rock. That this body was restored to life, and recovered his former wife, it was my skill accomplished it. I, therefore, should take the wife.'

"'But for the wooden bird,' said the mechanic, 'no one would ever have reached the wife. A numerous host attend upon the Chan; no one can approach the house wherein he resides. Through my wooden bird alone was the wife recovered. Let me, then, take her.'

"'The wife,' said the painter, 'never would have carried food to a wooden bird; therefore it was only through my skill in painting that she was recovered; I, therefore, claim her.'

"And when they had thus spoken, they drew their knives and slew one another."

"Alas! poor woman!" exclaimed the son of the Chan; and Ssidi said, "Ruler of Destiny, thou hast spoken words:—Ssarwala missbrod jackzang!" Thus spake he, and burst from the sack through the air.

Thus Ssidi's first tale treated of the adventures of the rich youth.

THE ADVENTURES OF THE BEGGAR'S SON.

When the Son of the Chan arrived as before at the cold Forest of Death, he exclaimed with threatening gestures at the foot of the amiri-tree, "Thou dead one, descend, or I will hew down the tree." Ssidi descended. The son of Chan placed him in the sack, bound the sack fast with the rope, ate of his provender, and journeyed forth with his burden. Then spake the dead one these words, "Since we have a long journey before us, do you relate a pleasant story by the way, or I will do so." But the Son of the Chan merely shook his head without speaking a word. Whereupon Ssidi commenced the following tale :—

"A long time ago there was a mighty Chan who was ruler over a country full of market-places. At the source of the river which ran through it there was an immense marsh, and in this marsh there dwelt two crocodile-frogs, who would not allow the water to run out of the marsh. And because there came no water over their fields, every year did both the good and the bad have cause to mourn, until such times as a man had been given to the frogs for the pests to devour. And at length the lot fell upon the Chan himself to be an offering to them, and needful as he was to the welfare of the kingdom, denial availed him not; therefore father and son communed sorrowfully together, saying, ' Which of us two shall go ?'

"I am an old man," said the father, "and shall leave no one to lament me. I will go, therefore. Do you remain here, my son, and reign according as it is appointed."

"'O Tângâri,' exclaimed the son, ' verily this is not as it should be! Thou hast brought me up with care, O my father! If the Chan and the wife

of the Chan remain, what need is there of their son ?
I then will go, and be as a feast for the frogs.'

" Thus spake he, and the people walked sorrowfully round about him, and then betook themselves back again. Now the son of the Chan had for his companion the son of a poor man, and he went to him and said, ' Walk ye according to the will of your parents, and remain at home in peace and safety. I am going, for the good of the kingdom, to serve as a sacrifice to the frogs.' At these words the son of the poor man said, weeping and lamenting, ' From my youth up, O Chan, thou hast carefully fostered me. I will go with thee, and share thy fate."

" Then they both arose and went unto the frogs ; and on the verge of the marsh they heard the yellow frog and the blue frog conversing with one another. And the frogs said, ' If the son of the Chan and his companion did but know that if they only smote off our heads with the sword, and the son of the Chan consumed me, the yellow frog, and the son of the poor man consumed thee, the blue frog, they would both cast out from their mouths gold and brass, then would the country be no longer compelled to find food for frogs.'

" Now, because the son of the Chan understood all sorts of languages, he comprehended the discourse of the frogs, and he and his companion smote the heads of the frogs with their swords ; and when they had devoured the frogs, they threw out from their mouths gold and brass at their heart's pleasure. Then said the wanderers, ' The frogs are both slain —the course of the waters will be hemmed in no more.   Let us then turn back unto our own country.' But the son of the Chan agreed not to this, and said, ' Let us not turn back into our own country, lest they say they are become spirits; therefore it is better that we journey further.'

" As they thereupon were walking over a mountain, they came to a tavern, in which dwelt two women, beautiful to behold—mother and daughter. Then said they, ' We would buy strong liquor that we might drink.'   The women replied, ' What have ye to give in exchange for strong liquor?'   Thereupon each of them threw forth gold and brass, and the women found pleasure therein, admitted them into their dwelling, gave them liquor in abundance, until they became stupid and slept, took from them what they had, and then turned them out of doors.'

" Now when they awoke the son of the Chan and his companion travelled along a river and arrived in a wood, where they found some children quarrelling one with another.   ' Wherefore,' inquired they, ' do you thus dispute?'

" ' We have,' said the children, ' found a cap in this wood, and every one desires to possess it.'

" ' Of what use is the cap?'

" ' The cap has this wonderful property, that whosoever places it on his head can be seen neither by the Tângâri, nor by men, nor by the Tschadkurrs' (evil spirits).

"'Now go all of ye to the end of the forest and run hither, and I will in the meanwhile keep the cap, and give it to the first of you who reaches me.'

"Thus spoke the son of the Chan; and the children ran, but they found not the cap, for it was upon the head of the Chan. 'Even now it was here,' said they, 'and now it is gone.' And after they had sought for it, but without finding it, they went away weeping.

"And the son of the Chan and his companion travelled onwards, and at last they came to a forest in which they found a body of Tschadkurrs quarrelling one with another, and they said, 'Wherefore do ye thus quarrel one with another?'

"'I,' exclaimed each of them, 'have made myself master of these boots.'

"'Of what use are these boots?' inquired the son of the Chan.

"'He who wears these boots,' replied the Tschadkurrs, 'is conveyed to any country wherein he wishes himself.'

"'Now,' answered the son of the Chan, 'go all of you that way, and he who first runs hither shall obtain the boots.'

"And the Tschadkurrs, when they heard these words, ran as they were told; but the son of the Chan had concealed the boots in the bosom of his companion, who had the cap upon his head. And the Tschadkurrs saw the boots no more; they sought them in vain, and went their way.

"And when they were gone, the prince and his companion drew on each of them one of the boots, and they wished themselves near the place of election in a Chan's kingdom. They wished their journey, laid themselves down to sleep, and on their awaking in the morning they found themselves in the hollow of a tree, right in the centre of the imperial place of election. It was, moreover, a day for the assembling of the people, to throw a Baling (a sacred figure of dough or paste) under the guidance of the Tângâri. 'Upon whose head even the Baling falls, he shall be our Chan.' Thus spake they as they threw it up; but the tree caught the Baling of Destiny. 'What means this?' exclaimed they all with one accord. 'Shall we have a tree for our Chan?'

"'Let us examine,' cried they one to another, 'whether the tree concealeth any stranger.' And when they approached the tree the son of the Chan and his companion stepped forth. But the people stood yet in doubt, and said one to another thus, 'Whosoever ruleth over the people of this land, this shall be decided to-morrow morning by what proceedeth from their mouths.' And when they had thus spoken, they all took their departure.

"On the following morning some drank water, and what they threw from their mouths was white; others ate grass, and what they threw from their mouths was green. In short, one threw one thing, and another another thing. But because the son of the Chan and his companion cast out from their mouths gold and brass, the people cried, 'Let the one be Chan of this people—let the other be his minister.' Thus were they nominated Chan and minister! And the daughter of the former Chan was appointed the wife of the new Chan.

"Now in the neighbourhood of the palace wherein the Chan dwelt was a lofty building, whither the wife of the Chan betook herself every day. 'Wherefore,' thought the minister, 'does the wife of the Chan betake herself to this spot every day?' Thus thinking, he placed the wonderful cap upon his head, and followed the Chan's wife through the open doors, up one step after another, up to the roof. Here the wife of the Chan gathered together silken coverlets and pillows, made ready various drinks and delicate meats, and burnt for their perfume tapers and frankincense. The minister being concealed by his cap, which made him invisible, seated himself by the side of the Chan's wife, and looked around on every side.

"Shortly afterwards a beautiful bird swept through the sky. The wife of the Chan received it with fragrance-giving tapers. The bird seated itself upon the roof and twittered with a pleasing voice; but out of the bird came Solangdu, the Son of the Tângâri, whose beauty was incomparable, and he laid himself on the silken coverlets and fed of the dainties prepared for him. Then spake the son of the Tângâri, 'Thou hast passed this morning with the husband whom thy fate has allotted to thee. What thinkest thou of him?' The wife of the Chan answered, 'I know too little of the prince to speak of his good qualities or his defects.' Thus passed the day, and the wife of the Chan returned home again.

"On the following day the minister followed the wife of the Chan as he had done before, and heard the son of the Tângâri say unto her, 'To-morrow I will come like a bird of Paradise to see thine husband.' And the wife of the Chan said, 'Be it so.'

"The day passed over, and the minister said to the Chan, 'In yonder palace lives Solangdu, the beauteous son of the Tângâri.' The minister then related all that he had witnessed, and said, 'To-morrow early the son of the Tângâri will seek thee, disguised like a bird of Paradise. I will seize the bird by the tail, and cast him into the fire; but you must smite him in pieces with the sword.'

"On the following morning, the Chan and the wife of the Chan were seated together, when the son of the Tângâri, transformed into a bird of

Paradise, appeared before them on the steps that led to the palace. The wife of the Chan greeted the bird with looks expressive of pleasure, but the minister, who had on his invisible-making cap, seized the bird suddenly by the tail, and cast him into the fire. And the Chan smote at him violently with his sword; but the wife of the Chan seized the hand of her husband, so that only the wings of the bird were scorched. 'Alas, poor bird!' exclaimed the wife of the Chan, as, half dead, it made its way, as well as it could, through the air.

"On the next morning the wife of the Chan went as usual to the lofty building, and this time, too, did the minister follow her. She collected together, as usual, the silken pillows, but waited longer than she was wont, and sat watching with staring eyes. At length the bird approached with a very slow flight, and came down from the bird-house covered with blood and wounds, and the wife of the Chan wept at the sight. 'Weep not,' said the son of the Tângâri; 'thine husband has a heavy hand. The fire has so scorched me that I can never come more.'

"Thus spoke he, and the wife of the Chan replied, 'Do not say so, but come as you are wont to do, at least come on the day of the full moon.' Then the son of the Tângâri flew up to the sky again, and the wife of the Chan began from that time to love her husband with her whole heart.

"Then the minister placed his wonderful cap upon his head, and, drawing near to a pagoda, he saw, through the crevice of the door, a man, who spread out a figure of an ass, rolled himself over and over upon the figure, thereupon took upon himself the form of an ass, and ran up and down braying like one. Then he began rolling afresh, and appeared in his human form. At last he folded up the paper, and placed it in the hand of a burchan (a Calmuc idol). And when the man came out the minister went in, procured the paper, and remembering the ill-treatment which he had formerly received, he went to the mother and daughter who had sold him the strong liquor, and said, with crafty words, 'I am come to you to reward you for your good deeds.' With these words he gave the women three pieces of gold; and the women asked him, saying, 'Thou art, indeed, an honest man, but where did you procure so much gold?' Then the minister answered, 'By merely rolling backwards and forwards over this paper did I procure this gold.' On hearing these words, the women said, 'Grant us that we too may roll upon it.' And they did so, and were changed into asses. And the minister brought the asses to the Chan, and the Chan said, 'Let them be employed in carrying stones and earth.'

"Thus spake he, and for three years were these two asses compelled to carry stones and earth; and their backs were sore wounded, and covered with bruises. Then saw the Chan their eyes filled with tears, and he said to the minister, 'Torment the poor brutes no longer.'

"Thereupon they rolled upon the paper, and after they had done so they were changed to two shrivelled women."

"Poor creatures!" exclaimed the Son of the Chan. Ssidi replied, "Ruler of Destiny, thou hast spoken words: Ssarwala missdood jakzank!" Thus spoke he, and flew out of the sack through the air.

And Ssidi's second relation treats of the adventures of the Poor Man's Son.

THE ADVENTURES OF MASSANG.

When the Son of the Chan arrived at the foot of the amiri-tree, and spoke as he had formerly done, Ssidi approached him, suffered himself to be placed in the sack, fastened with the rope, and carried away. Ssidi spoke as before, but the Son of the Chan shook his head, whereupon Ssidi began as follows :—

"A long time ago there lived in a certain country a poor man, who had nothing in the world but one cow; and because there was no chance of the cow's calving, he was sore grieved, and said, 'If my cow does not have a calf, I shall have no more milk, and I must then die of hunger and thirst.'

"But when a certain number of moons had passed, instead of the calf the poor man had looked for he found a man with horns, and with a long tail like a cow. And at the sight of this monster the owner of the beast was filled with vexation, and he lifted up his staff to kill him; but the horned man said, 'Kill me not, father, and your mercy shall be rewarded.'

"And with these words he retreated into the depth of a forest, and there he found among the trees a man of sable hue. 'Who art thou?' inquired Massang the horned. 'I was born of the forest,' was the reply, 'and am called Iddar. I will follow thee whithersoever thou goest.'

"And they journeyed forth together, and at last they reached a thickly-covered grassy plain, and there they beheld a green man. 'Who art thou?' inquired they. 'I was born of the grass,' replied the green man, 'and will bear thee company.'

"Thereupon they all three journeyed forth together, until they came to a sedgy marsh, and there they found a white man. 'Who art thou?' inquired they. 'I was born of the sedges,' replied the white man, 'and will bear thee company.'

"Thereupon they all four journeyed forth together, until they reached a desert country, where, in the very depths of the mountain, they found a hut; and because they found plenty both to eat and to drink in the hut, they abode there. Every day three of them went out hunting, and left the fourth in charge of the hut. On the first day, Iddar, the Son of the Forest, remained in the hut, and was busied preparing milk, and cooking meat for his companions, when a little old woman put up the ladder and came in at the door. 'Who's there?' exclaimed Iddar, and, upon looking round, he beheld an old woman about a span high, who carried on her back a little sack. 'Oh, what, there is somebody sitting there?' said the old woman, 'and you are cooking meat; let me, I beseech you, taste a little milk and a little meat.'

"And though she merely tasted a little of each, the whole of the food disappeared. When the old woman thereupon took her departure, the Son of the Forest was ashamed that the food had disappeared, and he arose and looked out of the hut. And as he chanced to perceive two hoofs of a horse, he made with them a number of horse's footmarks around the dwelling, and shot an arrow into the court; and when the hunters returned home and inquired of him, 'Where is the milk and the fatted meat?' he answered them, saying, 'There came a hundred horsemen, who pressed their way into the house, and took the milk and the flesh, and they have beaten me almost to death. Go ye out, and look around.' And his companions went out when they heard these words, looked around, saw the prints of the horses' feet and the arrow which he himself had shot, and said, 'The words which he spoke are true.'

"On the following day the Son of the Grass remained at home in the hut, and it befell him as it had befallen his companion on the previous day. But because he perceived the feet of two bullocks, he made with them the marks of the feet of many bullocks around the dwelling, and said to his companions, 'There came a hundred people with laden bullocks, and robbed me of the food I had prepared for you.'

' "Thus spake he falsely. On the third day the Son of the Sedges remained at home in the hut, and because he met with no better fortune, he made, with a couple of the feet of a mule, a number of prints of mules' feet around the dwelling, and said to his companions, 'A hundred men with laden mules surrounded the house, and robbed me of the food I had prepared for you.'

"Thus spake he falsely. On the following day Massang remained at home in the hut, and as he was sitting preparing milk and flesh for his companions, the little old woman stepped in as before and said, 'Oh, so there is somebody here this time? Let me, I pray you, taste a little of the milk and a little of the meat.' At these words Massang considered, 'Of a certainty this old woman has been here before. If I do what she requires of me, how do I know that there will be any left?' And having thus considered, he said to the old woman, 'Old woman, before thou tastest food, fetch me some water.' Thus spoke he, giving her a bucket, of which the bottom was drilled full of holes, to fetch water in. When the old woman was gone, Massang looked after her, and found that the span-high old woman, reaching now up to the skies, drew the bucket full of water again and again, but that none of the water remained in it. While she was thus occupied, Massang peeped into the little sack which she carried on her shoulders, and took out of it a coil of rope, an iron hammer, and a pair of iron pincers, and put in their place some very rotten cords, a wooden hammer, and wooden pincers.

" He had scarcely done so before the old woman returned, saying, 'I cannot draw water in your bucket. If you will not give me a little of your food to taste, let us try our strength against each other.' Then the old woman drew forth the coil of rotten cords, and bound Massang with them, but Massang put forth his strength and burst the cords asunder. But when Massang had bound the old woman with her own coil, and deprived her of all power of motion, she said unto him, 'Herein thou hast gotten the victory; now let us pinch each other with the pincers.'

" Whereupon Massang nipped hold of a piece of the old woman's flesh as big as one's head, and tore it forcibly from her. 'Indeed, youth,' cried the old woman, sighing, 'but thou hast gotten a hand of stone ; now let us hammer away at each other !'

"So saying, she smote Massang with the wooden hammer on his breast, but the hammer flew from the handle, and Massang was left without a wound. Then drew Massang the iron hammer out of the fire, and smote the old woman with it in such wise that she fled from the hut crying and wounded.

"Shortly after this, the three companions returned home, and said to Massang, 'Now, Massang, thou hast surely had something to suffer?' But Massang replied, 'Ye are all cowardly fellows, and have uttered lies; I have paid off the old woman. Arise, and let us follow her!'

"At these words they arose, followed her by the traces of her blood, and at length reached a gloomy pit in a rock. At the bottom of this pit there were ten double circular pillars, and on the ground lay the corpse of the old woman, among gold, brass, and armour, and other costly things. 'Will you three descend,' said Massang, 'and then pack together the costly things, and I will draw them up, or I will pack them, and you shall draw them out.' But the three companions said, 'We will not go down into the cavern, for of a verity the old woman is a Schumnu' (a witch). But Massang, without being dispirited, allowed himself to be let down into the cavern, and collected the valuables, which were then drawn forth by his companions. Then

his companions spoke with one another, saying, 'If
we draw forth Massang, he will surely take all these
treasures to himself. It were better, then, that we
should carry away these treasures, and leave Massang
behind in the cavern!'

"When Massang noticed that his three companions
treated him thus ungratefully, he looked about the
cavern in search of food, but between the pillars he
found nothing but some pieces of bark. Thereupon
Massang planted the bark in the earth, nourished
it as best he might, and said, 'If I am a true
Massang, then from this bark let there grow forth
three great trees. If I am not, then shall I die
here in this pit.'

"After these enchanting words, he laid himself
down, but from his having come in contact with the
corse of the old woman, he slept for many years.
When he awoke, he found three great trees which
reached to the mouth of the pit. Joyfully clambered
he up and betook himself to the hut, which was in
the neighbourhood. But, because there was no
longer any one to be found therein, he took his iron
bow and his arrows, and set forth in search of his
companions. These had built themselves houses
and taken wives. 'Where are your husbands?'
inquired Massang of their wives. 'Our husbands
are gone to the chase,' replied they. Then Massang
took arrow and bow, and set forth. His companions
were returning from the chase with venison, and

when they beheld Massang with arrow and bow, they cried, as with one accord, 'Thou art the well-skilled one! take thou our wives and property, we will now wander forth further!' At these words Massang said, 'Your behaviour was certainly not what it should have been; but I am going to reward my father—live on, therefore, as before.'

"By the way Massang discovered a brook, and out of the brook arose a beautiful maiden. The maiden went her way, and flowers arose out of her footsteps. Massang followed the maiden until he arrived in heaven, and when he was come there, Churmusta Tângâri (the Protector of the Earth) said unto him, 'It is well that thou art come hither, Massang. We have daily to fight with the host of Schumnu (witches). To-morrow look around; after to-morrow be companion unto us.'

"On the following day, when the white host were sore pressed by the black, Churmusta spake unto Massang: 'The white host are the host of the Tângâri, the black are the host of the Schumnu. To-day the Tângâri will be pressed by the Schumnu; draw, therefore, thy bow, and send an arrow into the eye of the leader of the black host.' Then Massang aimed at the eye of the leader of the black host, and smote him, so that he fled with a mighty cry. Then spake Churmusta to Massang, "Thy deed is deserving of reward; henceforward dwell with us for ever.' But Massang replied, 'I go to reward my father.'

"Hereupon Churmusta presented to Massang, Dschindamani, the wonder-stone of the Gods, and said unto him, 'By a narrow circuitous path you will reach the cave of the Schumnu. Go without fear or trembling therein. Knock at the door and say, "I am the human physician." They will then lead thee to the Schumnu Chan, that you may draw out the arrow from his eyes; then lay hands upon the arrow, scatter seven sorts of grain towards heaven, and drive the arrow yet deeper into his head.'

"Thus spake Churmusta authoritatively, and Massang obeyed his commands; reached, without erring, the cavern of the Schumnu, and knocked at the door. 'What hast thou learned?' inquired the woman. 'I am a physician,' answered Massang; and he was conducted into the building. He examined the wound of the Chan, and laid hands upon the arrow. 'Already,' said the Chan, 'my wound feels better.' But Massang suddenly drove the arrow further into the head, scattered the seven grains towards heaven, and a chain fell clattering from heaven down to earth.

"But while Massang was preparing to lay hands upon the chain, the Schumnu woman smote him with an iron hammer with such force, that from the blow there sprang forth seven stars."

"Then," said the Son of the Chan, "he was not able to reward his father."

"Ruler of Destiny, thou hast spoken words! Ssarwala missdood jonkzang." Thus spake Ssidi, and burst from the sack through the air.

Thus Ssidi's third relation treats of the adventures of Massang.

THE MAGICIAN WITH THE SWINE'S HEAD.

When the Son of the Chan had, as before, seized upon Ssidi, and was carrying him away, Ssidi spoke as formerly, but the Son of the Chan shook his head, without uttering a word, and Ssidi began the following relation :—

"A long while since there lived in a happy country a man and a woman. The man had many bad qualities, and cared for nothing but eating, drinking, and sleeping. At last his wife said unto him, 'By thy mode of life thou hast wasted all thine inheritance. Arise thee, then, from thy bed, and while I am in the fields, go you out and look about you!'

"As he, therefore, according to these words, was looking about him, he saw a multitude of people pass behind the pagoda with their herds; and birds, foxes, and dogs crowding and noising together around a particular spot. Thither he went, and there found a bladder of butter; so he took it home and placed it upon the shelf. When his wife returned and saw the bladder of butter upon the shelf, she asked, 'Where found you this bladder of butter?' To this he replied, 'I did according to your word, and found this.' Then said the woman 'Thou went out but for an instant, and hast already found thus much.'

"Then the man determined to display his abilities, and said, 'Procure me then a horse, some clothes, and a bloodhound.' The wife provided them accordingly; and the man taking with him, besides these, his bow, cap, and mantle, seated himself on horseback, led the hound in a leash, and rode forth at random. After he had crossed over several rivers he espied a fox. 'Ah,' thought he, 'that would serve my wife for a cap.'

"So saying, he pursued the fox, and when it fled into a hamster's hole, the man got off his horse, placed his bow, arrows, and clothes upon the saddle, fastened the bloodhound to the bridle, and covered the mouth of the hole with his cap. The next thing he did was to take a large stone, and hammer over the hole with it; this frightened the fox, which ran out and fled with the cap upon its head. The hound followed the fox, and drew the horse along with it, so that they both vanished in an instant, and the man was left without any clothes.

After he had turned back a long way, he reached the country of a mighty Chan, entered the Chan's stable, and concealed himself in a stack of hay, so that merely his eyes were left uncovered. Not long afterwards, the beloved of the Chan was walking out, and wishing to look at a favourite horse, she approached close to the hayrick, placed the talisman of life of the Chan's kingdom upon the ground, left it there, and returned back to the palace without recollecting it. The man saw the wonderful stone, but was too lazy to pick it up. At sunset the cows came by, and the stone was beaten into the ground. Some time afterwards a servant came and cleansed the place, and the wonderful stone was cast aside upon a heap.

"On the following day the people were informed, by the beating of the kettledrums, that the beloved of the Chan had lost the wonderful stone. At the same time, all the magicians and soothsayers and interpreters of signs were summoned, and questioned upon the subject. On hearing this, the man in the hayrick crept out as far as his breast, and when the people thronged around him and asked, 'What hast thou learned?' he replied, 'I am a magician.' On hearing these words they exclaimed, 'Because the wondrous stone of the Chan is missing, all the magicians in the country are summoned to appear before him. Do you then draw nigh unto the Chan.' The man said, 'I have no clothes.' Hereupon the whole crowd hastened to the Chan, and announced unto him thus: 'In the hayrick there lieth a magician who has no clothes. This magician would draw nigh unto you, but he has nought to appear in.' The Chan said, 'Send unto him this robe of cloth, and let him approach.' It was done.

"The man was fetched, and after he had bowed down to the Chan, he was asked what he needed for the performance of his magic charms. To this question he replied, 'For the performance of my magic charms, it is needful that I should have the head of a swine, some cloths of five colours, and some baling' (a sacred figure of dough or paste). When all these things were prepared, the magician deposited the swine's head at the foot of a tree, dressed it with the cloths of five colours, fastened on the large baling, and passed the whole of three nights in meditation. On the day appointed, all the people assembled, and the magician having put on a great durga (cloak), placed himself, with the swine's head in his hand, in the street. When they were all assembled together, the magician, showing the swine's head, said, 'Here not and there not.' All were gladdened at hearing these words. 'Because, therefore,' said the magician, 'the wonderful stone is not to be found among the people, we must seek for it elsewhere.'

"With these words the magician, still holding the swine's head in his hand, drew nigh unto the palace, and the Chan and his attendants followed him, singing songs of rejoicing. When, at last, the magician arrived at the heap, he stood suddenly still, and exclaimed, 'There lies the wonderful stone.' Then, first removing some of the earth, he drew forth the stone, and cleansed it. 'Thou art a mighty magician,' joyfully exclaimed all who beheld it. 'Thou art the master of magic with the swine's head. Lift up thyself that thou mayest receive thy reward.' The Chan said, 'Thy reward shall be whatsoever thou wilt.' The magician, who thought only of the property he had lost, said, 'Give unto me a horse, with saddle and bridle, a bow and arrows, a cap, a mantle, a hound, and a fox. Such things give unto me.' At these words the Chan exclaimed, 'Give him all that he desireth.' This was done, and the magician returned home with all that he desired, and with two elephants, one carrying meat, and the other butter.

"His wife met him close to his dwelling, with brandy for him to drink, and said, 'Now, indeed, thou art become a mighty man.' Thereupon they went into the house, and when they had laid themselves down to sleep, the wife said to him, 'Where hast thou found so much flesh and so much butter?' Then her husband related to her circumstantially the whole affair, and she answered him saying, 'Verily, thou art a stupid ass. To-morrow I will go with a letter to the Chan.'

"The wife accordingly wrote a letter, and in the letter were the following words:—'Because it was known unto me that the lost wondrous stone retained some evil influence over the Chan, I have, for the obviating of that influence, desired of him the dog and the fox. What I may receive for my reward depends upon the pleasure of the Chan.'

"The Chan read the letter through, and sent costly presents to the magician. And the magician lived pleasantly and happily.

"Now in a neighbouring country there dwelt seven Chans, brethren. Once upon a time they betook themselves, for pastime, to an extensive forest, and there they discovered a beauteous maiden with a buffalo, and they asked, ' What are you two doing here? Whence come you?' The maiden answered, ' I come from an eastern country, and am the daughter of a Chan. This buffalo accompanies me.' At these words these others replied, ' We are the seven brethren of a Chan, and have no wife. Wilt thou be our wife?'[1] The maiden answered, ' So be it.' But the maiden and the buffalo were two Mangusch (a species of evil spirit like the Schumnu), and were seeking out men whom they might devour. The male Mangusch was a buffalo, and the female, she who became wife to the brethren.

"After the Mangusch had slain, yearly, one of the brethren of the Chan, there was only one re-

---

[1] It is in accordance with the customs of Thibet for a woman of that country to have several husbands.

maining. And because he was suffering from a grievous sickness, the ministers consulted together and said, 'For the sickness of the other Chans we have tried all means of cure, and yet have found no help, neither do we in this case know what to advise. But the magician with the swine's head dwells only two mountains off from us, and he is held in great estimation; let us, without further delay, send for him to our assistance.'

"Upon this four mounted messengers were despatched for the magician, and when they arrived at his dwelling, they made known to him the object of their mission. 'I will,' said the magician, ' consider of this matter in the course of the night, and will tell you in the morning what is to be done.'

"During the night he related to his wife what was required of him, and his wife said, 'You are looked upon, up to this time, as a magician of extraordinary skill; but from this time there is an end to your reputation. However, it cannot be helped, so go you must.'

"On the following morning the magician said to the messengers, 'During the night-time I have pondered upon this matter, and a good omen has presented itself to me in a dream. Let me not tarry any longer but ride forth to-day.' The magician, thereupon, equipped himself in a large cloak, bound his hair together on the crown of his head, carried in his left hand the rosary, and in his right the swine's head, enveloped in the cloths of five colours.

"When in this guise he presented himself before the dwelling-place of the Chan, the two Mangusch were sorely frightened, and thought to themselves, 'This man has quite the appearance, quite the countenance, of a man of learning.' Then the magician, first placing a baling on the pillow of the bed, lifted up the swine's head, and muttered certain magic words.

"The wife of the Chan seeing this discontinued tormenting the soul of the Chan, and fled in all haste out of the room. The Chan, by this conduct being freed from the pains of sickness, sank into a sound sleep. 'What is this?' exclaimed the magician, filled with affright. 'The disease has grown worse, the sick man uttereth not a sound; the sick man hath departed.' Thus thinking, he cried, 'Chan, Chan!' But because the Chan uttered no sound, the magician seized the swine's head, vanished through the door, and entered the treasure-chamber. No sooner had he done so, than 'Thief, thief!' sounded in his ears, and the magician fled into the kitchen; but the cry of 'Stop that thief! stop that thief!' still followed him. Thus pursued the magician thought to himself, 'This night it is of no use to think of getting away, so I will, therefore, conceal myself in a corner of the stable.' Thus thinking, he opened the door, and there found a buffalo, that lay there as if wearied with a long journey. The magician took the swine's head, and struck the buffalo three times between the horns, whereupon the buffalo sprang up and fled like the wind.

"But the magician followed after the buffalo, and when he approached the spot where he was, he heard the male Mangusch say to his female companion, 'Yonder magician knew that I was in the stable; with his frightful swine's head he struck me three blows—so that it was time for me to escape from him.' And the Chan's wife replied, 'I too am so afraid, because of his great knowledge, that I would not willingly return; for, of a certainty, things will go badly with us. To-morrow he will gather together the men with weapons and arms, and will say unto the women, "Bring hither firing;" when this is done he will say, "Lead the buffalo hither." And when thou appearest, he will say unto thee, "Put off the form thou hast assumed." And because all resistance would be useless, the people perceiving thy true shape will fall upon thee with swords, and spears, and stones; and when they have put thee to death, they will consume thee with fire. At last the magician will cause me to be dragged forth and consumed with fire. Oh, but I am sore afraid!'

"When the magician heard these words, he said to himself, 'After this fashion may the thing be easily accomplished.' Upon this he betook himself, with the swine's head to the Chan, lifted up the baling, murmured his words of magic, and asked, 'How is it now with the sickness of the Chan?' And the Chan replied, 'Upon the arrival of the master of magic the sickness passed away, and I have slept soundly.' Then the magician spake as follows: 'To-morrow, then, give this command to thy ministers, that they collect the whole of the people together, and that the women be desired to bring firing with them.'

"When, in obedience to these directions, there were two lofty piles of fagots gathered together, the magician said, 'Place my saddle upon the buffalo.' Then the magician rode upon the saddled buffalo three times around the assembled people, then removed the saddle from the buffalo, smote it three times with the swine's head, and said, 'Put off the form thou hast assumed.'

"At these words the buffalo was transformed into a fearful ugly Mangusch. His eyes were blood-shot, his upper tusks descended to his breast, his bottom tusks reached up to his eyelashes, so that he was fearful to behold. When the people had hewed this Mangusch to pieces with sword and with arrow, with spear and with stone, and his body was consumed upon one of the piles of fagots, then said the magician, 'Bring forth the wife of the Chan.' And with loud cries did the wife of the

Chan come forth, and the magician smote her with
the swine's head, and said, 'Appear in thine own
form!' Immediately her long tusks and bloodshot
eyes exhibited the terrific figure of a female Mangusch.

"After the wife of the Chan had been cut in
pieces, and consumed by fire, the magician mounted
his horse; but the people bowed themselves before
him, and strewed grain over him, presented him
with gifts, and regaled him so on every side, that
he was only enabled to reach the palace of the Chan
on the following morning. Then spake the Chan,
full of joy, to the magician, 'How can I reward you
for the great deed that thou hast done?' And the
magician answered, 'In our country there are but
few nose-sticks for oxen to be found. Give me, I
pray you, some of these nose-sticks.' Thus spake
he, and the Chan had him conducted home with
three sacks of nose-sticks, and seven elephants
bearing meat and butter.

"Near unto his dwelling his wife came with
brandy to meet him; and when she beheld the
elephants, she exclaimed, 'Now, indeed, thou art
become a mighty man.' Then they betook themselves to their house, and at night-time the wife of
the magician asked him, 'How camest thou to be
presented with such gifts?' The magician replied,
'I have cured the sickness of the Chan, and consumed with fire two Mangusch.' At these words

she replied, 'Verily, thou hast behaved very foolishly. After such a beneficial act, to desire nothing but nose-sticks for cattle! To-morrow I myself will go to the Chan.'

"On the morrow the wife drew near unto the Chan, and presented unto him a letter from the magician, and in this letter stood the following words:—'Because the magician was aware that of the great evil of the Chan a lesser evil still remained behind, he desired of him the nose-sticks. What he is to receive as a reward depends upon the pleasure of the Chan.'

"'He is right,' replied the Chan, and he summoned the magician, with his father and mother, and all his relations before him, and received them with every demonstration of honour. 'But for you I should have died; the kingdom would have been annihilated; the ministers and all the people consumed as the food of the Mangusch. I, therefore, will honour thee,' and he bestowed upon him proofs of his favour."

"Both man and wife were intelligent," exclaimed the Son of the Chan.

"Ruler of Destiny," replied Ssidi, "thou hast spoken words! Swarwala missdood jakzang!" Thus spake he, and burst from the sack through the air.

Ssidi's fourth relation treats of the Magician with the head of the Swine.

The History of Sunshine and his Brother.

As the Chan's Son was journeying along as before, laden with Ssidi, Ssidi inquired of him as formerly who should tell a tale. But the Son of the Chan shook his head without speaking a word, and Ssidi began as follows :—

"Many years ago Guchanasschang reigned over a certain happy land. This Chan had a wife and a son, whose name was Sunshine (Narrani Garral). Upon the death of his first wife the Chan married a second; and by her likewise he had a son, and the name of his second son was Moonshine (Ssarrani Garral). And when both these sons were grown up, the wife of the Chan thought to herself, 'So long as Sunshine, the elder brother, lives, Moonshine, the younger, will never be Chan over this land.'

"Some time after this the wife of the Chan fell sick, and tossed and tumbled about on her bed from the seeming agony she endured. And the Chan inquired of her, 'What can be done for you, my noble spouse?' To these words the wife of the Chan replied, 'Even at the time I dwelt with my parents I was subject to this sickness. But now it is become past bearing. I know, indeed, but one way of removing it; and that way is so impracticable, that there is nothing left for me but to die.' Hereupon spake the Chan, 'Tell unto me this way of help, and though it should cost me half my kingdom thou shalt have it. Tell me what thou requirest.' Thus spake he, and his wife replied with the following words, 'If the heart of one of the Chan's sons were roasted in the fat of the Gunsa (a beast); but thou wilt not, of course, sacrifice Sunshine for this purpose; and I myself bare Moonshine, his heart I will not consume. So that there is now nothing left for me but to die.' The Chan replied, 'Of a surety Sunshine is my son, and inexpressibly dear unto me; but in order that I may not lose thee, I will to-morrow deliver him over to the Jargatschi' (the servants of Justice).

"Moonshine overheard these words and hastened to his brother, and said, 'To-morrow they will murder thee.' When he had related all the circumstances, the brother replied, 'Since it is so, do you remain at home, honouring your father and mother. The time of my flight is come.' Then said Moonshine with a troubled heart, 'Alone I will not remain, but I will follow thee whithersoever thou goest.'

"Because the following day was appointed for the murder, the two brothers took a sack with baling-cakes from the altar, crept out at night, for it was the night of the full moon, from the palace, and journeyed on day and night through the mountainous country, until they at length arrived at the course of a dried-up river. Because their provender was finished, and the river afforded no water,

Moonshine fell to the earth utterly exhausted. Then spake the elder brother, full of affliction, 'I will go and seek water; but do you watch an instant until I come down from the high places.'

"After some vain attempts Sunshine returned, and found that his brother had departed this life. After he had with great tenderness covered the body of his brother with stones, he wandered over high mountains, and then arrived at the entrance of a cave. Within the cave sat an aged Arschi. 'Whence comest thou?' inquired the old man, 'thy countenance betokeneth deep affliction.' And when the youth had related all that had passed, the old man, taking with him the means of awakening the dead, went with the youth to the grave, and called Moonshine back to life. 'Will ye be unto me as sons?' Thus spake the old man, and the two young men became as sons unto him.

"Not far from this place there reigned a mighty Chan of fearful power; and the time was approaching in this country when the fields were watered, but the crocodiles prevented this. The crocodiles frequented a marsh at the source of the river, and would not allow the water to stream forth until such times as a Son of the Tiger-year[1] had been offered to them as food. After a time it happened

[1] Among the Calmucs every year has its peculiar name, and persons born in any year are called the children of that year.

that when search had been made in vain for a Son of the Tiger-year, certain people drew nigh unto the Chan, and said, 'Near unto the source of the river dwelleth the old Arschi, and with him a Son of the Tiger-year. Thither led we our cattle to drink, and we saw him.'

"When he heard this, the Chan said, 'Go and fetch him.'

" Accordingly the messengers were despatched for him, and when they arrived at the entrance of the cave, the Arschi himself came forth. 'What is it that ye seek here?' inquired the aged Arschi. ' The Chan,' replied they, 'speaketh to thee thus: Thou hast a Son of the Tiger-year. My kingdom hath need of him: send him unto me.' But the Arschi said, 'Who could have told you so? who, indeed, would dwell with an old Arschi?'

"Thus speaking he retired into his cave, closed the door after him, and concealed the youth in a stone chest, placed the lid on him, and cemented up the crevices with clay, as if it was from the distillation of arrack. But the messengers having broken down the door, thrust themselves into the cave, searched it, and then said, 'Since he whom we sought is not here, we are determined that nothing shall be left in the cave.' Thus speaking, they drew their swords; and the youth said, out of fear for the Arschi, 'Hurt not my father; I am here.'

"And when the youth was come forth, the mes-

sengers took him with them; but the Arschi they
left behind them weeping and sorrowing. When
the youth entered into the palace of the Chan, the
daughter of the Chan beheld him and loved him,
and encircled his neck with her arms. But the
attendants addressed the Chan, saying, 'To-day is
the day appointed for the casting of the Son of the
Tiger-year into the waters.' Upon this the Chan
said, 'Let him then be cast into the waters!' But
when they would have led him forth for that purpose, the daughter of the Chan spake and said,
'Cast him not into the waters, or cast me into the
waters with him.'

"And when the Chan heard these words, he was
angered, and said, 'Because this maiden careth so
little for the welfare of the kingdom, over which I
am Chan, let her be bound fast unto the Son of the
Tiger-year, and let them be cast together into the
waters.' And the attendants said, 'It shall be
according as you have commanded.'

"And when the youth was bound fast, and with
the maiden cast into the waters, he cried out, 'Since
I am the Son of the Tiger-year, it is certainly lawful
for them to cast me into the waters; but why
should this charming maiden die, who so loveth
me?' But the maiden said, 'Since I am but an
unworthy creature, it is certainly lawful for them
to cast me into the waters; but wherefore do they
cast in this beauteous youth?'

"Now the crocodiles heard these words, felt compassion, and placed the lovers once more upon the shore. And no sooner had this happened than the streams began to flow again. And when they were thus saved, the maiden said to the youth, 'Come with me, I pray you, unto the palace?' and he replied, 'When I have sought out my father Arschi, then will I come, and we will live together unsevered as man and wife.'

"Accordingly the youth returned to the cave of the old Arschi, and knocked at the door. 'I am thy son,' said he. 'My son,' replied the old man, 'has the Chan taken and slain; therefore it is that I sit here and weep.' At these words the son replied, 'Of a verity I am thy son. The Chan indeed bade them cast me into the waters; but because the crocodiles devoured me not, I am returned unto you. Weep not, O my father!'

"Arschi then opened the door, but he had suffered his beard and the hair of his head to grow, so that he looked like a dead man. Sunshine washed him therefore with milk and with water, and aroused him by tender words from his great sorrow.

"Now when the maiden returned back again to the palace, the Chan and the whole people were exceedingly amazed. 'The crocodiles,' they exclaimed, 'have, contrary to their wont, felt compassion for this maiden and spared her. This is indeed a very wonder.' So the whole people passed around the maiden, bowing themselves down before her. But the Chan said, 'That the maiden is returned is indeed very good. But the Son of the Tiger-year is assuredly devoured.' At these words his daughter replied unto him, 'The Son of the Tiger-year assuredly is not devoured. On account of his goodness his life was spared him.'

"And when she said this, all were more than ever surprised. 'Arise!' said the Chan to his ministers, 'lead this youth hither.' Agreeably to these commands, the ministers hastened to the cave of the aged Arschi. Both Arschi and the youth arose, and when they approached unto the dwelling of the Chan, the Chan said, 'For the mighty benefits which this youth has conferred upon us, and upon our dominions, we feel ourselves bound to go forth to meet him.'

"Thus spake he, and he went forth to meet the youth, and led him into the interior of the palace, and placed him upon one of the seats appropriated to the nobles. 'O thou most wondrous youth!' he exclaimed, 'art thou indeed the son of Arschi?' The youth replied, 'I am the Son of a Chan. But because my stepmother, out of the love she bare to her own son, sought to slay me, I fled, and, accompanied by my younger brother, arrived at the cave of the aged Arschi.'

"When the Son of the Chan related all this, the

Chan loaded him with honours, and gave his daughters for wives unto the two brothers, and sent them, with many costly gifts and a good retinue, home to their own kingdom. Thither they went, drew nigh unto the palace, and wrote a letter as follows :—'To the Chan their father, the two brothers are returned back again.'

"Now the father and mother had for many years bewailed the loss of both their sons, and their sorrows had rendered them so gloomy that they remained ever alone.

"On receipt of this letter they sent forth a large body of people to meet their children. But because the wife of the Chan saw both the youths approaching with costly gifts and a goodly retinue, so great was her envy that she died."

"She was very justly served!" exclaimed the Son of the Chan.

"Ruler of Destiny, thou hast spoken words! Ssarwala missdood jonkzang." Thus spake Ssidi, and burst from the sack through the air.

Thus Ssidi's fifth relation treats of Sunshine and his brother.

The Wonderful Man who overcame the Chan.

When the Son of the Chan had proceeded as formerly to seize the dead one, then spake he the threatening words, seized upon Ssidi, thrust him into the sack, tied the sack fast, ate of the butter-cakes, and journeyed forth with his burden. After Ssidi had as before asked who should tell the tale, and the Son of the Chan had replied by merely shaking his head, Ssidi began the following relation :—

"A long, long time ago there lived in the land of Barschiss, a wild, high-spirited man, who would not allow any one to be above him. Then spake the Chan of the kingdom to him, full of displeasure, 'Away with thee, thou good-for-nothing one ! Away with thee to some other kingdom !' Thus spake he, and the wild man departed forth out of the country.

"On his journey he arrived about mid-day at a forest, where he found the body of a horse, which had been somehow killed, and he accordingly cut off its head, fastened it to his girdle, and climbed up a tree.

"About midnight there assembled a host of Tschadkurrs (evil spirits) mounted upon horses of bark, wearing likewise caps of bark, and they placed themselves around the tree. Afterwards there assembled together other Tschadkurrs, mounted upon horses of paper, and having caps of paper on their heads, and they likewise placed themselves around the tree.

"During the time that those who were assembled were partaking of various choice wines and liquors, the man peeped anxiously down from the tree, and as he was doing so, the horse's head fell down from his belt. The Tschadkurrs were thereby exceedingly alarmed; so much that they fled hither and thither uttering fearful cries.

"On the following morning the man descended from the tree, and said, 'This night there was in this spot many choice viands and liquors, and now they are all vanished.' And while he was thus speaking, he found a brandy flask, and as he was anxious for something to drink, he immediately applied the flask which he had found to his lips; when suddenly there sprang out of it meat and cakes and other delicacies fit for eating. 'This flask,' cried he, 'is of a surety a wishing flask, which will procure him who has it everything he desires. I will take the flask with me.'

"And when he had thus spoken, he continued his journey until he met with a man holding a sword in his hand. 'Wherefore,' cried he, 'dost thou carry that sword in thine hand?' And the man answered, 'This sword is called Kreischwinger; and when I say to it, "Kreischwinger, thither goes a man who has taken such a thing from me, follow him and bring it back," Kreischwinger goes forth, kills the man, and brings my property back again.' To this the first replied, 'Out of this vessel springeth everything you desire; let us exchange.' So accordingly they made an exchange; and when the man went away with the flask, he who now owned the sword said, 'Kreischwinger, go forth now and bring me back my flask.' So the sword went forth, smote his former master dead, and brought the golden vessel back again.

"When he had journeyed a little further, he met a man holding in his hand an iron hammer. 'Wherefore,' cried he, 'dost thou hold this hammer in thy hand?' To this question the other replied, 'When I strike the earth nine times with this hammer, there immediately arises a wall of iron, nine pillars high.' Then said the first, 'Let us make an exchange.' And when the exchange was made, he cried out, 'Kreischwinger, go forth and bring me back my golden vessel!'

· "After Kreischwinger had slain the man, and brought back the golden vessel, the man journeyed on until he encountered another man, carrying in his bosom a sack, made of goatskin, and he asked him, 'Wherefore keepest thou that sack?' To this question the other replied, 'This sack is a very wonderful thing. When you shake it, it rains heavily; and if you shake it very hard, it rains very heavily.' Hereupon the owner of the flask said, 'Let us change,' and they changed accordingly; and the sword went forth, slew the man, and returned back to its master with the golden vessel.

"When the man found himself in the possession of all these wonderful things, he said unto himself, 'The Chan of my country is indeed a cruel man;

nevertheless I will turn back unto my native land.'
When he had thus considered, he turned back again,
and concealed himself in the neighbourhood of the
royal palace.

"About midnight he struck the earth nine times
with his iron hammer, and there arose an iron wall
nine pillars high.

"On the following morning the Chan arose, and
said, 'During the night I have heard a mighty tock,
tock at the back of the palace.' Thereupon the wife
of the Chan looked out, and said, 'At the back of
the palace there stands an iron wall nine pillars
high.' Thus spake she; and the Chan replied, full
of anger, 'The wild, high-spirited man has of a surety
erected this iron wall; but we shall see whether he
or I will be the conqueror.'

"When he had spoken these words the Chan
commanded all the people to take fuel and bellows,
and make the iron wall red-hot on every side.
Thereupon there was an immense fire kindled, and
the Wonderful Man found himself, with his mother,
within the wall of iron. He was himself upon the
upper pillars, but his mother was on the eighth.
And because the heat first reached the mother, she
exclaimed unto her son, 'The fires which the Chan
has commanded the people to kindle will destroy
the iron wall, and we shall both die.' The son
replied, 'Have no fear, mother, for I can find means
to prevent it.'

"When he had spoken these words he shook the sack of goatskin, and there descended heavy rain and extinguished the fire. After that he shook the sack still more forcibly, and there arose around them a mighty sea, which carried away both the fuel and the bellows which the people had collected."

"Thus, then, the Wonderful gained the mastery over the Chan," exclaimed the Son of the Chan.

"Ruler of Destiny, thou hast spoken words! Ssarwala missdood jakzang!" Thus spake Ssidi, and burst from the sack through the air.

Thus Ssidi's sixth relation treats of the Wonderful Man who overpowered the Chan.

THE BIRD-MAN.

When the Son of the Chan had done as formerly, spoken the threatening words, and carried off Ssidi, Ssidi asked him as before to tell a tale; but the Son of the Chan shook his head without speaking a word, and Ssidi began as follows :—

"In times gone by there lived in a fair country the father of a family, whose three daughters had daily by turns to watch over the calves. Now it once happened, during the time that the eldest sister should have been watching the calves, that she fell asleep, and one of them was lost. When the maiden awoke and missed the calf, she arose and went forth to seek it, and wandered about until she reached a large house with a red door.

"She went in, and then came to a golden door, next to that to a silver one, and last of all to a brazen door. After she had likewise opened this door she found, close to the entrance of it, a cage decorated with gold and all manner of costly jewels, and within it, on a perch, there stood a white bird.

"'I have lost a calf,' said the maiden, 'and am come hither to seek it.' At these words the bird said, 'If thou wilt become my wife I will find the calf for you, but not without.' But the maiden said, 'That may not be; among men birds are looked upon but as wild creatures. Therefore I will not become your wife, even though, through refusing, I lose the calf for ever.' And when she had thus spoken she returned home again.

"On the following day the second sister went forth to tend the calves, and she likewise lost one of them. And it happened unto her as it had done unto the eldest sister, and she too refused to become the wife of the bird.

"At last the youngest sister went forth with the calves, and when she missed one she too wandered on until she reached the house wherein the bird resided. The bird said unto her likewise, 'If thou wilt become my wife, I will procure for thee the calf which thou hast lost.' 'Be it according to thy will.' Thus spake she, and became the wife of the bird.

"After some time it happened that a mighty thirteen days' feast was held at a large pagoda in

the neighbourhood, and upon this occasion a number
of persons assembled together, amongst the rest
the wife of the bird. And she was the foremost
among the women; but among the men the most
noticed was an armed man, who rode upon a white
horse three times round the assemblage. And all
who saw him exclaimed, ' He is the first.'

" And when the woman returned home again the
white bird demanded of her, ' Who were the foremost among the men· and the women who were
there assembled together ? ' Then said the woman,
'The foremost among the men was seated upon a
white horse, but I knew him not. The foremost of
the women was myself.'

" And for eleven days did these things so fall out.
But on the twelfth day, when the wife of the bird
went to the assemblage, she sat herself down near
an old woman. ' Who,' said the old woman, ' is
the first in the assemblage this day ? ' To this
question the wife of the bird replied, ' Among the
men, the rider upon the white horse is beyond all
comparison the foremost. Among the women, I
myself am so. Would that I were bound unto this
man, for my husband is numbered among wild
creatures since he is nothing but a bird.'

" Thus spake she, weeping, and the old woman
replied as follows :—' Speak ye no more words like
unto these. Amongst the assembled women thou
art in all things the foremost. But the rider upon

the white horse is thine own husband. To-morrow is the thirteenth day of the feast. Come not to-morrow unto the feast, but remain at home behind the door until thine husband opens his birdhouse, takes his steed from the stable, and rides to the feast. Take ye, then, the open birdhouse and burn it. And when thou hast done this thy husband will remain henceforth and for ever in his true form.'

"The wife of the bird, thereupon, did as she had been told ; and when the birdhouse was opened, and her husband had departed, she took the birdhouse and burnt it upon the hearth. When the sun bowed down towards the west the bird returned home, and said to his wife, ' What, art thou already returned?' and she said, ' I am already returned.' Then said her husband, ' Where is my birdhouse?' And the wife replied, ' I have burnt it.' And he said, ' Barama, that is a pretty business—that birdhouse was my soul.'

"And his wife was troubled, and said, ' What is now to be done?' To these words the bird replied, ' There is nothing can be done now, except you seat yourself behind the door, and there by day and night keep clattering a sword. But if the clattering sword ceases, the Tschadkurrs will carry me away. Seven days and seven nights must ye thus defend me from the Tschadkurrs and from the Tângâri.'

" At these words the wife took the sword, propped

open her eyelids with little sticks, and watched for the space of six nights. On the seventh night her eyelids closed for an instant, but in that instant the Tschadkurrs and Tângâri suddenly snatched her husband away.

" Weeping bitterly, and despising all nourishment, the distracted wife ran about everywhere, crying unceasingly, ' Alas, my bird-husband! Alas, my bird-husband ! '

" When she had sought for him day and night without finding him, she heard from the top of a mountain the voice of her husband. Following the sound, she discovered that the voice proceeded from the river. She ran to the river, and then discovered her husband with a load of tattered boots upon his back. ' Oh! my heart is greatly rejoiced,' said the husband, ' at seeing thee once more. I am forced to draw water for the Tschadkurrs and the Tângâri, and have worn out all these boots in doing so. If thou wishest to have me once again, build me a new birdhouse, and dedicate it to my soul; then I shall come back again.'

" With these words he vanished into the air. But the woman betook herself home to the house again, made a new birdhouse, and dedicated it to the soul of her husband. At length the bird-man appeared and perched himself on the roof of the house."

" Truly, his wife was an excellent wife!" exclaimed the Son of the Chan.

"Ruler of Destiny, thou hast spoken words! Ssarwala missdood jakzang!' Thus spake Ssidi, and burst from the sack through the air.

Thus Ssidi's seventh relation treats of the Bird-man.

The Painter and the Wood-carver.

When the Son of the Chan had, as on all the former occasions, spoken the words of threatening, placed the dead one in the sack, and journeyed forth with him, Ssidi spake this time also as follows:— 'The day is long, and the distant journey will tire us: do you relate a tale unto me, or I will relate one unto you." But the Son of the Chan shook his head without saying a word, and Ssidi began as follows:—

"Many years ago there lived in the land of Gujassmunn a Chan, whose name was Gunisschang. This Chan, however, died, and his son Chamuk Sakiktschi was elected Chan in his place. Now there lived among the people of that country a painter and a wood-carver, who bore similar names, and were evilly disposed towards each other.

"Once upon a time the painter, Gunga, drew nigh unto the Chan, and said unto him, 'Thy father hath been borne into the kingdom of the Tângâri, and hath said unto me, "Come unto me!" Thither I went, and found thy father in great power and

splendour; and I have brought for you this letter
from him.' With these words the painter delivered
unto the Chan a forged letter, the contents of which
were as follows :—

" ' This letter is addressed to my son Chamuk
Sakiktschi.

" ' When I departed this life, I was borne to the
kingdom of the Tângâri. An abundance of all
things reigns in this land; but since I am desirous
of erecting a pagoda, and there are no wood-carvers
to be found here, do you despatch unto me Cunga,
the wood-carver. The means by which he is to
reach this place he may learn from the painter.'

" After he had perused this letter, the Chan of
Gujassmunn said, 'If my father has really been
carried into the realms of the Tângâri, that would
indeed be a good thing. Call hither the wood-
carver ?' The wood-carver was called, and appeared
before the Chan, and the Chan said unto him, 'My
father has been carried into the realms of the
Tângâri. He is desirous of erecting a pagoda, and
because there are no wood-carvers there he is
desirous that you should be despatched unto him.'

" With these words the Chan displayed the forged
letter, and when he had read it, the wood-carver
said unto himself, 'Of a surety Gunga, the painter,
has played me this trick; but I will try if I cannot
overreach him.'

" Thus thinking, he inquired of the painter, 'By

what means can I reach the kingdom of the Tângâri ?'

"To these words the painter replied, 'When thou hast prepared all thy tools and implements of trade, then place thyself upon a pile of fagots, and when thou hast sung songs of rejoicing and set light to the pile of fagots, thus wilt thou be able to reach the kingdom of the Tângâri.' Thus spake he, and the seventh night from that time was appointed for the carver's setting forth on his journey.

"When the wood-carver returned home unto his wife, he spake unto her these words :—'The painter hath conceived wickedness in his mind against me ; yet I shall try means to overreach him.'

"Accordingly he secretly contrived a subterranean passage, which reached from his own house into the middle of his field. Over the aperture in the field he placed a large stone, covered the stone with earth, and when the seventh night was come, the Chan said, 'This night let the wood-carver draw nigh unto the Chan, my father.' Thereupon, agreeably to the commands of the Chan, every one of the people brought out a handful of the fat of the Gunsa (a beast). A huge fire was kindled, and the wood-cutter, when he had sung the songs of rejoicing, escaped by the covered way he had made back to his own house.

"Meanwhile the painter was greatly rejoiced, and pointed upwards with his finger, and said, 'There

rideth the wood-carver up to heaven.' All who had
been present, too, betook themselves home, thinking
in their hearts, 'The wood-carver is dead, and gone
up above to the Chan.'

"The wood-carver remained concealed at home
a whole month, and allowed no man to set eyes
upon him, but washed his head in milk every day,
and kept himself always in the shade. After that
he put on a garment of white silk, and wrote a
letter, in which stood the following words:—

"'This letter is addressed to my son Chamuk
Sakiktschi. That thou rulest the kingdom in
peace; it is very good. Since thy wood-carver has
completed his work, it is needful that he should be
rewarded according to his deserts. Since, moreover, for the decoration of the pagoda, many
coloured paintings are necessary, send unto me the
painter, as thou hast already sent this man.'

"The wood-carver then drew nigh unto the Chan
with this letter. 'What!' cried the Chan, 'art
thou returned from the kingdom of the Tângâri?'
The wood-carver handed the letter unto him, and
said, 'I have, indeed, been in the kingdom of the
Tângâri, and from it I am returned home again.'

"The Chan was greatly rejoiced when he heard
this, and rewarded the wood-carver with costly
presents. 'Because the painter is now required,'
said the Chan, 'for the painting of the pagoda, let
him now be called before me.'

"The painter drew nigh accordingly, and when he saw the wood-carver, fair, and in white-shining robes, and decorated with gifts, he said unto himself, 'Then he is not dead!' And the Chan handed over to the painter the forged letter, with the seal thereto, and said, 'Thou must go now.'

"And when the seventh night from that time arrived, the people came forward as before with a contribution of the fat of the Gunsa; and in the midst of the field a pile of fagots was kindled. The painter seated himself in the midst of the fire, with his materials for painting, and a letter and gifts of honour for the Chan Gunisschang, and sang songs of rejoicing; and as the fire kept growing more and more intolerable, he lifted up his voice and uttered piercing cries; but the noise of the instruments overpowered his voice, and at length the fire consumed him."

"He was properly rewarded!" exclaimed the Son of the Chan.

"Ruler of Destiny, thou hast spoken words! Ssarwala missdood jakzang!" Thus spake Ssidi, and burst from the sack through the air.

Thus Ssidi's eighth relation treats of the Painter and the Wood-carver.

THE STEALING OF THE HEART.

When the Son of the Chan was, as formerly, carrying Ssidi away in the sack, Ssidi inquired of him as before; but the Son of the Chan shook his head without speaking a word, so Ssidi proceeded as follows :—

"Many, many years ago there ruled over a certain kingdom a Chan named Guguluktschi. Upon the death of this Chan his son, who was of great reputation and worth, was elected Chan in his place.

"One berren (a measure of distance) from the residence of the Chan dwelt a man, who had a daughter of wonderful abilities and extraordinary beauty. The son of the Chan was enamoured of this maiden, and visited her daily; until, at length, he fell sick of a grievous malady, and died, without the maiden being made aware of it.

"One night, just as the moon was rising, the maiden heard a knocking at the door, and the face of the maiden was gladdened when she beheld the son of the Chan; and the maiden arose and went to meet him, and she led him in and placed arrack and cakes before him. 'Wife,' said the son of the Chan, 'come with me!'

"The maiden followed, and they kept going further and further, until they arrived at the dwelling of the Chan, from which proceeded the sound of cymbals and kettledrums.

"'Chan, what is this?' she asked. The son of the Chan replied to these inquiries of the maiden, 'Do you not know that they are now celebrating the feast of my funeral?' Thus spake he; and the maiden replied, 'The feast of thy funeral! Has anything then befallen the Chan's son?' And the son of the Chan replied, 'He is departed. Thou wilt, however, bear a son unto him. And when the season is come, go into the stable of the elephant, and let him be born there. In the palace there will arise a contention betwixt my mother and her attendants, because of the wonderful stone of the kingdom. The wonderful stone lies under the table of sacrifice. After it has been discovered, do you and my mother reign over this kingdom until such time as my son comes of age.'

"Thus spake he, and vanished into air. But his beloved fell, from very anguish, into a swoon. 'Chan! Chan!' exclaimed she sorrowfully, when she came to herself again. And because she felt that the time was come, she betook herself to the stable of the elephants, and there gave birth to a son.

"On the following morning, when the keeper of the elephants entered the stable, he exclaimed, 'What! has a woman given birth to a son in the stable of the elephants? This never happened before. This may be an injury to the elephants.'

"At these words the maiden said, 'Go unto the mother of the Chan, and say unto her, "Arise! something wonderful has taken place."'

"When these words were told unto the mother of the Chan, then she arose and went unto the stable,

and the maiden related unto her all that had
happened. 'Wonderful!' said the mother of the
Chan. 'Otherwise the Chan had left no successors.
Let us go together into the house.'

"Thus speaking, she took the maiden with her
into the house, and nursed her, and tended her
carefully. And because her account of the wonderful
stone was found correct, all the rest of her story was
believed. So the mother of the Chan and his wife
ruled over the kingdom.

"Henceforth, too, it happened that every month,
on the night of the full moon, the deceased Chan
appeared to his wife, remained with her until
morning dawned, and then vanished into air. And
the wife recounted this to his mother, but his mother
believed her not, and said, 'This is a mere invention.
If it were true my son would, of a surety, show himself likewise unto me. If I am to believe your
words, you must take care that mother and son
meet one another.'

"When the son of the Chan came on the night
of the full moon, his wife said unto him, 'It is well
that thou comest unto me on the night of every full
moon, but it were yet better if thou camest every
night.' And as she spake thus, with tears in her
eyes, the son of the Chan replied, 'If thou hadst
sufficient spirit to dare its accomplishment, thou
mightest do what would bring me every night; but
thou art young and cannot do it.' 'Then,' said she,

'if thou wilt but come every night, I will do all that is required of me, although I should thereby lose both flesh and bone.'

"Thereupon the son of the Chan spake as follows : 'Then betake thyself on the night of the full moon a berren from this place to the iron old man, and give unto him arrack. A little further you will come unto two rams, to them you must offer batschimak cakes. A little further on you will perceive a host of men in coats of mail and other armour, and there you must share out meat and cakes. From thence you must proceed to a large black building, stained with blood; the skin of a man floats over it instead of a flag. Two aerliks (fiends) stand at the entrance. Present unto them both offerings of blood. Within the mansion thou wilt discover nine fearful exorcists, and nine hearts upon a throne. "Take me! take me!" will the eight old hearts exclaim; and the ninth heart will cry out, "Do not take me!" But leave the old hearts and take the fresh one, and run home with it without looking round.'

"Much as the maiden was alarmed at the task which she had been enjoined to perform, she set forth on the night of the next full moon, divided the offerings, and entered the house. 'Take me not!' exclaimed the fresh heart; but the maiden seized the fresh heart and fled with it. The exorcists fled after her, and cried out to those who were watching, 'Stop the thief of the heart!' And the two aerlic (fiends) cried, 'We have received offerings of blood!' Then each of the armed men cried out, ¡Stop the thief!' But the rams said, 'We have received batschimak cakes.' Then they called out to the iron old man, 'Stop the thief with the heart!' But the old man said, 'I have received arrack from her, and shall not stop her.'

"Thereupon the maiden journeyed on without fear until she reached home; and she found upon entering the house the Chan's son, attired in festive garments. And the Chan's son drew nigh, and threw his arms about the neck of the maiden."

"The maiden behaved well indeed!" exclaimed the Son of the Chan.

"Ruler of Destiny, thou hast spoken words! Ssarwala missdood jakzang." Thus spake Ssidi, and burst from the sack through the air.

Thus Ssidi's ninth relation treats of the Stealing of the Heart.

The Man and his Wife.

When Ssidi had been captured as before, and was being carried away in the sack, he inquired, as he had always done, as to telling a tale; but the Son of the Chan shook his head without speaking a word. Whereupon Ssidi began the following relation:—

"Many, many years since, there lived in the kingdom of Olmilsong two brothers, and they were both married. Now the elder brother and his wife were niggardly and envious, while the younger brother was of quite a different disposition.

"Once upon a time the elder brother, who had contrived to gather together abundance of riches, gave a great feast, and invited many people to partake of it. When this was known, the younger thought to himself, 'Although my elder brother has hitherto not treated me very well, yet he will now, no doubt, since he has invited so many people to his feast, invite also me and my wife.' This he certainly expected, but yet he was not invited. 'Probably,' thought he, 'my brother will summon me to-morrow morning to the brandy-drinking.' Because, however, he was not even invited unto that, he grieved very sore, and said unto himself, 'This night, when my brother's wife has drunk the brandy, I will go unto the house and steal somewhat.'

"When, however, he had glided into the treasure-chamber of his brother, there lay the wife of his brother near her husband; but presently she arose and went into the kitchen, and cooked meat and sweet food, and went out of the door with it. The concealed one did not venture at this moment to steal anything, but said unto himself, 'Before I steal anything, I will just see what all this means.'

"So saying, he went forth and followed the

woman to a mountain where the dead were wont to be laid. On the top, upon a green mound, lay a beautiful ornamental tomb over the body of a dead man. This man had formerly been the lover of the woman. Even when afar off she called unto the dead man by name, and when she had come unto him she threw her arms about his neck; and the younger brother was nigh unto her, and saw all that she did.

"The woman next handed the sweet food which she had prepared to the dead man, and because the teeth of the corse did not open, she separated them with a pair of brazen pincers, and pushed the food into his mouth. Suddenly the pincers bounced back from the teeth of the dead man, and snapped off the tip of the woman's nose; while, at the same time, the teeth of the dead man closed together and bit off the end of the woman's tongue. Upon this the woman took up the dish with the food and went back to her home.

"The younger brother thereupon followed her home, and concealed himself in the treasure-chamber, and the wife laid herself down again by her husband. Presently the man began to move, when the wife immediately cried out, 'Woe is me! woe is me! was there ever such a man?' And the man said, 'What is the matter now?' The wife replied, 'The point of my tongue, and the tip of my nose, both these thou hast bitten off. What can a woman do without these two things? To-morrow the Chan shall be made acquainted with this conduct.' Thus spake she, and the younger brother fled from the treasure-chamber without stealing anything.

" On the following morning the woman presented herself before the Chan, and addressed him, saying, ' My husband has this night treated me shamefully. Whatsoever punishment may be awarded to him, I myself will see it inflicted.'

" But the husband persisted in asserting, ' Of all this I know nothing!' Because the complaint of the wife.seemed well-founded, and the man could not exculpate himself, the Chan said, ' Because of his evil deeds, let this man be burnt."

" When the younger brother heard what had befallen the elder, he went to see him. And after the younger one had related to him all the affair, he betook himself unto the Chan, saying, ' That the evil-doer may be really discovered, let both the woman and her husband be summoned before you ; I will clear up the mystery.'

" When they were both present, the younger brother related the wife's visit to the dead man, and because the Chan would not give credence unto his story, he said : ' In the mouth of the dead man you will find the end of the woman's tongue ; and the blood-soiled tip of her nose you will find in the pincers of brass. Send thither, and see if it be not so.'

"Thus spake he, and people were sent to the place, and confirmed all that he had asserted. Upon this the Chan said, 'Since the matter stands thus, let the woman be placed upon the pile of fagots and consumed with fire.' And the woman was placed upon the pile of fagots and consumed with fire."

"That served her right!" said the Son of the Chan.

"Ruler of Destiny, thou hast spoken words! Ssarwala missdood jakzang!" Thus spake Ssidi, and burst from the sack through the air.

Thus Ssidi's tenth relation treats of the Man and his Wife.

Of the Maiden Ssuwarandari.

When the Son of the Chan was carrying off Ssidi, as formerly, Ssidi related the following tale :—

"A long while ago, there was in the very centre of a certain kingdom an old pagoda, in which stood the image of Choschim Bodissadoh (a Mongolian idol), formed of clay. Near unto this pagoda stood a small house, in which a beautiful maiden resided with her aged parents. But at the mouth of the river, which ran thereby, dwelt a poor man, who maintained himself by selling fruit, which he carried in an ark upon the river.

"Now it happened once, that as he was returning

home he was benighted in the neighbourhood of the pagoda. He listened at the door of the house in which the two old people dwelt, and heard the old woman say unto her husband, 'We are both grown exceedingly old; could we now but provide for our daughter, it would be well.'

"'That we have lived so long happily together,' said the old man, 'we are indebted to the talisman of our daughter. Let us, however, offer up sacrifice to Bodissadoh, and inquire of him to what condition we shall dedicate our daughter—to the spiritual or to the worldly. To-morrow, at the earliest dawn, we will therefore lay our offering before the Burchan.'

"'Now know I what to do,' said the listener; so in the night-time he betook himself to the pagoda, made an opening in the back of the idol, and concealed himself therein. When on the following morning the two old people and the daughter drew nigh and made their offering, the father bowed himself to the earth and spake as follows :—

"'Deified Bodissadoh! shall this maiden be devoted to a spiritual or worldly life? If she is to be devoted to a worldly life, vouchsafe to point out now or hereafter, in a dream or vision, to whom we shall give her to wife.'

"Then he who was concealed in the image exclaimed, 'It is better that thy daughter be devoted to a worldly life. Therefore, give her to wife to the first man who presents himself at thy door in the morning.'

"The old people were greatly rejoiced when they heard these words; and they bowed themselves again and again down to the earth, and walked around the idol.

"On the following morning the man stepped out of the idol and knocked at the door of the aged couple. The old woman went out, and when she saw that it was a man, she turned back again, and said to her husband, 'The words of the Burchan are fulfilled; the man has arrived.'

"'Give him entrance!' said the old man. The man came in accordingly, and was welcomed with food and drink; and when they had told him all that the idol had said, he took the maiden with the talisman to wife.

"When he was wandering forth and drew nigh unto his dwelling, he thought unto himself, 'I have with cunning obtained the daughter of the two old people. Now I will place the maiden in the ark, and conceal the ark in the sand.'

"So he concealed the ark, and went and said unto the people, 'Though I have ever acted properly, still it has never availed me yet. I will therefore now seek to obtain liberal gifts through my prayers.' Thus spake he, and after repeating the Zoka-prayers (part of the Calmuc ritual), he obtained food and gifts, and said, 'To-morrow I will again wander around, repeat the appointed Zoka-prayers, and seek food again.'

"In the meanwhile it happened that the son of the Chan and two of his companions, with bows and arrows in their hands, who were following a tiger, passed by unnoticed, and arrived at the sand-heap of the maiden Ssuwarandari. 'Let us shoot at that heap!' cried they. Thus spake they, and shot accordingly, and lost their arrows in the sand. As they were looking after the arrows, they found the ark, opened it, and drew out the maiden with the talisman.

"'Who art thou, maiden?' inquired they. 'I am the daughter of Lu.' The Chan's son said, 'Come with me, and be my wife.' And the maiden said, 'I cannot go unless another is placed in the ark instead of me.' So they all said, 'Let us put in the tiger.' And when the tiger was placed in the ark, the Chan's son took away with him the maiden, and the talisman with her.

"In the meanwhile the beggar ended his prayers; and when he had done so, he thought unto himself, 'If I take the talisman, slay the maiden, and sell the talisman, of a surety I shall become rich indeed.' Thus thinking he drew nigh unto the sand-heap, drew forth the ark, carried it home with him, and said unto his wife, who he thought was within the ark, 'I shall pass this night in repeating the Zoka-prayers.' He threw off his upper garment. And when he had done so, he lifted off the cover of the ark, and said, 'Maiden, be not alarmed?' When he was thus speaking, he beheld the tiger.

"When some persons went into the chamber on the following morning, they found a tiger with his tusks and claws covered with blood, and the body of the beggar torn into pieces.

"And the wife of the Chan gave birth to three sons, and lived in the enjoyment of plenty of all things. But the ministers and the people murmured, and said, 'It was not well of the Chan that he drew forth his wife out of the earth. Although the wife of the Chan has given birth to the sons of the Chan, still she is but a low-born creature.' Thus spoke they, and the wife of the Chan received little joy therefrom. 'I have borne three sons,' said she, 'and yet am noways regarded; I will therefore return home to my parents.'

"She left the palace on the night of the full moon, and reached the neighbourhood of her parents at noontide. Where there had formerly been nothing to be seen she saw a multitude of workmen busily employed, and among them a man having authority, who prepared meat and drink for them. 'Who art thou, maiden?' inquired this man. 'I come far from hence,' replied the wife of the Chan; 'but my parents formerly resided upon this mountain, and I have come hither to seek them.'

"At these words the young man said, 'Thou art

then their daughter?' and he received for answer, 'I am their daughter.'

"'I am their son,' said he. 'I have been told that I had a sister older than myself. Art thou she? Sit thee down, partake of this meat and this drink, and we will then go together unto our parents.'

"When the wife of the Chan arrived at the summit of the mountain, she found in the place where the old pagoda stood a number of splendid buildings, with golden towers full of bells. And the hut of her parents was changed into a lordly mansion. 'All this,' said her brother, 'belongs to us, since you took your departure. Our parents lived here in health and peace.'

"In the palace there were horses and mules, and costly furniture in abundance. The father and mother were seated on rich pillows of silk, and gave their daughter welcome, saying, 'Thou art still well and happy. That thou hast returned home before we depart from this life is of a surety very good.'

"After various inquiries had been made on both sides, relative to what had transpired during the separation of the parties, the old parents said, 'Let us make these things known unto the Chan and his ministers.'

"So the Chan and his ministers were loaded with presents, and three nights afterwards they were welcomed with meat and drink of the best. But the Chan said, 'Ye have spoken falsely, the wife of the Chan had no parents.'   Now the Chan departed with his retinue, and his wife said, 'I will stop one more night with my parents, and then I will return unto you.'

" On the following morning the wife of the Chan found herself on a hard bed, without pillows or coverlets.   'What is this?' exclaimed she; 'was I not this night with my father and mother—and did I not retire to sleep on a bed of silk ?'

" And when she rose up she beheld the ruined hut of her parents.   Her father and mother were dead, and their bones mouldered; their heads lay upon a stone.   Weeping loudly, she said unto herself, 'I will now look after the pagoda.'   But she saw nothing but the ruins of the pagoda and of the Burchan.   'A godly providence,' exclaimed she, ' has resuscitated my parents.   Now since the Chan and the ministers will be pacified, I will return home again.'

On her arrival in the kingdom of her husband, the ministers and the people came forth to meet her, and walked around her.   'This wife of the Chan,' cried they, ' is descended from noble parents, has borne noble sons, and is herself welcome, pleasant, and charming.'   Thus speaking, they accompanied the wife of the Chan to the palace."

" Her merits must have been great."   Thus spake the Son of the Chan.

"Ruler of Destiny, thou hast spoken words, Ssarwala missdood jakzang !' Thus spake Ssidi, and burst from the sack through the air.

Thus Ssidi's eleventh relation treats of the Maiden Ssuwarandari.

THE TWO CATS.

I$_N$ former days there was an old woman, who lived
in a hut more confined than the minds of the ignorant, and more dark than the tombs of misers. Her
companion was a cat, from the mirror of whose
imagination the appearance of bread had never been
reflected, nor had she from friends or strangers ever
heard its name. It was enough that she now and
then scented a mouse, or observed the print of its
feet on the floor; when, blessed by favouring stars
or benignant fortune, one fell into her claws—

> "She became like a beggar who discovers a treasure of
> gold;
> Her cheeks glowed with rapture, and past grief was
> consumed by present joy."

This feast would last for a week or more; and while
enjoying it she was wont to exclaim—

> " Am I, O God, when I contemplate this, in a dream or
> awake?
> Am I to experience such prosperity after such ad-
> versity? "

But as the dwelling of the old woman was in
general the mansion of famine to this cat, she was

always complaining, and forming extravagant and fanciful schemes. One day, when reduced to extreme weakness, she, with much exertion, reached the top of the hut; when there she observed a cat stalking on the wall of a neighbour's house, which, like a fierce tiger, advanced with measured steps, and was so loaded with flesh that she could hardly raise her feet. The old woman's friend was amazed to see one of her own species so fat and sleek, and broke out into the following exclamation :—

> "Your stately strides have brought you here at last ; pray tell me from whence you come ?
> From whence have you arrived with so lovely an appearance ?
> You look as if from the banquet of the Khan of Khatai.
> Where have you acquired such a comeliness? and how came you by that glorious strength ?"

The other answered, "I am the Sultan's crumb-eater. Each morning, when they spread the convivial table, I attend at the palace, and there exhibit my address and courage. From among the rich meats and wheat-cakes I cull a few choice morsels; I then retire and pass my time till next day in delightful indolence."

The old dame's cat requested to know what rich meat was, and what taste wheat-cakes had? "As for me," she added, in a melancholy tone, "during my life I have neither eaten nor seen anything but the old woman's gruel and the flesh of mice." The other, smiling, said, " This accounts for the difficulty

I find in distinguishing you from a spider. Your shape and stature is such as must make the whole generation of cats blush; and we must ever feel ashamed while you carry so miserable an appearance abroad.

> You certainly have the ears and tail of a cat,
> But in other respects you are a complete spider.

Were you to see the Sultan's palace, and to smell his delicious viands, most undoubtedly those withered bones would be restored; you would receive new life; you would come from behind the curtain of invisibility into the plane of observation—

> When the perfume of his beloved passes over the tomb of
> a lover,
> Is it wonderful that his putrid bones should be re-animated?"

The old woman's cat addressed the other in the most supplicating manner: "O my sister!" she exclaimed, "have I not the sacred claims of a neighbour upon you? are we not linked in the ties of kindred? What prevents your giving a proof of friendship, by taking me with you when next you visit the palace? Perhaps from your favour plenty may flow to me, and from your patronage I may attain dignity and honour.

> Withdraw not from the friendship of the honourable;
> Abandon not the support of the elect."

The heart of the Sultan's crumb-eater was melted

by this pathetic address; she promised her new
friend should accompany her on the next visit to
the palace.   The latter, overjoyed, went down immediately from the terrace, and communicated every
particular to the old woman, who addressed her
with the following counsel :—

"Be not deceived, my dearest friend, with the
worldly language you have listened to; abandon
not your corner of content, for the cup of the covetous is only to be filled by the dust of the grave,
and the eye of cupidity and hope can only be closed
by the needle of mortality and the thread of fate.

> It is content that makes men rich;
> Mark this, ye avaricious, who traverse the world :
> He neither knows nor pays adoration to his God
> Who is dissatisfied with his condition and fortune."

But the expected feast had taken such possession
of poor puss's imagination, that the medicinal counsel
of the old woman was thrown away.

> "The good advice of all the world is like wind in a cage,
>   Or water in a sieve, when bestowed on the headstrong."

To conclude: next day, accompanied by her companion, the half-starved cat hobbled to the Sultan's
palace.   Before this unfortunate wretch came, as it
is decreed that the covetous shall be disappointed,
an extraordinary event had occurred, and, owing to
her evil destiny, the water of disappointment was
poured on the flame of her immature ambition.
The case was this: a whole legion of cats had the

day before surrounded the feast, and made so much noise that they disturbed the guests; and in consequence the Sultan had ordered that some archers armed with bows from Tartary should, on this day, be concealed, and that whatever cat advanced into the field of valour, covered with the shield of audacity, should, on eating the first morsel, be overtaken with their arrows. The old dame's puss was not aware of this order. The moment the flavour of the viands reached her, she flew like an eagle to the place of her prey.

Scarcely had the weight of a mouthful been placed in the scale to balance her hunger, when a heart-dividing arrow pierced her breast.

A stream of blood rushed from the wound.
She fled, in dread of death, after having exclaimed,
"Should I escape from this terrific archer,
I will be satisfied with my mouse and the miserable
hut of my old mistress.
My soul rejects the honey if accompanied by the sting.
Content, with the most frugal fare, is preferable "

LEGEND OF DHURRUMNATH.

DURING the reign of a mighty rajah named Guddeh Sing, a celebrated, and as it is now supposed, deified priest, or hutteet, called Dhurrumnath, came, and in all the characteristic humility of his sect established a primitive and temporary resting-place within a few miles of the rajah's residence at Runn, near Mandavie. He was accompanied by his adopted son, Ghurreeb Nath.

From this spot Dhurrumnath despatched his son to seek for charitable contributions from the inhabitants of the town. To this end Ghurreeb Nath made several visits; but being unsuccessful, and at the same time unwilling that his father should know of the want of liberality in the city, he at each visit purchased food out of some limited funds of his own. At length, his little hoard failing, on the sixth day he was obliged to confess the deceit he had practised.

Dhurrumnath, on being acquainted with this, became extremely vexed, and vowed that from that day all the rajah's putteen cities should become desolate and ruined. The tradition goes on to state that in due time these cities were destroyed; Dhurrumnath, accompanied by his son, left the neighbourhood, and proceeded to Denodur. Finding it a desirable place, he determined on performing Tupseeah, or penance, for twelve years, and chose the form of standing on his head.

On commencing to carry out this determination, he dismissed his son, who established his Doonee in the jungles, about twenty miles to the north-west of Bhooj. After Dhurrumnath had remained Tupseeah for twelve years, he was visited by all the angels from heaven, who besought him to rise; to which he replied, that if he did so, the portion of the country on which his sight would first rest would become barren: if villages, they would disappear; if woods or fields, they would equally be destroyed. The angels then told him to turn his head to the north-east, where flowed the sea. Upon this he resumed his natural position, and, turning his head in the direction he was told, opened his eyes, when immediately the sea disappeared, the stately ships became wrecks, and their crews were destroyed, leaving nothing behind but a barren, unbroken desert, known as the Runn.

Dhurrumnath, too pure to remain on the earth, partook of an immediate and glorious immortality, being at once absorbed into the spiritual nature of the creating, the finishing, the indivisible, all-pervading Brum.

This self-imposed penance of Dhurrumnath has shed a halo of sanctity around the hill of Denodur, and was doubtless the occasion of its having been selected as a fitting site for a Jogie establishment, the members of which, it is probable, were originally the attendants on a small temple that had been erected, and which still remains, on the highest point of the hill, on the spot where the holy Dhurrumnath is said to have performed his painful Tupseeah.

THE TRAVELLER'S ADVENTURE.

IT is related that a man, mounted upon a camel, in the course of travelling arrived at a place where others from the same caravan had lighted a fire before proceeding on their journey. The fan-like wind, breathing on the embers, had produced a flame; and the sparks, flying over the jungle, the dry wood had become ignited, and the whole plain glowed like a bed of tulips.

In the midst of this was an enormous snake, which, encircled by the flames, possessed no means of escape, and was about to be broiled like a fish, or kabobed like a partridge for the table. Blood oozed from its poison-charged eyes; and, seeing the man and the camel, it thus supplicated for assistance—

"What if in kindness thou vouchsafe me thy pity;
Loosen the knot with which my affairs are entangled."

Now the traveller was a good man, and one who feared God. When he heard the complaint of the snake, and saw its pitiable condition, he reasoned thus with himself: "This snake is, indeed, the enemy of man, but being in trouble and perplexity, it would be most commendable in me to drop the seed of compassion, the fruit of which is prosperity in this world, and exaltation in the next." Thus convinced, he fastened one of his saddle-bags to the end of his spear, and extended it to the snake, which, delighted at escape, entered the bag, and was rescued from the flames. The man then opening the mouth of the bag, addressed it thus: "Depart whither thou wilt, but forget not to offer up thanksgiving for thy preservation; henceforth seek the corner of retirement, and cease to afflict mankind, for they who do so are dishonest in this world and the next—

> Fear God—distress no one;
> This indeed is true salvation."

The snake replied, "O young man, hold thy peace, for truly I will not depart until I have wounded both thee and this camel."

The man cried out, "But how is this? Have I not rendered thee a benefit? Why, then, is such to be my recompense?

> On my part there was faithfulness,
> Why then this injustice upon thine?"

The snake said, "True, thou hast shown mercy, but it was to an unworthy object; thou knowest me to be an agent of injury to mankind, consequently, when thou savedst me from destruction, thou subjectedst thyself to the same rule that applies to the punishment due for an evil act committed against a worthy object.

"Again, between the snake and man there is a long-standing enmity, and they who employ foresight hold it as a maxim of wisdom to bruise the head of an enemy; to thy security my destruction was necessary, but, in showing mercy, thou hast forfeited vigilance. It is now necessary that I should wound thee, that others may learn by thy example."

The man cried, "O snake, call but in the counsel of justice; in what creed is it written, or what practice declares, that evil should be returned for good, or that the pleasure of conferring benefits should be returned by injury and affliction?"

The snake replied, "Such is the practice amongst men. I act according to thy own decree; the same commodity of retribution I have purchased from thee I also sell.

Buy for one moment that which thou sell'st for years."

In vain did the traveller entreat, the snake ever replying, "I do but treat thee after the manner of men." This the man denied. "But," said he, "let us call witnesses: if thou prove thy assertion, I will yield to thy will." The snake, looking round, saw a cow grazing at a distance, and said, "Come, we will ask this cow the rights of the question." When they came up to the cow, the snake, opening its mouth, said, "O cow, what is the recompense for benefits received?"

The cow said, "If thou ask me after the manner of men, the return of good is always evil. For instance, I was for a long time in the service of a farmer; yearly I brought forth a calf; I supplied his house with milk and ghee; his sustenance, and the life of his children, depended upon me. When I became old, and no longer produced young, he ceased to shelter me, and thrust me forth to die in a jungle. After finding forage, and roaming at my ease, I grew fat, and my old master, seeing my plump condition, yesterday brought with him a butcher, to whom he has sold me, and to-day is appointed for my slaughter."

The snake said, "Thou hast heard the cow; prepare to die quickly." The man cried, "It is not lawful to decide a case on the evidence of one witness, let us then call another." The snake looked about and saw a tree, leafless and bare, flinging up its wild branches to the sky. "Let us," said it, "appeal to this tree." They proceeded together to the tree; and the snake, opening its mouth, said, "O tree, what is the recompense for good?"

The tree said, "Amongst men, for benefits are returned evil and injury. I will give you a proof of what I assert. I am a tree which, though growing on one leg in this sad waste, was once flourishing

and green, performing service to every one. When
any of the human race, overcome with heat and
travel, came this way, they rested beneath my shade,
and slept beneath my branches; when the weight of
repose abandoned their eyelids, they cast up their
eyes to me, and said to each other, ' Yon twig would
do well for an arrow; that branch would serve for
a plough; and from the trunk of this tree what
beautiful planks might be made!' If they had an
axe or a saw, they selected my branches, and carried
them away. Thus they to whom I gave ease and
rest rewarded me only with pain and affliction.

Whilst my care overshadows him in perplexity,
He meditates only how best to root me up."

"Well," said the snake, "here are two witnesses;
therefore, form thy resolution, for I must wound
thee." The man said, "True; but the love of life
is powerful, and while strength remains, it is difficult
to root the love of it from the heart. Call but one
more witness, and then I pledge myself to submit to
his decree." Now it so wonderfully happened that
a fox, who had been standing by, had heard all the
argument, and now came forward. The snake on
seeing it exclaimed, "Behold this fox, let us ask
it." But before the man could speak the fox
cried out, "Dost thou not know that the recompense
for good is always evil? But what good hast thou
done in behalf of this snake, to render thee worthy

of punishment ?"   The man related his story.   The fox replied, "Thou seemest an intelligent person, why then dost thou tell me an untruth ?

How can it be proper for him that is wise to speak falsely?
How can it become an intelligent man to state an untruth ?"

The snake said, "The man speaks truly, for behold the bag in which he rescued me." The fox, putting on the garb of astonishment, said, "How can I believe this thing ?   How could a large snake such as thou be contained in so small a space ?" The snake said, "If thou doubt me, I will again enter the bag to prove it."   The fox said, "Truly if I saw thee there, I could believe it, and afterwards settle the dispute between thee and this man."   On this the traveller opened the bag, and the snake, annoyed at the disbelief of the fox, entered it; which observing, the fox cried out, "O young man, when thou hast caught thine enemy, show him no quarter.

When an enemy is vanquished, and in thy power,
It is the maxim of the wise to show him no mercy."

The traveller took the hint of the fox, fastened the mouth of the bag, and, dashing it against a stone, destroyed the snake, and thus saved mankind from the evil effects of its wicked propensities.

THE SEVEN STAGES OF ROOSTEM.

Persia was at peace, and prosperous; but its king, Ky-Kâoos, could never remain at rest. A favourite singer gave him one day an animated account of the beauties of the neighbouring kingdom of Mazenderan : its ever-blooming roses, its melodious nightingales, its verdant plains, its mountains shaded with lofty trees, and adorned to their summits with flowers which perfumed the air, its clear murmuring rivulets, and, above all, its lovely damsels and valiant warriors.

All these were described to the sovereign in such glowing colours that he quite lost his reason, and declared he should never be happy till his power extended over a country so favoured by Nature. It was in vain that his wisest ministers and most attached nobles dissuaded him from so hazardous an enterprise as that of invading a region which had, besides other defenders, a number of Deevs, or demons, who, acting under their renowned chief, Deev-e-Seffeed, or the White Demon, had hitherto defeated all enemies.

Ky-Kâoos would not listen to his nobles, who in despair sent for old Zâl, the father of Roostem, and prince of Seestan. Zâl came, and used all his efforts, but in vain; the monarch was involved in clouds of pride, and closed a discussion he had with Zâl by exclaiming, " The Creator of the world is my friend; the chief of the Deevs is my prey." This impious boasting satisfied Zâl he could do no good; and he even refused to become regent of Persia in the absence of Ky-Kâoos, but promised to aid with his counsel.

The king departed to anticipated conquest; but the prince of Mazenderan summoned his forces, and, above all, the Deev-e-Seffeed and his band. They came at his call: a great battle ensued, in which the Persians were completely defeated. Ky-Kâoos was made prisoner, and confined in a strong fortress under the guard of a hundred Deevs, commanded by Arjeng, who was instructed to ask the Persian monarch every morning how he liked the roses, nightingales, flowers, trees, verdant meadows, shady mountains, clear streams, beautiful damsels, and valiant warriors of Mazenderan.

The news of this disaster soon spread over Persia, and notwithstanding the disgust of old Zâl at the headstrong folly of his monarch, he was deeply afflicted at the tale of his misfortune and disgrace. He sent for Roostem, to whom he said, " Go, my son, and with thy single arm, and thy good horse,

Reksh, release our sovereign." Roostem instantly obeyed. There were two roads, but he chose the nearest, though it was reported to be by far the most difficult and dangerous.

Fatigued with his first day's journey, Roostem lay down to sleep, having turned Reksh loose to graze in a neighbouring meadow, where he was attacked by a furious lion; but this wonderful horse, after a short contest, struck his antagonist to the ground with a blow from his fore-hoof, and completed the victory by seizing the throat of the royal animal with his teeth. When Roostem awoke, he was surprised and enraged. He desired Reksh never again to attempt, unaided, such an encounter. "Hadst thou been slain," asked he of the intelligent brute, "how should I have accomplished my enterprise?"

At the second stage Roostem had nearly died of thirst, but his prayers to the Almighty were heard. A fawn appeared, as if to be his guide; and following it, he was conducted to a clear fountain, where, after regaling on the flesh of a wild ass, which he had killed with his bow, he lay down to sleep. In the middle of the night a monstrous serpent, seventy yards in length, came out of its hiding-place, and made at the hero, who was awaked by the neighing of Reksh; but the serpent had crept back to its hiding-place, and Roostem, seeing no danger, abused his faithful horse for disturbing his repose. Another attempt of the serpent was defeated in the same way; but as the monster had again concealed itself, Roostem lost all patience with Reksh, whom he threatened to put to death if he again awaked him by any such unseasonable noises. The faithful steed, fearing his master's rage, but strong in his attachment, instead of neighing when the serpent again made his appearance, sprang upon it, and commenced a furious contest. Roostem, hearing the noise, started up and joined in the combat. The serpent darted at him, but he avoided it, and, while his noble horse seized their enemy by the back, the hero cut off its head with his sword.

When the serpent was slain, Roostem contemplated its enormous size with amazement, and, with that piety which always distinguished him, returned thanks to the Almighty for his miraculous escape.

Next day, as Roostem sat by a fountain, he saw a beautiful damsel regaling herself with wine. He approached her, accepted her invitation to partake of the beverage, and clasped her in his arms as if she had been an angel. It happened, in the course of their conversation, that the Persian hero mentioned the name of the great God he adored. At the sound of that sacred word the fair features and shape of the female changed, and she became black, ugly, and deformed. The astonished Roostem seized her, and after binding her hands, bid her declare who she was. "I am a sorceress," was the reply, "and have been employed by the evil spirit Aharman for thy destruction; but save my life, and I am powerful to do thee service." "I make no compact with the devil or his agents," said the hero, and cut her in twain. He again poured forth his soul in thanksgiving to God for his deliverance.

On his fourth stage Roostem lost his way. While wandering about he came to a clear rivulet, on the banks of which he lay down to take some repose, having first turned Reksh loose into a field of grain. A gardener who had charge of it came and awoke the hero, telling him in an insolent tone that he would soon suffer for his temerity, as the field in which his horse was feeding belonged to a pehloovân, or warrior, called Oulâd. Roostem, always irascible, but particularly so when disturbed in his slumbers, jumped up, tore off the gardener's ears, and gave him a blow with his fist that broke his nose and teeth. "Take these marks of my temper to your master," he said, "and tell him to come here, and he shall have a similar welcome."

Oulâd, when informed of what had passed, was excited to fury, and prepared to assail the Persian hero, who, expecting him, had put on his armour and mounted Reksh. His appearance so dismayed Oulâd that he dared not venture on the combat till he had summoned his adherents. They all fell upon Roostem at once; but the base-born caitiffs were scattered like chaff before the wind; many were slain, others fled, among whom was their chief. Him Roostem came up with at the fifth stage, and having thrown his noose over him, took him prisoner. Oulâd, in order to save his life, not only gave him full information of the place where his sovereign was confined, and of the strength of the Deev-e-Seffeed, but offered to give the hero every aid in the accomplishment of his perilous enterprise. This offer was accepted, and he proved a most useful auxiliary.

On the sixth day they saw in the distance the city of Mazenderan, near which the Deev-e-Seffeed resided. Two chieftains, with numerous attendants, met them; and one had the audacity to ride up to Roostem, and seize him by the belt. That chief's fury at this insolence was unbounded; he disdained, however, to use his arms against such an enemy, but, seizing the miscreant's head, wrenched it from the body, and hurled it at his companions, who fled in terror and dismay at this terrible proof of the hero's prowess.

Roostem proceeded, after this action, with his guide to the castle where the king was confined. The Deevs who guarded it were asleep, and Ky-Kâoos was found in a solitary cell, chained to the ground. He recognised Roostem, and bursting into tears, pressed his deliverer to his bosom. Roostem immediately began to knock off his chains. The noise occasioned by this awoke the Deevs, whose leader, Beedâr-Reng, advanced to seize Roostem ; but the appearance and threats of the latter so overawed him that he consented to purchase his own safety by the instant release of the Persian king and all his followers.

After this achievement Roostem proceeded to the last and greatest of his labours, the attack of the Deev-e-Seffeed. Oulâd told him that the Deevs watched and feasted during the night, but slept during the heat of the day, hating (according to our narrator) the sunbeams. Roostem, as he advanced, saw an immense army drawn out; he thought it better, before he attacked them, to refresh himself by some repose. Having laid himself down, he soon fell into a sound sleep, and at daylight he awoke quite refreshed. As soon as the sun became warm, he rushed into the camp. The heavy blows of his mace soon awoke the surprised and slumbering guards of the Deev-e-Seffeed; they collected in myriads, hoping to impede his progress, but all in vain. The rout became general, and none escaped but those who fled from the field of battle.

When this army was dispersed, Roostem went in search of the Deev-e-Seffeed, who, ignorant of the fate of his followers, slumbered in the recess of a cavern, the entrance to which looked so dark and gloomy that the Persian hero hesitated whether he should advance; but the noise of his approach had roused his enemy, who came forth, clothed in complete armour. His appearance was terrible; but Roostem, recommending his soul to God, struck a desperate blow, which separated the leg of the Deev from his body. This would on common occasions have terminated the contest, but far different was the result on the present. Irritated to madness by the loss of a limb, the monster seized his enemy in his arms, and endeavoured to throw him down. The struggle was for some time doubtful; but Roostem, collecting all his strength, by a wondrous effort dashed his foe to the ground, and seizing him by one of the horns, unsheathed his dagger and stabbed him to the heart. The Deev-e-Seffeed instantly expired; and Roostem, on looking round to the entrance of the cavern, from whence the moment before he had seen numberless Deevs issuing to the aid of their lord, perceived they were all dead. Oulâd, who stood at a prudent distance from the scene of combat, now advanced and informed the hero that the lives of all the Deevs depended upon that of their chief. When he was slain, the spell which created and preserved this band was broken, and they all expired.

Roostem found little difficulty after these seven days of toil, of danger, and of glory, in compelling Mazenderan to submit to Persia. The king of the country was slain, and Oulâd was appointed its governor as a reward for his fidelity.

The success of his arms had raised Ky-Kâoos to the very plenitude of power; not only men, but Deevs, obeyed his mandates. The latter he employed in building palaces of crystal, emeralds, and rubies, till at last they became quite tired of their toil and abject condition. They sought, therefore, to destroy him; and to effect this they consulted with the devil, who, to forward the object, instructed a Deev, called Dizjkheem, to go to Ky-Kâoos and raise in his mind a passion for astronomy, and to promise him a nearer view of the celestial bodies than had ever yet been enjoyed by mortal eyes. The Deev fulfilled his commission with such success that the king became quite wild with a desire to attain perfection in this sublime science. The devil then instructed Dizjkheem to train some young vultures to carry a throne upwards; this was done by placing spears round the throne, on the points of which pieces of flesh were fixed in view of the vultures, who were fastened at the bottom. These voracious birds, in their efforts to reach the meat, raised the throne.

Though he mounted rapidly for a short time, the vultures became exhausted, and finding their efforts to reach the meat hopeless, discontinued them; this altered the direction and equilibrium of the machine, and it tossed to and fro. Ky-Kâoos would have been cast headlong and killed had he not clung to it. The vultures, not being able to disengage themselves, flew an immense way, and at last landed the affrighted monarch in one of the woods of China. Armies marched in every direction to discover and release the sovereign, who, it was believed, had again fallen into the hands of Deevs. He was at last found and restored to his capital. Roostem, we are told, upbraided his folly, saying—

" Have you managed your affairs so well on earth
That you must needs try your hand in those of heaven ?"

THE MAN WHO NEVER LAUGHED.

THERE was a man, of those possessed of houses and riches, who had wealth and servants and slaves and other possessions ; and he departed from the world to receive the mercy of God (whose name be exalted !), leaving a young son. And when the son grew up, he took to eating and drinking, and the hearing of instruments of music and songs, and was liberal and gave gifts, and expended the riches that his father had left to him until all the wealth had gone. He then betook himself to the sale of the male black slaves, and the female slaves, and other possessions, and expended all that he had of his father's wealth and other things, and became so poor that he worked with the labourers. In this state he remained for a period of years. While he was sitting one day beneath a wall, waiting to see who would hire him, lo ! a man of comely countenance and apparel drew near to him and saluted him. So the youth said to him, "O uncle, hast thou known me before now ?" The man answered him, "I have not known thee, O my son, at all ;

but I see the traces of affluence upon thee, though thou art in this condition." The young man replied, "O uncle, what fate and destiny have ordained hath come to pass. But hast thou, O uncle, O comely-faced, any business in which to employ me?" The man said to him, "O my son, I desire to employ thee in an easy business." The youth asked, "And what is it, O uncle?" And the man answered him, "I have with me ten sheykhs in one abode, and we have no one to perform our wants. Thou shalt receive from us, of food and clothing, what will suffice thee, and shalt serve us, and thou shalt receive of us thy portion of benefits and money. Perhaps, also, God will restore to thee thine affluence by our means." The youth therefore replied, "I hear and obey." The sheykh then said to him, "I have a condition to impose upon thee." "And what is thy condition, O uncle?" asked the youth. He answered him, "O my son, it is that thou keep our secret with respect to the things that thou shalt see us do; and when thou seest us weep, that thou ask us not respecting the cause of our weeping." And the young man replied, "Well, O uncle."

So the sheykh said to him, "O my son, come with us, relying on the blessing of God (whose name be exalted!)." And the young man followed the sheykh until the latter conducted him to the bath; after which he sent a man, who brought him a comely garment of linen, and he clad him with it, and went with him to his abode and his associates. And when the young man entered, he found it to be a high mansion, with lofty angles, ample, with chambers facing one another, and saloons; and in each saloon was a fountain of water, and birds were warbling over it, and there were windows overlooking, on every side, a beautiful garden within the mansion. The sheykh conducted him into one of the chambers, and he found it decorated with coloured marbles, and its ceiling ornamented with blue and brilliant gold, and it was spread with carpets of silk; and he found in it ten sheykhs sitting facing one another, wearing the garments of mourning, weeping, and wailing. So the young man wondered at their case, and was about to question the sheykh who had brought him, but he remembered the condition, and therefore withheld his tongue. Then the sheykh committed to the young man a chest containing thirty thousand pieces of gold, saying to him, "O my son, expend upon us out of this chest, and upon thyself, according to what is just, and be thou faithful, and take care of that wherewith I have intrusted thee." And the young man replied, "I hear and obey." He continued to expend upon them for a period of days and nights, after which one of them died; whereupon his companions took him, and washed him and shrouded him, and buried him in a garden behind the mansion. And death ceased not to take of them one after another, until there remained only the sheykh who had hired the young man. So he remained with the young man in that mansion, and there was not with them a third; and they remained thus for a period of years. Then the sheykh fell sick; and when the young man despaired of his life, he addressed him with courtesy, and was grieved for him, and said to him, "O uncle, I have served you, and not failed in your service one hour for a period of twelve years, but have acted faithfully to you, and served you according to my power and ability." The sheykh replied, "Yes, O my son, thou hast served us until these sheykhs have been taken unto God (to whom be ascribed might and glory!), and we must inevitably die." And the young man said, "O my master, thou art in a state of peril, and I desire of thee that thou inform me what hath been the cause of your weeping, and the continuance of your wailing and your mourning and your sorrow." He replied, "O my son, thou hast no concern with that, and require me not to do what I am unable; for I have begged God (whose name be exalted!) not to afflict any one with my affliction. Now if thou desire to be safe from that into which we have fallen, open not that door," and he pointed to it with his hand, and cautioned him against it; "and if thou desire that what hath befallen us should befall thee, open it, and thou wilt know the cause of that which thou hast beheld in our conduct; but thou wilt repent, when repentance will not avail thee." Then the illness increased upon the sheykh, and he died; and the young man washed him with his own hands, and shrouded him, and buried him by his companions.

He remained in that place, possessing it and all the treasure; but notwithstanding this, he was uneasy, reflecting upon the conduct of the sheykhs. And while he was meditating one day upon the words of the sheykh, and his charge to him not to open the door, it occurred to his mind that he might look at it. So he went in that direction, and searched until he saw an elegant door, over which the spider had woven its webs, and upon it were four locks of steel. When he beheld it, he remembered how the sheykh had cautioned him, and he departed from it. His soul desired him to open the door, and he restrained it during a period of seven days; but on the eighth day his soul overcame him, and he said, "I must open that door, and see what will happen to me in consequence; for nothing will repel what God (whose name be exalted!) decreeth and predestineth, and no event will happen but by His will." Accordingly he arose and opened the door, after he had broken the locks. And when he had opened the door he saw a narrow passage, along which he walked for the space of three hours; and lo! he came forth upon the bank of a great river. At this the young man wondered. And he walked along the bank, looking to the right and left; and behold! a great eagle descended from the sky, and taking up the young man with its talons, it flew with him, between heaven and earth, until it conveyed him to an island in the midst of the sea. There it threw him down, and departed from him.

So the young man was perplexed at his case, not knowing whither to go; but while he was sitting one day, lo! the sail of a vessel appeared to him upon the sea, like the star in the sky; wherefore the heart of the young man became intent upon the vessel, in the hope that his escape might be effected in it. He continued looking at it until it came near unto him; and when it arrived, he beheld a bark of ivory and ebony, the oars of which were of sandal-wood and aloes-wood, and the whole of it was encased with plates of brilliant gold. There were also in it ten damsels, virgins, like moons. When the damsels saw him, they landed to him from the bark, and kissed his hands, saying to him, "Thou art the king, the bridegroom." Then there advanced to him a damsel who was like the shining sun in the clear sky, having in her hand a kerchief of silk, in which were a royal robe, and a crown of gold set with varieties of jacinths. Having advanced to him, she clad him and crowned him; after which the damsels carried him in their arms to the bark, and he found in it varieties of carpets of silk of divers colours. They then spread the sails, and proceeded over the depths of the sea.

"Now when I proceeded with them," says the young man, "I felt sure that this was a dream, and knew not whither they were going with me. And when they came in sight of the land, I beheld it filled with troops, the number of which none knew but God (whose perfection be extolled, and whose name be exalted!) clad in coats of mail. They brought forward to me five marked horses, with saddles of gold, set with varieties of pearls and precious stones; and I took a horse from among these and mounted it. The four others proceeded with me; and when I mounted, the ensigns and banners were set up over my head, the drums and the cymbals were beaten, and the troops disposed themselves in two divisions, right and left. I wavered in opinion as to whether I were asleep or awake, and ceased not to advance, not believing in the reality of my stately procession, but imagining that it was the result of confused dreams, until we came in sight of a verdant meadow, in which were palaces and gardens, and trees and rivers and flowers, and birds proclaiming the perfection of God, the One, the Omnipotent. And now there came forth an army from among those palaces and gardens, like the torrent when it poureth down, until it filled the meadow. When the troops drew near to me, they hailed, and lo! a king advanced from among them, riding alone, preceded by some of his chief officers walking."

The king, on approaching the young man, alighted from his courser; and the young man, seeing him do so, alighted also; and they saluted each other with the most courteous salutation. Then they mounted their horses again, and the king said to the young man, "Accompany us; for thou art my guest." So the young man proceeded with him, and they conversed together, while the stately trains in orderly disposition went on before them to the palace of the king, where they alighted, and all of them entered, together with the king and the young man, the young man's hand being in the hand of the king, who thereupon seated him on the throne of gold and seated himself beside him. When the king removed the litham from his face, lo! this supposed king was a damsel, like the shining sun in the clear sky, a lady of beauty and loveliness, and elegance and perfection, and conceit and amorous dissimulation. The young man beheld vast affluence and great prosperity, and wondered at the beauty and loveliness of the damsel. Then the damsel said to him, "Know, O king, that I am the queen of this land, and all these troops that thou hast seen, including every one, whether of cavalry or infantry, are women. There are not among them any men. The men among us, in this land, till and sow and reap, employing themselves in the cultivation of the land, and the building and repairing of the towns, and in attending to the affairs of the people, by the pursuit of every kind of art and trade; but as to the women, they are the governors and magistrates and soldiers." And the young man wondered at this extremely. And while they were thus conversing, the vizier entered; and lo! she was a grey-haired old woman, having a numerous retinue, of venerable and dignified appearance; and the queen said to her, "Bring to us the Kádee and the witnesses." So the old woman went for that purpose. And the queen turned towards the young man, conversing with him and cheering him, and dispelling his fear by kind words; and, addressing him courteously, she said to him, "Art thou content for me to be thy wife?" And thereupon he arose and kissed the ground before her; but she forbade him; and he replied, "O my mistress, I am less than the servants who serve thee." She then said to him, "Seest thou not these servants and soldiers and wealth and treasures and hoards?" He answered her, "Yes." And she said to him, "All these are at thy disposal; thou shalt make use of them, and give and bestow as seemeth fit to thee." Then she pointed to a closed door, and said to him, "All these things thou shalt dispose of; but this door thou shalt not open; for if thou open it, thou wilt repent, when repentance will not avail thee." Her words were not

ended when the vizier, with the Kádee and the
witnesses, entered, and all of them were old women,
with their hair spreading over their shoulders, and
of venerable and dignified appearance.   When they
came before the queen, she ordered them to perform the ceremony of the marriage-contract.   So
they married her to the young man.   And she prepared the banquets and collected the troops ; and
when they had eaten and drunk, the young man
took her as his wife.   And he resided with her
seven years, passing the most delightful, comfortable,
and agreeable life.

But he meditated one day upon opening the door,
and said, "Were it not that there are within it
great treasures, better than what I have seen, she
had not prohibited me from opening it."   He then
arose and opened the door, and lo! within it was
the bird that had carried him from the shore of the
great river, and deposited him upon the island.
When the bird beheld him, it said to him, "No
welcome to a face that will never be happy!"   So,
when he saw it and heard its words, he fled from it;
but it followed him and carried him off, and flew
with him between heaven and earth for the space of
an hour, and at length deposited him in the place
from which it had carried him away; after which it
disappeared.   He thereupon sat in that place, and,
returning to his reason, he reflected upon what he
had seen of affluence and glory and honour, and the

riding of the troops before him, and commanding and forbidding; and he wept and wailed. He remained upon the shore of the great river, where that bird had put him, for the space of two months, wishing that he might return to his wife; but while he was one night awake, mourning and meditating, some one spoke (and he heard his voice, but saw not his person), calling out, "How great were the delights! Far, far from thee is the return of what is passed! And how many therefore will be the sighs!" So when the young man heard it, he despaired of meeting again that queen, and of the return to him of the affluence in which he had been living. He then entered the mansion where the sheykhs had resided, and knew that they had experienced the like of that which had happened unto him, and that this was the cause of their weeping and their mourning; wherefore he excused them. Grief and anxiety came upon the young man, and he entered his chamber, and ceased not to weep and moan, relinquishing food and drink and pleasant scents and laughter, until he died; and he was buried by the side of the sheykhs.

THE FOX AND THE WOLF.

A FOX and a wolf inhabited the same den, resorting thither together, and thus they remained a long time. But the wolf oppressed the fox; and it so happened that the fox counselled the wolf to assume benignity, and to abandon wickedness, saying to him, " If thou persevere in thine arrogance, probably God will give power over thee to a son of Adam; for he is possessed of stratagems, and artifice, and guile; he captureth the birds from the sky, and the fish from the sea, and cutteth the mountains and transporteth them; and all this he accomplisheth through his stratagems. Betake thyself, therefore, to the practice of equity, and relinquish evil and oppression; for it will be more pleasant to thy taste." The wolf, however, received not his advice; on the contrary, he returned him a rough reply, saying to him, " Thou hast no right to speak on matters of magnitude and importance." He then gave the fox such a blow that he fell down senseless; and when he recovered, he smiled in the wolf's face, apologising for his shameful words, and recited these two verses :—

"If I have been faulty in my affection for you, and committed a deed of a shameful nature,
I repent of my offence, and your clemency will extend to the evildoer who craveth forgiveness."

So the wolf accepted his apology, and ceased from ill-treating him, but said to him, "Speak not of that which concerneth thee not, lest thou hear that which will not please thee." The fox replied, "I hear and obey. I will abstain from that which pleaseth thee not; for the sage hath said, 'Offer not information on a subject respecting which thou art not questioned; and reply not to words when thou art not invited; leave what concerneth thee not, to attend to that which *doth* concern thee; and lavish not advice upon the evil, for they will recompense thee for it with evil.'"

When the wolf heard these words of the fox, he smiled in his face; but he meditated upon employing some artifice against him, and said, "I must strive to effect the destruction of this fox." As to the fox, however, he bore patiently the injurious conduct of the wolf, saying within himself, "Verily, insolence and calumny occasion destruction, and betray one into perplexity; for it hath been said, 'He who is insolent suffereth injury, and he who is ignorant repenteth, and he who feareth is safe: moderation is one of the qualities of the noble, and good manners are the noblest gain.' It is advisable to behave with dissimulation towards this tyrant, and he will inevitably be overthrown." He then said to the wolf, "Verily the Lord pardoneth and becometh propitious unto His servant when he hath sinned; and I am a weak slave, and have committed a transgression in offering thee advice. Had I foreknown the pain that I have suffered from thy blow, I had known that the elephant could not withstand nor endure it; but I will not complain of the pain of that blow, on account of the happiness that hath resulted unto me from it; for, if it had a severe effect upon me, its result was happiness; and the sage hath said, 'The beating inflicted by the preceptor is at first extremely grievous; but in the end it is sweeter than clarified honey!'" So the wolf said, "I forgive thine offence, and cancel thy fault; but beware of my power, and confess thyself my slave; for thou hast experienced my severity unto him who showeth me hostility." The fox, therefore, prostrated himself before him, saying to him, "May God prolong thy life, and mayest thou not cease to subdue him who opposeth thee!" And he continued to fear the wolf, and to dissemble towards him.

After this the fox went one day to a vineyard, and saw in its wall a breach; but he suspected it, saying unto himself, "There must be some cause for this breach, and it hath been said, 'Whoso seeth a hole in the ground, and doth not shun it, and be

cautious of advancing to it boldly, exposeth himself
to danger and destruction.' It is well known that
some men make a figure of the fox in the vineyard,
and even put before it grapes in plates, in order
that a fox may see it, and advance to it, and fall
into destruction. Verily I regard this breach as a
snare; and it hath been said, 'Caution is the half
of cleverness.' Caution requireth me to examine this
breach, and to see if I can find there anything that
may lead to perdition. Covetousness doth not
induce me to throw myself into destruction." He
then approached it, and, going round about examining it warily, beheld it; and lo! there was a
deep pit, which the owner of the vineyard had dug
to catch in it the wild beasts that despoiled the
vines; and he observed over it a slight covering.
So he drew back from it, and said, "Praise be to
God that I regarded it with caution! I hope that
my enemy, the wolf, who hath made my life miserable, may fall into it, so that I alone may enjoy
absolute power over the vineyard, and live in it
securely." Then, shaking his head, and uttering a
loud laugh, he merrily sang these verses—

"Would that I beheld at the present moment in this
    well a wolf,
    Who hath long afflicted my heart, and made me drink
    bitterness perforce!
    Would that my life might be spared, and that the wolf
    might meet his death!
    Then the vineyard would be free from his presence,
    and I should find in it my spoil."

Having finished his song, he hurried away until he came to the wolf, when he said to him, " Verily God hath smoothed for thee the way to the vineyard without fatigue. This hath happened through thy good fortune. Mayest thou enjoy, therefore, that to which God hath granted thee access, in smoothing thy way to that plunder and that abundant sustenance without any difficulty ! " So the wolf said to the fox, " What is the proof of that which thou hast declared ? " The fox answered, " I went to the vineyard, and found that its owner had died ; and I entered the garden, and beheld the fruits shining upon the trees."

So the wolf doubted not the words of the fox, and in his eagerness he arose and went to the breach. His cupidity had deceived him with vain hopes, and the fox stopped and fell down behind him as one dead, applying this verse as a proverb suited to the case—

"Dost thou covet an interview with Leyla ? It is covetousness that causeth the loss of men's heads."

When the wolf came to the breach, the fox said to him, " Enter the vineyard ; for thou art spared the trouble of breaking down the wall of the garden, and it remaineth for God to complete the benefit." So the wolf walked forward, desiring to enter the vineyard, and when he came to the middle of the covering of the hole, he fell into it ; whereupon the fox was violently excited by happiness and joy, his anxiety and grief ceased, and in merry tones he sang these verses—

"Fortune hath compassionated my case, and felt pity for
    the length of my torment,
  And granted me what I desired, and removed that which
    I dreaded.
  I will, therefore, forgive its offences committed in former
    times ;
  Even the injustice it hath shown in the turning of my
    hair grey.
  There is no escape for the wolf from utter annihilation ;
  And the vineyard is for me alone, and I have no stupid
    partner."

He then looked into the pit, and beheld the wolf weeping in his repentance and sorrow for himself, and the fox wept with him. So the wolf raised his head towards him, and said, " Is it from thy compassion for me that thou hast wept, O Abu-l-Hoseyn ?" " No," answered the fox, " by him who cast thee into this pit; but I weep for the length of thy past life, and in my regret at thy not having fallen into this pit before the present day. Hadst thou fallen into it before I met with thee, I had experienced refreshment and ease. But thou hast been spared to the expiration of thy decreed term and known period." The wolf, however, said to him, " Go, O evildoer, to my mother, and acquaint her with that which hath happened to me ; perhaps she will contrive some means for my deliverance." But the fox replied, " The excess of thy covetousness and eager desire has entrapped thee into destruction, since thou hast fallen into a pit from which thou wilt never be saved. Knowest thou not, O ignorant wolf, that the author of the proverb saith, 'He who thinks not of results will not be secure from perils?'"   "O Abu-l-Hoseyn!" rejoined the wolf, "thou wast wont to manifest an affection for me, and to desire my friendship, and fear the greatness of my power. Be not, then, rancorous towards me for that which I have done unto thee; for he who hath one in his power, and yet forgiveth, will receive a recompense from God, and the poet hath said—

> "'Sow good, even on an unworthy soil; for it will not be
>   fruitless wherever it is sown.
> Verily, good, though it remained long buried, none will
>   reap but him who sowed it.'"

"O most ignorant of the beasts of prey!" said the fox, "and most stupid of the wild beasts of the regions of the earth, hast thou forgotten thy haughtiness, and insolence, and pride, and thy disregarding the rights of companionship, and thy refusing to be advised by the saying of the poet?—

> "'Tyrannise not, if thou hast the power to do so; for the
>   tyrannical is in danger of revenge,
> Thine eye will sleep while the oppressed, wakeful, will
>   call down curses on thee, and God's eye sleepeth not.'"

"O Abu-l-Hoseyn!" exclaimed the wolf, "be not angry with me for my former offences, for forgiveness is required of the generous, and kind conduct is among the best means of enriching one's-self. How excellent is the saying of the poet—

"'Haste to do good when thou art able ; for at every season thou hast not the power.'"

He continued to abase himself to the fox, and said to him, "Perhaps thou canst find some means of delivering me from destruction." But the fox replied, "O artful, guileful, treacherous wolf! hope not for deliverance ; for this is the recompense of thy base conduct, and a just retaliation." Then, shaking his jaws with laughing, he recited these two verses—

"No longer attempt to beguile me ; for thou wilt not attain thy object.
What thou seekest from me is impossible. Thou hast sown, and reap, then, vexation."

"O gentle one among the beasts of prey !" resumed the wolf, "thou art in my estimation more faithful than to leave me in this pit." He then shed tears, and repeated this couplet—

"O thou whose favours to me have been many, and whose gifts have been more than can be numbered !
No misfortune hath ever yet befallen me but I have found thee ready to aid me in it."

The fox replied, "O stupid enemy, how art thou reduced to humility, submissiveness, abjectness, and obsequiousness, after thy disdain, pride, tyranny, and haughtiness ! I kept company with thee through fear of thine oppression, and flattered thee without a hope of conciliating thy kindness; but now terror hath affected thee, and punishment hath overtaken thee." And he recited these two verses—

"O thou who seekest to beguile! thou hast fallen in thy
   base intention.
  Taste, then, the pain of shameful calamity, and be with
   other wolves cut off."

The wolf still entreated him, saying, "O gentle one! speak not with the tongue of enmity, nor look with its eye; but fulfil the covenant of fellowship with me before the time for discovering a remedy shall have passed. Arise and procure for me a rope, and tie one end of it to a tree, and let down to me its other end, that I may lay hold of it. Perhaps I may so escape from my present predicament, and I will give thee all the treasures that I possess." The fox, however, replied, "Thou hast prolonged a conversation that will not procure thy liberation. Hope not, therefore, for thy escape through my means; but reflect upon thy former wicked conduct, and the perfidy and artifice which thou thoughtest to employ against me, and how near thou art to being stoned. Know that thy soul is about to quit the world, and to perish and depart from it: then wilt thou be reduced to destruction, and an evil abode is it to which thou goest!" "O Abu-l-Hoseyn!" rejoined the wolf, "be ready in returning to friendship, and be not so rancorous.

Know that he who delivereth a soul from destruction hath saved it alive, and he who saveth a soul alive is as if he had saved the lives of all mankind. Follow not a course of evil, for the wise abhor it; and there is no evil more manifest than my being in this pit, drinking the suffocating pains of death, and looking upon destruction, when thou art able to deliver me from the misery into which I have fallen." But the fox exclaimed, " O thou barbarous, hard-hearted wretch! I compare thee, with respect to the fairness of thy professions and the baseness of thine intention, to the falcon with the partridge." "And what," asked the wolf, " is the story of the falcon and the partridge ? "

The fox answered, "I entered a vineyard one day to eat of its grapes, and while I was there, I beheld a falcon pounce upon a partridge; but when he had captured him, the partridge escaped from him and entered his nest, and concealed himself in it; whereupon the falcon followed him, calling out to him, ' O idiot! I saw thee in the desert hungry, and, feeling compassion for thee, I gathered for thee some grain, and took hold of thee that thou mightest eat; but thou fleddest from me, and I see no reason for thy flight unless it be to mortify. Show thyself, then, and take the grain that I have brought thee and eat it, and may it be light and wholesome to thee.' So when the partridge heard these words of the falcon, he believed him and came forth to him; and the falcon stuck his talons into him, and got possession of him. The partridge therefore said to him, 'Is this that of which thou saidst that thou hadst brought for me from the desert, and of which thou saidst to me, "Eat it, and may it be light and wholesome to thee?" Thou hast lied unto me; and may God make that which thou eatest of my flesh to be a mortal poison in thy stomach!' And when he had eaten it, his feathers fell off, and his strength failed, and he forthwith died."

The fox then continued, "Know, O wolf, that he who diggeth a pit for his brother soon falleth into it himself; and thou behavedst with perfidy to me first." "Cease," replied the wolf, "from addressing me with this discourse, and propounding fables, and mention not unto me my former base actions. It is enough for me to be in this miserable state, since I have fallen into a calamity for which the enemy would pity me, much more the true friend. Consider some stratagem by means of which I may save myself, and so assist me. If the doing this occasion thee trouble, thou knowest that the true friend endureth for his own true friend the severest labour, and will suffer destruction in obtaining his deliverance; and it hath been said, 'An affectionate friend is even better than a brother.' If thou procure means for my escape, I will collect for thee such things as shall be a store for thee against the time of want, and then I will teach thee extraordinary stratagems by which thou shalt make the plenteous vineyards accessible, and shalt strip the fruitful trees : so be happy and cheerful." But the fox said, laughing as he spoke, "How excellent is that which the learned have said of him who is excessively ignorant like thee!" "And what have the learned said?" asked the wolf. The fox answered, "The learned have observed that the rude in body and in disposition is far from intelligence, and nigh unto ignorance; for thine assertion, O perfidious idiot! that the true friend undergoeth trouble for the deliverance of his own true friend is just as thou hast said; but acquaint me, with thine ignorance and thy paucity of sense, how I should bear sincere friendship towards thee with thy treachery. Hast thou considered me a true friend unto thee when I am an enemy who rejoiceth in thy misfortune? These words are more severe than the piercing of arrows, if thou understand. And as to thy saying that thou wilt give me such things as will be a store for me against the time of want, and will teach me stratagems by which I shall obtain access to the plenteous vineyards and strip the fruitful trees—how is it, O guileful traitor! that thou knowest not a stratagem by means of which to save thyself from destruction? How far, then, art thou from profiting thyself, and how far am I from receiving thine advice? If thou know of stratagems, employ them to save thyself from this predicament from which I pray God to make thine escape far distant. See, then, O idiot! if thou know any stratagem, and save thyself by its means from slaughter, before thou lavish instruction upon another. But thou art like a man whom a disease attacked, and to whom there came a man suffering from the same disease to cure him, saying to him, 'Shall I cure thee of thy disease?' The first man, therefore, said to the other, 'Why hast thou not begun by curing thyself?' So he left him and went his way. And thou, O wolf, art in the same case. Remain, then, in thy place, and endure that which hath befallen thee."

Now when the wolf heard these words of the fox, he knew that he had no kindly feeling for him; so he wept for himself, and said, " I have been careless of myself; but if God deliver me from this affliction, I will assuredly repent of my overbearing conduct unto him that is weaker than I; and I will certainly wear wool, and ascend the mountains, commemorating the praises of God (whose name be exalted!) and fearing His punishment; and I will separate myself from all the other wild beasts, and verily I will feed the warriors in defence of the religion and the poor." Then he wept and lamented; and thereupon the heart of the fox was moved with tenderness for him. On hearing his humble expressions, and the words which indicated his repenting of arrogance and pride, he was affected with compassion for him, and, leaping with joy, placed himself at the brink of the pit, and sat upon his hind-legs and hung down his tail into the cavity. Upon this the wolf arose, and stretched forth his paw towards the fox's tail, and pulled him down to him; so the fox was with him in the pit. The wolf then said to him, "O fox of little compassion! wherefore didst thou rejoice in my misfortune? Now thou hast become my companion, and in my power. Thou hast fallen into the pit with me, and punishment hath quickly overtaken thee. The sages have said, 'If any one of you reproach his brother for deriving his nourishment from miserable means, he shall experience the same necessity,' and how excellent is the saying of the poet—

> " ' When fortune throweth itself heavily upon some, and encampeth by the side of others,
> Say to those who rejoice over us, "Awake: the rejoicers over us shall suffer as *we* have done." ' "

"I must now," he continued, "hasten thy slaughter, before thou beholdest mine." So the fox said within himself, "I have fallen into the snare with this tyrant, and my present case requireth the employment of artifice and frauds. It hath been said that the woman maketh her ornaments for the day of festivity; and, in a proverb, 'I have not reserved thee, O my tear, but for the time of my difficulty!' and if I employ not some stratagem in the affair of this tyrannical wild beast, I perish inevitably. How good is the saying of the poet—

   "'Support thyself by guile; for thou livest in an age
      whose sons are like the lions of the forest ;
    And brandish around the spear of artifice, that the
      mill of subsistence may revolve ;
    And pluck the fruits ; or if they be beyond thy reach,
      then content thyself with herbage.' "

He then said to the wolf, "Hasten not to kill me, lest thou repent, O courageous wild beast, endowed with might and excessive fortitude! If thou delay, and consider what I am about to tell thee, thou wilt know the desire that I formed; and if thou hasten to kill me, there will be no profit to thee in thy doing so, but we shall die here together." So the wolf said, "O thou wily deceiver! how is it that thou hopest to effect my safety and thine own, that thou askest me to give thee a delay? Acquaint me with the desire that thou formedst." The fox replied, "As to the desire that I formed, it was such as requireth thee to recompense me for it well, since, when I heard thy promises, and thy confession of thy past conduct, and thy regret at not having before repented and done good; and when I heard thy vows to abstain from injurious conduct to thy companions and others, and to relinquish the eating of the grapes and all other fruits, and to impose upon thyself the obligation of humility, and to clip thy claws and break thy dog-teeth, and to wear wool and offer sacrifice to God (whose name be exalted!) if He delivered thee from thy present state, I was affected with compassion for thee, though I was before longing for thy destruction. So when I heard thy profession of repentance, and what thou vowedst to do if God delivered thee, I felt constrained to save thee from thy present predicament. I therefore hung down my tail that thou mightest catch hold of it and make thine escape. But thou wouldst not relinquish thy habit of severity and violence, nor desire escape and safety for thyself by gentleness. On the contrary, thou didst pull me in such a way that I thought my soul had departed, so I became a companion with thee of the abode of destruction and death; and nothing will effect the escape of myself and thee but one plan. If thou approve of this plan that I have to propose, we shall both save ourselves; and after that, it will be incumbent on thee to fulfil that which thou hast vowed to do, and I will be thy companion." So the wolf said, "And what is thy proposal that I am to accept?" The fox answered, "That thou raise thyself upright; then I will place myself upon thy head, that I may approach the surface of the earth, and when I am upon its surface I will go forth and bring thee something of which to take hold, and after that thou wilt deliver thyself." But the wolf replied, "I put no confidence in thy words; for the sages have said, 'He who confideth when he should hate is in error'; and it hath been said, 'He who confideth in the faithless is deceived, and he who maketh trial of the trier will repent.' How excellent also is the saying of the poet—

"'Let not your opinion be otherwise than evil; for ill opinion is among the strongest of intellectual qualities.
Nothing casteth a man into a place of danger like the practice of good, and a fair opinion!'

"And the saying of another—

"'Always hold an evil opinion, and so be safe.
Whoso liveth vigilantly, his calamities will be few.
Meet the enemy with a smiling and an open face; but raise for him an army in the heart to combat him.'

"And that of another—

"'The most bitter of thine enemies is the nearest whom thou trustest in: beware then of men, and associate with them wilily.
Thy favourable opinion of fortune is a weakness: think evil of it, therefore, and regard it with apprehension!'"

"Verily," rejoined the fox, "an evil opinion is not commendable in every case; but a fair opinion is among the characteristics of excellence, and its result is escape from terrors. It is befitting, O wolf, that thou employ some stratagem for thine escape from the present predicament; and it will be better for us both to escape than to die. Relinquish, therefore, thine evil opinion and thy malevolence; for if thou think favourably of me, I shall not fail to do one of two things; either I shall bring thee something of which to lay hold, and thou wilt escape from thy present situation, or I shall act perfidiously towards thee, and save myself and leave thee; but this is a thing that cannot be, for I am not secured from meeting with some such affliction as that which thou hast met with, and that would be the punishment of perfidy. It hath been said in a proverb, 'Fidelity is good, and perfidy is base.' It is fit, then, that thou trust in me, for I have not been ignorant of misfortunes. Delay not, therefore, to contrive our escape, for the affair is too strait for thee to prolong thy discourse upon it."

The wolf then said, "Verily, notwithstanding my little confidence in thy fidelity, I knew what was in thy heart, that thou desiredst my deliverance when thou wast convinced of my repentance; and I said within myself, 'If he be veracious in that which he asserteth, he hath made amends for his wickedness; and if he be false, he will be recompensed by his Lord.' So now I accept thy proposal to me, and if thou act perfidiously towards me, thy perfidy will be the means of thy destruction." Then the wolf raised himself upright in the pit, and took the fox upon his shoulders, so that his head reached the surface of the ground. The fox thereupon sprang from the wolf's shoulders, and found himself upon the face of the earth, when he fell down senseless. The wolf now said to him, "O my friend! forget not my case, nor delay my deliverance."

The fox, however, uttered a loud laugh, and replied, "O thou deceived! it was nothing but my jesting with thee and deriding thee that entrapped me into thy power; for when I heard thy profession of repentance, joy excited me, and I was moved with delight, and danced, and my tail hung down into the pit; so thou didst pull me, and I fell by thee.   Then God (whose name be exalted!) delivered me from thy hand.   Wherefore, then, should I not aid in thy destruction when thou art of the associates of the devil?   Know that I dreamt yesterday that I was dancing at thy wedding, and I related the dream to an interpreter, who said to me, 'Thou wilt fall into a frightful danger, and escape from it.'   So I knew that my falling into thy power and my escape was the interpretation of my dream.   Thou, too, knowest, O deceived idiot! that I am thine enemy.   How, then, dost thou hope, with thy little sense and thine ignorance, that I will deliver thee, when thou hast heard what rude language I used?   And how shall I endeavour to deliver thee, when the learned have said that by the death of the sinner are produced ease to mankind and purgation of the earth?   Did I not fear that I should suffer, by fidelity to thee, such affliction as would be greater than that which may result from perfidy, I would consider upon means for thy deliverance."   So when the wolf heard the words of the fox, he bit his paw in repentance.   He then spoke softly to him, but obtained nothing thereby.   With a low voice he said to him, "Verily, you tribe of foxes are the sweetest of people in tongue, and the most pleasant in jesting, and this is jesting in thee; but every time is not convenient for sport and joking." "O idiot!" replied the fox, "jesting hath a limit which its employer transgresseth not. Think not that God will give thee possession of me after He hath delivered me from thy power." The wolf then said to him, "Thou art one in whom it is proper to desire my liberation, on account of the former brotherhood and friendship that subsisted between us; and if thou deliver me, I will certainly recompense thee well." But the fox replied, "The sages have said, 'Take not as thy brother the ignorant and wicked, for he will disgrace thee, and not honour thee; and take not as thy brother the liar, for if good proceed from thee he will hide it, and if evil proceed from thee he will publish it!' And the sages have said, 'For everything there is a stratagem, excepting death; and everything may be rectified excepting the corruption of the very essence; and everything may be repelled excepting destiny.' And as to the recompense which thou assertest that I deserve of thee, I compare thee, in thy recompensing, to the serpent fleeing from the Háwee, when a man saw her in a state of terror, and said to her, 'What is the matter with thee, O serpent?' She answered, 'I have fled from the Háwee, for he seeketh me; and if thou deliver me from him, and conceal me with thee, I will recompense thee well, and do thee every kindness.' So the man took her, to obtain the reward, and eager for the recompense, and put her into his pocket; and when the Háwee had passed and gone his way, and what she feared had quitted her, the man said to her, 'Where is the recompense, for I have saved thee from that which thou fearedst and didst dread?' The serpent answered him, 'Tell me in what member I shall bite thee; for thou knowest that we exceed not this recompense.' She then inflicted upon him a bite, from which he died. And thee, O idiot!" continued the fox, "I compare to that serpent with that man. Hast thou not heard the saying of the poet?—

"'Trust not a person in whose heart thou hast made anger to dwell, nor think his anger hath ceased.
Verily, the vipers, though smooth to the touch, show graceful motions, and hide mortal poison.'"

"O eloquent and comely-faced animal!" rejoined the wolf, "be not ignorant of my condition, and of the fear with which mankind regard me. Thou knowest that I assault the strong places, and strip the vines. Do, therefore, what I have commanded thee, and attend to me as the slave attendeth to his master." "O ignorant idiot! who seekest what is vain," exclaimed the fox, "verily I wonder at thy stupidity, and at the roughness of thy manner, in thine ordering me to serve thee and to stand before thee as though I were a slave. But thou shalt soon see what will befall thee, by the splitting of thy head with stones, and the breaking of thy treacherous dog-teeth."

The fox then stationed himself upon a mound overlooking the vineyard, and cried out incessantly to the people of the vineyard until they perceived him and came quickly to him. He remained steady before them until they drew near unto him, and unto the pit in which was the wolf, and then he fled. So the owners of the vineyard looked into the pit, and when they beheld the wolf in it, they instantly pelted him with heavy stones, and continued throwing stones and pieces of wood upon him, and piercing him with the points of spears, until they killed him, when they departed. Then the fox returned to the pit, and standing over the place of the wolf's slaughter, saw him dead; whereupon he shook his head in the excess of his joy, and recited these verses—

" Fate removed the wolf's soul, and it was snatched
    away.
  Far distant from happiness be his soul that hath
    perished.
  How long hast thou striven, Abos Tirhán, to destroy
    me !
  But now have burning calamities befallen thee.
  Thou hast fallen into a pit into which none shall de-
    scend without finding in it the blasts of death."

After this the fox remained in the vineyard alone, and in security, fearing no mischief.

THE SHEPHERD AND THE JOGIE.

IT is related that during the reign of a king of
Cutch, named Lakeh, a Jogie lived, who was a wise
man, and wonderfully skilled in the preparation of
herbs. For years he had been occupied in searching for a peculiar kind of grass, the roots of which
should be burnt, and a man be thrown into the
flames. The body so burnt would become gold, and
any of the members might be removed without the
body sustaining any loss, as the parts so taken
would always be self-restored.

It so occurred that this Jogie, whilst following a
flock of goats, observed one amongst them eating of
the grass he was so anxious to procure. He immediately rooted it up, and desired the shepherd who
was near to assist him in procuring firewood.
When he had collected the wood and kindled a
flame, into which the grass was thrown, the Jogie,
wishing to render the shepherd the victim of his
avarice, desired him, under some pretence, to make
a few circuits round the fire. The man, however,
suspecting foul play, watched his opportunity, and,

seizing the Jogie himself, he threw him into the fire and left him to be consumed. Next day, on returning to the spot, great was his surprise to behold the golden figure of a man lying amongst the embers. He immediately chopped off one of the limbs and hid it. The next day he returned to take another, when his astonishment was yet greater to see that a fresh limb had replaced the one already taken. In short, the shepherd soon became wealthy, and revealed the secret of his riches to the king, Lakeh, who, by the same means, accumulated so much gold that every day he was in the habit of giving one lac and twenty-five thousand rupees in alms to fakirs.

THE PERFIDIOUS VIZIER.

A KING of former times had an only son, whom he contracted in marriage to the daughter of another king. But the damsel, who was endowed with great beauty, had a cousin who had sought her in marriage, and had been rejected; wherefore he sent great presents to the vizier of the king just mentioned, requesting him to employ some stratagem by which to destroy his master's son, or to induce him to relinquish the damsel. The vizier consented. Then the father of the damsel sent to the king's son, inviting him to come and introduce himself to his daughter, to take her as his wife; and the father of the young man sent him with the treacherous vizier, attended by a thousand horsemen, and provided with rich presents. When they were proceeding over the desert, the vizier remembered that there was near unto them a spring of water called Ez-zahra, and that whosoever drank of it, if he were a man, became a woman. He therefore ordered the troops to alight near it, and induced the prince to go thither with him. When they arrived at the spring, the king's son dismounted from his courser, and washed his hands, and drank; and lo! he became a woman; whereupon he cried out and wept until he fainted. The vizier asked him what had befallen him, so the young man informed him; and on hearing his words, the vizier affected to be grieved for him, and wept. The king's son then sent the vizier back to his father to inform him of this event, determining not to proceed nor to return until his affliction should be removed from him, or until he should die.

He remained by the fountain during a period of three days and nights, neither eating nor drinking, and on the fourth night there came to him a horseman with a crown upon his head, appearing like one of the sons of the kings. This horseman said to him, "Who brought you, O young man, unto this place?" So the young man told him his story; and when the horseman heard it, he pitied him, and said to him, "The vizier of thy father is the person who hath thrown thee into this calamity; for no one of mankind knoweth of this spring excepting one man." Then the horseman ordered him to mount with him. He therefore mounted; and the horseman said to him, "Come with me to my abode: for thou art my guest this night." The young man replied, "Inform me who thou art before

I go with thee." And the horseman said, "I am the son of a king of the Jinn, and thou art son of a king of mankind. And now, be of good heart and cheerful eye on account of that which shall dispel thine anxiety and thy grief, for it is unto me easy."

So the young man proceeded with him from the commencement of the day, forsaking his troops and soldiers (whom the vizier had left at their halting-place), and ceased not to travel on with his conductor until midnight, when the son of the king of the Jinn said to him, "Knowest thou what space we have traversed during this period?" The young man answered him, "I know not." The son of the king of the Jinn said, "We have traversed a space of a year's journey to him who travelleth with diligence." So the young man wondered thereat, and asked, "How shall I return to my family?" The other answered, "This is not thine affair. It is my affair; and when thou shalt have recovered from thy misfortune, thou shalt return to thy family in less time than the twinkling of an eye, for to accomplish that will be to me easy." The young man, on hearing these words from the Jinnee, almost flew with excessive delight. He thought that the event was a result of confused dreams, and said, "Extolled be the perfection of him who is able to restore the wretched, and render him prosperous!" They ceased not to proceed until morning, when they arrived at a verdant, bright land, with tall trees, and warbling birds, and gardens of surpassing beauty, and fair palaces; and thereupon the son of the king of the Jinn alighted from his courser, commanding the young man also to dismount. He therefore dismounted, and the Jinnee took him by the hand, and they entered one of the palaces, where the young man beheld an exalted king and a sultan of great dignity, and he remained with them that day, eating and drinking, until the approach of night. Then the son of the king of the Jinn arose and mounted with him, and they went forth, and proceeded during the night with diligence until the morning. And lo! they came to a black land, not inhabited, abounding with black rocks and stones, as though it were a part of hell; whereupon the son of the king of men said to the Jinnee, "What is the name of this land?" And he answered, "It is called the Dusky Land, and belongeth to one of the kings of the Jinn, whose name is Zu-l-Jenáheyn. None of the kings can attack him, nor doth any one enter his territory unless by his permission, so stop in thy place while I ask his permission." Accordingly the young man stopped, and the Jinn was absent from him for a while, and then returned to him; and they ceased not to proceed until they came to a spring flowing from black mountains. The Jinnee said to the young man, "Alight." He therefore alighted from his courser, and the Jinnee said to him, "Drink of this spring."

The young prince drank of it, and immediately became again a man, as he was at first, by the power of God (whose name be exalted!), whereat he rejoiced with great joy, not to be exceeded. And he said to the Jinn, " O my brother, what is the name of this spring?" The Jinnee answered, "It is called the Spring of the Women : no woman drinketh of it but she becometh a man; therefore praise God, and thank Him for thy restoration, and mount thy courser." So the king's son prostrated himself, thanking God (whose name be exalted!). Then he mounted, and they journeyed with diligence during the rest of the day until they had returned to the land of the Jinnee, and the young man passed the night in his abode in the most comfortable manner; after which they ate and drank until the next night, when the son of the king of the Jinn said to him, "Dost thou desire to return to thy family this night?" The young man answered, "Yes." So the son of the king of the Jinn called one of his father's slaves, whose name was Rájiz, and said to him, "Take this young man hence, and carry him upon thy shoulders, and let not the dawn overtake him before he is with his father-in-law and his wife." The slave replied, "I hear and obey, and with feelings of love and honour will I do it."

Then the slave absented himself for a while, and approached in the form of an 'Efreet. And when the young man saw him his reason fled, and he was stupefied; but the son of the king of the Jinn said to him, "No harm shall befall thee. Mount thy courser. Ascend upon his shoulders." The young man then mounted upon the slave's shoulders, and the son of the king of the Jinn said to him, "Close thine eyes." So he closed his eyes, and the slave flew with him between heaven and earth, and ceased not to fly along with him while the young man was unconscious, and the last third of the night came not before he was on the top of the palace of his father-in-law. Then the 'Efreet said to him, "Alight." He therefore alighted. And the 'Efreet said to him, "Open thine eyes; for this is the palace of thy father-in-law and his daughter." Then he left him and departed. And as soon as the day shone, and the alarm of the young man subsided, he descended from the roof of the palace; and when his father-in-law beheld him, he rose to him and met him, wondering at seeing him descend from the top of the palace, and he said to him, "We see other men come through the doors, but thou comest down from the sky." The young man replied, "What God (whose perfection be extolled, and whose name be exalted!) desired hath happened." And when the sun rose, his father-in-law ordered his vizier to prepare great banquets, and the wedding was celebrated; the young man remained there two months, and then departed with his wife to the city of his father. But as to the cousin of the damsel, he perished by reason of his jealousy and envy.

Printed by T. and A. Constable, Printers to Her Majesty,
at the Edinburgh University Press.